TERRA'S
WORLD

Also by Mitch Benn from Gollancz:

Terra

Mitch Benn

TERRA'S WORLD

GOLLANCZ

LONDON

The right of Mitch Benn to be identified as the author of this
work has been asserted by him in accordance with the
Copyright, Designs and Patents Act 1988.

First published in Great Britain in 2014 by Gollancz
An imprint of the Orion Publishing Group
Orion House, 5 Upper St Martin's Lane, London WC2H 9EA
An Hachette UK Company

A CIP catalogue record for this book
is available from the British Library

ISBN 978 0 575 13212 2 (Cased)
ISBN 978 0 575 13213 9 (Export Trade Paperback)

1 3 5 7 9 10 8 6 4 2

Typeset by Deltatype Ltd, Birkenhead, Merseyside

Printed in Great Britain by Clays Ltd, St Ives plc

The Orion Publishing Group's policy is to use papers that
are natural, renewable and recyclable products and made from
wood grown in sustainable forests. The logging and manufacturing
processes are expected to conform to the environmental
regulations of the country of origin.

www.mitchbenn.com
www.orionbooks.co.uk
www.gollancz.co.uk

For Mike Benn, for sending me on this adventure.

- Hi, Mitch here again.

- Once again, a note on notation:

'Dialogue presented as it's spoken will be formatted like this.'

- Dialogue translated from the languages of the planet Fnrr (and other planets) will be formatted like this.

- Nice to see you again. Hope you enjoy yourself.

M xx

Fear of a Black Planet

The Coshrai people of the planet Sagaska were the first to see it.

A rogue planet, adrift in deep space. It came within range of their long-range astroscopes in the second cycle of what, in the Coshrai's rather idiosyncratic calendar, was denoted the year 5-Black-7-Tree-4.

As it approached, the Coshrai astrographers refocused and retuned their imaging devices, trying to make out some features of the planet's surface.

It had none. It was black.

No land mass, no ocean, no ice cap, not even so much as a crater could be seen. The planet was featureless and black, like a hole in the fabric of space. And still it approached.

Coshrai probes were launched from Sagaska to take a closer look, and saw nothing. The rogue planet seemed to be covered in a thick layer of black dust. The planet was silent, dead, black.

The scientific communities of neighbouring worlds were consulted. Intrigued, they sent delegations to observe the approach of the black planet, which was now predicted to pass right through Sagaska's home system.

On Sagaska itself, expectations ranged from indifference to apocalyptic terror. The Obscure and Ancient Order of Scryers, a society of mystics and soothsayers to whom scant attention had been paid for centuries, enjoyed a resurgence in popularity as a bewildered populace turned to them for guidance.

After due consideration, divination and meditation the Order of Scryers decreed that the conjunction of the appearance of a black planetoid with a black calendar year (only one year in twenty-three was designated 'black' in the Coshrai calendar; that's how idiosyncratic it was) must clearly be of great significance.

When pressed further on what that significance might be, the Order of Scryers considered, divined and meditated some more before announcing that the black planet was a good and auspicious omen, heralding a time of peace and prosperity for Sagaska, and requesting that all further enquiries be made via their newly engaged publicity agent.

The scientific delegations from Sagaska's neighbouring worlds began to arrive: astrographers from Binda Prime; xenologists from Shaa; stellar physicists from Ch'Kesh Ch'Kesh.

The black planet was now visible – in as much as a black non-reflective object can ever be said to be visible – in Sagaska's night sky, a patch of pure darkness among the stars. The rogue planet's trajectory had been plotted; contrary to the more hysterical predictions of the panickier elements of Coshrai society, it was not expected to smash into Sagaska, nor would it pass by so closely as to cause any great gravitational disturbances. Rather, at around midday on the fifth day of the fourth cycle of the year 5-Black-7-Tree-4, it would pass within a few thousand macrofurlongs of Sagaska's upper atmosphere, before moving on into space.

As Sagaska watched, the rogue planet drifted ever closer, silent, dead, black.

At midday on the fifth day of the fourth cycle of the year 5-Black-7-Tree-4, the whole population of Sagaska, both native and visiting, looked to the skies in awe and excitement.

Just after midday on the fifth day of the fourth cycle of the year 5-Black-7-Tree-4, all contact with the planet Sagaska was lost.

The first ships from Shaa and Ch'kesh Ch'kesh arrived a few days later. Their initial thought was that Sagaska had simply disappeared. The rogue planet was there, as silent, dead and black as ever, but of Sagaska there was no sign.

It was only when they studied the size and orbit of the black planet that the dreadful truth became clear.

The rogue planet had clearly moved on, straight through Sagaska's system and out into deep space. The planet they were now looking at was Sagaska itself, but of the Coshrai, their cities, their culture, there remained not a trace. Just dust. Thick black dust.

Sagaska was silent. Sagaska was dead. Sagaska was black.

PART ONE

Ordinary World

Billy Dolphin really missed science fiction.

There wasn't much of it about these days, not like when Billy was younger.

His dad had introduced him to science fiction, or sci-fi, or just SF (the brevity of the name you gave it was, Billy had always thought, an indicator of how 'into' it you were) at the age of four or five, sitting him down in front of the TV to watch *Star Trek* reruns, or *Doctor Who*, or maybe one of the more kid-friendly SF movies like *Star Wars* (original trilogy, obviously; even at that age Billy's taste in SF had been quite discerning, although as he got older he realised that *Star Wars* wasn't really science fiction at all so much as heroic fantasy with spaceships and lasers, but at least it had spaceships and lasers).

From movies and TV shows Billy had graduated to SF books; at first, novelisations of the movies and TV shows and, later, original SF classics. They were pretty much all Billy read, and reading was pretty much all Billy did.

Billy Dolphin consumed science fiction like most people consumed food. He would start with perhaps some contemporary, cyber-punky SF as an appetiser, move on to a satisfying main course of Proper Big Idea SF – Clarke or Asimov or one of their later disciples – then indulge in a couple of cheerfully violent SF comics for dessert.

That's not to say Billy didn't consume actual food as well. In fact, what with his healthy appetite and his sedentary lifestyle he had, throughout his childhood, developed a physique which well-meaning medical professionals and clothing store assistants would refer to as 'well built', as they looked him up and down with expressions of concern and disapproval. Billy always wished they'd just call him fat. The whole 'well built' nonsense just meant they thought not only that he was fat but also too emotionally fragile to handle being called fat.

His parents would occasionally use the f-word to describe Billy's condition, but his mother, in particular, had always prefaced it with 'puppy' – reassuring Billy (or whomever else she was talking to) that this was merely childhood chubbiness which he would grow out of in time. Now, at the age of fourteen, Billy was beginning to suspect that his mother was wrong. He was growing and developing as young boys do at that age, and his excess bodyweight was growing and developing right along with him. Billy wasn't 'stretching out'; he was just expanding.

This, combined with Billy Dolphin's unusual surname, was not making for a happy time at school. In his first year at Latimer Lane Comprehensive (established 1974, 623 pupils, ranked number three in the district according to Ofsted), Billy had been at pains to point out that 'Dolphin' was a corruption of the French 'Dauphin' (meaning Prince), and as such Billy was distantly related to European royalty and NOT to aquatic mammals (yes, MAMMALS, not fish, Gary Bassett). This information was ignored by his classmates. Between his weight and his name they'd already found the perfect nickname for him, and no amount of linguistic or zoological pedantry on his part would dissuade them from using it. He was Billy the Whale.

Billy the Whale, useless at football, Billy the Whale, dressed by his mum, Billy the Whale, rubbish with girls (although, hello? Hadn't anyone noticed his best friend was a girl? Okay, so Lydia was a bit boyish, and she was rather grumpy and she did have short purple hair, but she STILL COUNTED AS A GIRL, so there).

But none of that mattered, not his name, not his weight, not school, not Gary Bassett, because there was always science fiction. Sci-fi, to make his heart race and his mind soar. SF, to take him away.

Or there had been.

Until that stupid Terra girl turned up and ruined everything.

* * *

Two years earlier, on the day when the Earth had, to borrow a phrase, stood still, Billy Dolphin had been as excited as everyone else.

He and his dad had sat rooted to the spot in front of the TV for hours as the drama unfolded. Mealtimes had come and gone, food was brought out and sat cooling and ignored in front of them. Even hunger couldn't tear Billy's attention from the screen.

This was, after all, Billy's dream coming true. An honest-to-goodness alien spaceship, piloted by an honest-to-goodness alien from an honest-to-goodness alien planet. Billy and his dad hugged each other, their hearts racing and their minds wonderfully blown, amazed at the new world in which they found themselves and overcome with excitement at what it might contain.

It was with a gradual lurching disappointment over the next few months that Billy Dolphin realised that one thing this brave new world would NOT contain was science fiction.

Before the arrival of the lemon-shaped spaceship, of the lost Terra girl and her alien stepfather whose name Billy could never remember (or pronounce), space had been, from a storytelling point of view, a blank slate. A virgin canvas onto which the science fiction author could project whatever his (or her) fancy conjured forth. Since nobody knew what or who was out there, anything was possible. There were no limits imposed upon science fiction's collective imagination.

But now it was different. Now everyone not only knew that there was indeed life on other planets, they knew on which other planets, what these planets were called and what the inhabitants looked like. Thus far humanity might only have encountered one alien race – the Fnrrns – but scientists were now learning more about other extra-terrestrial civilisations. Indeed, the very fact that alien life was now being defined, catalogued, UNDERSTOOD by human beings meant that space simply wasn't the playground for the imagination it had once been. Sci-fi was subject to a whole new set of rules, rules that were making it less fun – and less popular, hence less commercial – than it used to be.

This began to be reflected in popular culture; some of Billy's favourite SF television shows were cancelled – or simply 'not renewed' – and no new ones took their place. The lists of forthcoming movies were bereft of futuristic or space-based titles. Visiting his beloved local bookshop, Billy would notice the science fiction section slowly dwindling down to a single shelf, containing only the 'classic SF' authors – Wells, Verne and the like – whose continued presence in the store owed more to the 'classic' part of their status than to the 'SF' bit.

There was still fantasy to be had, of the fictitious realm swords n' sorcerers type, but Billy had never been a fan of tales with 'magic' in them (it always felt like cheating to him) and, of course, there was no shortage of horror fiction, though that seemed to have been swamped by endless ranks of interchangeable Romantic Vampire Novels. Since when were vampires romantic? (Billy would ponder.) What was romantic about sleeping in a coffin and sucking the blood out of people? Vampires were supposed to be zombie serial killers, not dreamy-eyed, high-cheekboned, lovelorn poets. And even if a several-centuries-old man LOOKS seventeen, isn't a love story between a several-centuries-old man and a teenage girl a bit, well, you know, dodgy? Lydia at least was with him on that one.

But sci-fi, good old spaceshippy, lasery, robotty distant planets and/or distant future capital S capital F – nobody seemed to want that any more. Not since that day. Not since the space girl arrived. Not since Terra.

And then, as if to add cosmic insult to cultural injury, she'd disappeared.

A few months after the spaceship's arrival, Terra and her human family suddenly faded from public view. There was no more mention of them on the news, no more public appearances, the expected regular visits from alien delegations never happened, the eagerly anticipated leaps forward in technology never materialised. By now, many people had forgotten all about Terra the space girl, and of those who remembered, some were beginning to suspect that the whole thing had been an elaborate hoax. As far as Billy Dolphin could tell, the only lasting legacy of the whole Terra incident had been the end of his beloved science fic—

'You know what I think? I think you're jealous,' said Lydia.

They were waiting for the bus at the end of what had been an extremely Tuesdayish Tuesday.

'Jealous?' replied Billy, plucking one earphone out. Was that actually what Lydia had said?

'Yes, jealous,' said Lydia, yanking Billy's other earphone out. Led Zeppelin dangled squeakily around Billy's midriff as Lydia went on. 'All day, every day, Terra this, Terra that, she ruined sci-fi, she ruined my life—'

'I wasn't even talking,' protested Billy, fumbling for his earphones.

'No, but you were thinking about it,' grumped Lydia. 'Your lips were moving and your eyebrows were doing that thing.'

'Was singing along,' muttered Billy, rummaging in his pocket to silence Robert Plant.

'You're jealous because that Terra girl actually did the things you dream of doing. She travelled in space. She met aliens.'

'She grew up with aliens,' added Billy wistfully.

'Exactly,' said Lydia. 'Don't tell me this is all about a couple of cancelled TV shows. This is envy, pure and simple.'

'Maybe,' mumbled Billy, looking down at his feet.

'It's not like it's her fault anyway,' persisted Lydia. 'She wasn't to know what would happen, she just wanted to come home.'

Billy raised his eyes to the gunmetal-grey clouded sky. 'Well, I promise not to give her a hard time if I ever run into her,' he said with a grudging smile.

Lydia sat next to him on the bus stop bench and kicked her legs. 'No one knows where she is anyway,' she reminded him, removing her woolly hat and ruffling her purple hair, 'I reckon she's naffed off back to the planet Whatsit.'

The first drop of inevitable rain struck Billy between the eyes and trickled down his nose. 'Can't say I blame her,' he said, stuffing Led Zeppelin back into his ears. Lydia sighed and resigned herself to waiting for the bus in silence.

Billy registered Lydia's disappointment. He was sure she'd get over it. In time, the bus squeaked to a halt and they slouched on board, taking seats at the back. Billy closed his eyes and let 'Kashmir' bounce around the inside of his skull. Billy had inherited his love of classic rock from his dad, along with his love of science fiction. Thinking about it, Billy wasn't sure he owned a single album by a band which didn't have at least one dead member. He knew his musical tastes were decades out of date, and he didn't care. He was only dimly aware of what kind of music his contemporaries were listening to. The brief bursts he'd heard coming from their mobile phones were enough to put him off any further investigation.

Billy had no idea what sort of music Lydia listened to. Lydia didn't play music on her phone, she would just fiddle with it endlessly with varying degrees of annoyance. Glancing across at her, Billy noticed that she was frowning at her phone right now. Billy was never rude enough to loom over Lydia's shoulder to spy on what she was doing, but in the year or so he'd known her he'd never seen her look happy while staring at that phone. Perhaps she was having a tense conversation over some social network or another, or just losing a game rather badly. Lydia's phone seemed to be a source of great irritation to her; Billy wondered why she bothered with it.

Billy's stop came first. 'Bye, then,' he mumbled to Lydia. Lydia, glowering at her phone, may or may not have mumbled something back; Billy still had his earphones in. As he watched the bus slosh away into the damp evening light, Billy wondered what might be on TV that night. Something about lawyers, probably. Or hospitals. Or lawyers in hospital.

Billy Dolphin REALLY missed science fiction.

I.2

'**W**hat?'

Billy was dumbfounded on several levels at once. He had no idea what the strikingly pretty blonde girl had just said to him, he had no idea who the strikingly pretty blonde girl was, and, most perplexingly, he had absolutely no idea why this strikingly pretty blonde girl would be talking to him.

He'd missed the girl's question for the same reason he rarely heard anything anyone said to him the first time. He'd had his earphones in – Van Halen on this occasion (pre-Sammy Hagar era, obviously) – and what remained of his attention was focused on the book in his hands. This was how he spent most morning breaks, and unless Lydia had something particularly irritating to get off her chest, he generally spent this small nugget of private time unmolested, having staked out his territory on the steps leading up to the school's refectory. Not this time, though. During a lull between album tracks he suddenly became aware that someone was talking to him, and looking up, he was startled to see who – indeed, what – it was.

It was a girl. An actual proper girl-type girl. She had bright, excited blue eyes, and tumbling honey-blonde hair. She was dressed in a shiny blue sweater and jeans. (Latimer Lane had renounced school uniforms a few years before Billy's arrival, under the regime of a previous, rather progressive and liberal, head teacher. This head teacher had subsequently left under something of a cloud when it transpired he'd been a bit too progressive and liberal with regard to the school's finances, but the decree abolishing uniforms still stood.) She looked to be about Billy's own age and was pointing at his book.

Billy tugged his earphones out and the girl repeated her question.

'Is that William Gibson?'

'Erm …' (Say something, Billy, say something.) 'Yes, er, *Mona Lisa Overdrive.*'

'Cool!' The girl smiled. 'I've never read that one. Only *Neuromancer.*'

Was this actually happening? Even if Billy was imagining things, he liked the things he was imagining. He decided to go on imagining them.

'You can … borrow this if you want.'

'Really?' Wow. What a smile. I did that, thought Billy. I did that smile.

'Yeah, I've read it four or five times already.'

Billy handed her the book and the girl turned it over excitedly, reading the front and back covers. 'He's amazing, isn't he? To think he was writing about all this stuff before anyone even had email. He saw so many things coming.'

This was fast becoming Billy's All-Time Number One Favourite Conversation. 'He pushed his luck a bit with the whole everyone having a USB port in the back of their heads thing,' he said with a smile, and the laugh this provoked from the girl made his insides go gooey. 'I think that's next,' Billy continued, encouraged. 'People are gonna get so lazy even touch screens will seem like too much effort. They won't be happy till they can have the Internet injected straight into their brains.' And there was the laugh again.

The bell rang to announce the end of break and the start of late morning class. Billy had never resented a sound so violently in his life. He stood up.

'That was … I have to, I mean we have – EVERYBODY has to—'

She cut him off. He was so glad she cut him off.

'I'm Tracey,' she said.

'Billy,' said Billy, extending his hand for her to shake, a gesture which immediately struck him as so utterly lame that he was relieved when she ignored it and skipped away.

Just as Tracey reached the door of the school building she turned and held up the book. 'Thanks for this,' she said, and was gone.

* * *

'What's got you so happy?' asked Lydia as they waited for the bus at the end of what, as far as she could tell, had been a fairly averagely Wednesdayish Wednesday.

'Hm?' said Billy, not listening, and just for once not listening to his earphones either.

'That big dumb grin on your face,' persisted Lydia. 'What's it in aid of?'

'Have you met a girl called Tracey?' asked Billy.

'I've met HUNDREDS of girls called Tracey. Be more specific,' huffed Lydia.

'Blonde. About our age. I think she's new,' Billy elaborated.

'Pretty?' asked Lydia, peering at him through her purple fringe.

'I suppose ...'

Lydia hopped off the bus stop bench and stood right in front of him. 'Pathetic,' she spat. 'If you think she's pretty just SAY so.'

'Okay,' mumbled Billy, 'she's pretty.'

'There,' said Lydia, sitting back down. 'Wasn't so hard, was it?'

'AND she's into sci-fi,' Billy said after a moment's pause.

'Really?' A note of incredulity.

'Yeah, really. Lent her one of me William Gibsons.'

'Which one?'

'*Mona Lisa Overdrive.*'

'Ha.' Lydia snorted. 'She reckons she's into sci-fi and she's never read *Mona Lisa Overdrive*?'

'She's read *Neuromancer*,' protested Billy.

'EVERYONE's read *Neuromancer*. Your MUM's read *Neuromancer*.'

Billy burst out laughing. Lydia joined in. After a few seconds they fell silent, an awkward sort of silence such as there'd never been between them before.

Lydia broke it. 'Gonna ask her out, then?'

'I might,' said Billy. And he genuinely believed it was possible.

1.3

In the event, Billy didn't have to ask Tracey out.

He arrived at school on the Friday morning, having spent most of the Thursday contemplating how exactly to broach the subject with Tracey so as to minimise the humiliation when the inevitable rejection came.

He was shuffling through the corridor, just running through one such scenario in his mind ('No, that's okay, it was just a thought, no, it's fine, really') when Tracey appeared in front of him, beaming. She held out his copy of *Mona Lisa Overdrive*.

'Thank you so much, it's amazing. I think it's my favourite one of his,' she said.

Billy took the book. 'That's okay. If you want to borrow any other – what's this?'

There was a long strip of card wedged between the pages of the book. He opened it and the card fell out. He bent down to pick it up.

It was a ticket. A ticket to the Cinéaste Society screening of *Silent Running* at the Picturedrome cinema the very next night. Billy stared at it in excited bewilderment.

'It's my way of saying thank you,' said Tracey, a little bashfully. 'You are free, aren't you?'

Of COURSE I'm free, thought Billy. 'Well, I don't have anything special on,' said Billy. 'Nothing I can't get out of, certainly.'

'That's brilliant!' said Tracey with an excited laugh. She reached into her pocket and produced a similar ticket, waving it happily. 'Have you seen it? It's my favourite movie ever.'

'I have seen it, and it's MY favourite movie ever.' Billy

smiled. Billy's favourite movie ever was in fact *Blade Runner* (original 1982 theatrical cut), but he wasn't about to bring that up now.

'Fantastic, I'll see you there,' said Tracey, and skipped off in that delightful skipping-off way she had of skipping off.

Billy stood, wordless and grinning, for what might have been five minutes.

'You're going to be late,' said a voice.

'What?'

'School,' said Lydia. 'You're in school. It involves going to classes and stuff. Not just standing in a corridor with a big stupid smile on your face.'

'She asked me out!' said Billy, finally snapping out of his daze. 'Tracey! She asked me!'

'I know,' muttered Lydia. 'I was watching.'

'*Silent Running*! Tomorrow night! The Picturedrome!' Billy held up his ticket.

'Hm,' grunted Lydia.

'Oh,' said Billy as they walked towards their first class of the day, 'did you want to go to see it as well? Cos, you know, you still could, I'm sure it'd be—'

'Don't be ridiculous,' said Lydia.

I.4

B illy sat in the dark with a beautiful, interesting girl, and the best thing was he didn't have to say a thing.

In some regards *Silent Running* was an even more upsetting film now than when it had come out in the early 1970s; they'd made a profound and heartfelt warning about the dangers of Earth's ecosystem collapsing and all animal and plant life being destroyed. In the early 1970s. They hadn't seen anything yet, Billy reflected.

Silent Running was not the sort of movie which you watched to feel happy. But there in the dark with a beautiful, interesting girl, Billy was happier than he could ever remember being.

It wasn't just that Tracey had suggested *Silent Running*. It was that she really seemed to GET *Silent Running*. And anyone who 'got' *Silent Running*, Billy thought, had a chance of 'getting' him.

She didn't snuggle into him or hold his hand. He didn't try to hold hers. But he was sure he heard a tearful sniff at 'Take good care of the forest, Dewey', and that was enough for him.

The lights came up as Joan Baez sang, and Billy saw that there were indeed tears in Tracey's eyes. 'Come on,' he said, 'I'll get us some pizza.'

They strolled out into the cold night. The city's lights seemed brighter than Billy had ever noticed them before. They walked side by side, without speaking.

'It always makes me cry, that movie,' said Tracey.

'Me too,' said Billy without thinking, and instantly wished he could take it back. Cry? Really? He could have said it made him SAD, certainly, but cry?

'Do you cry a lot at movies?' asked Tracey.

'Oh yes,' said Billy, thinking his best bet now was to make a joke out of the topic. 'I wept buckets at the end of *Dumb and Dumber*.'

Tracey laughed. Billy loved that laugh.

A moment's silence. They walked on.

'So ...' said Tracey.

'So ...?' replied Billy.

'You're not ...' Tracey paused.

'Not what?'

Tracey looked away for a moment, then looked back at him. 'You're not going out with anyone at the moment, are you?'

Billy gave an involuntary high-pitched yelp of laughter, and was immediately horrified at the sound he made. 'No,' he said in an unusually deep tone, 'no, I'm not. Unless you include this.' He gestured back and forth between Tracey and himself.

'I see,' said Tracey, maddeningly neither confirming nor denying whether she included this. 'It's just ...'

Billy couldn't tell whether this was going to be the best or worst conversation of his young life. 'Just what?'

'Well,' began Tracey, 'everyone seems to think that you and Lydia are ...'

Billy gave the yelp of high-pitched laughter again, contemplated punching himself hard in the face, decided against it and replied, 'What, me and Lydia? No, no way,' in the deepest voice he could manage.

'You're just friends, then?' Tracey smiled.

'Hardly even that really,' snorted Billy.

'It's just you spend so much time together. How long have you known her?'

'Oh, I don't know,' said Billy, wondering quite how this evening had become about Lydia, 'a year or so, since she started at the school.'

'What school did she go to before?'

'She's never said. Never thought to ask. Where are we?'

Billy had only just noticed that they'd walked round the back of the cinema and were now standing in a dark alley. Had Tracey led them there or had he just wandered aimlessly with her following? It added to his unease. 'Do we have to talk about Lydia?' he asked, annoyed at how whiny he sounded.

Tracey smiled, a smile Billy had dreamed about seeing on the face of a real live girl for as long as he could remember.

'We don't have to talk about anything,' she said.

She took his hand. Billy realised it was the first time he'd touched her. Her hand felt strangely cold and hard. It was a chilly night, thought Billy. Oh my, thought Billy, this is actually happening.

'Close your eyes,' said Tracey softly.

Billy closed his eyes, parted his lips and waited.

He felt Tracey's other hand on the back of his head, the fingers – cold again – running through his hair. Then the fingers clamped hard on the back of his neck.

'Ow! Tracey, not so—'

The hand, surprisingly strong – impossibly strong, in fact – forced him to his knees. His excitement evaporated, replaced by confusion and fear.

'What are you do—? Ahh!'

The fingers tightened on his neck and he found he couldn't speak any more. A cold metallic something was pushed against the back of his head. He winced and thrashed.

'This will hurt a lot less if you keep still,' said Tracey, her voice as cold as the metal object.

The metal something now became warmer. It seemed to vibrate, and the vibrations passed through his skull and straight into his brain.

Images began to run through his mind like a video being fast-scanned. His own life was flashing before him: his childhood, school, adolescence – even sped up, it was boring.

Billy had the feeling of being drained, hollowed, emptied out.

Billy felt that even if he had any idea how to fight against this, soon there wouldn't be enough of him left to fight.

Billy's eyes struggled to focus. Tracey was behind him, holding him down. Someone else was there. Running towards him. He saw baggy jeans, a woolly hat, a purple fringe …

Lydia was there, and she had something in her hand. Something shiny, spherical …

There was a flash, a low whooshing sound, and the vibrations in his head stopped. His vision cleared. He staggered to his feet and looked around. Tracey lay unconscious on top of a pile of bin bags, a flat metal disc hanging from her limp fingers. Lydia stood brandishing the spherical object like the weapon it obviously was.

'Y-you …' he fought to get the words out.

'You're welcome,' said Lydia, taking her rucksack off her shoulder and stuffing the sphere-thingy into it.

'You shot her!' said Billy at last.

'Whatever it is, I seriously doubt it's a her,' said Lydia, pointing at the unconscious Tracey. Billy stared down. At first he thought his vision was failing again; Tracey seemed to blur and phase as he looked at her. Then Billy realised that Tracey actually WAS phasing and blurring. She distorted and fragmented like an interrupted digital TV picture … and then Tracey wasn't there at all. What WAS there made Billy recoil so violently he fell over his own feet and landed in a sitting position.

'What … what is it?' he stammered.

'Looks like a Craa, or possibly a Tastak. Some sort of highly evolved insectoid, anyway,' said Lydia. She began to cover the black, glistening, segmented body with the bin bags. Billy struggled to maintain any sort of grip on proceedings, and his dinner.

'We need to get out of here,' said Lydia, peering at her phone. It was the first sentiment that had made sense to Billy for quite a while. 'Ah – there we go. Up there,' said Lydia, looking up towards the roof of the cinema. 'Come on,' she said, 'it won't stay unconscious for long.'

Before Billy could protest, Lydia put her arm around his waist. She fiddled with something on her belt and they were enveloped in a sparkling field of energy. Billy felt a curious fluttering in his insides, as if he'd become weightless, and then suddenly he found that he was indeed weightless, and that he and Lydia were rising effortlessly into the air. He found his voice at last.

'What's going ON, Lydia?'

'My name's not Lydia,' she said. 'It's Terra.'

Few civilisations ever heard of the Jek-E-Lek people of the planet Kelejek, but many of those who did would come to envy them. Of all the worlds to encounter the Black Planet, their fate had been the most merciful. The Jek-E-Lek simply never knew what hit them.

The Jek-E-Lek had never progressed beyond a pastoral, agriculture-based existence because they hadn't needed to. The extraordinarily fertile soils and temperate climate of Kelejek provided everything they could want. They'd never industrialised, never developed their technology past simple devices required to till their fields and harvest their crops. They'd never considered the stars to be anything more than decorations in the night sky; they'd never attempted to escape the confines of their own world, or to communicate with any other world, because it had never occurred to them that there might be anything out there to communicate with.

They'd had no means of detecting the Black Planet's approach. When it appeared in the mist-shrouded night sky, no one even noticed a disc of pure darkness among the hazy stars. And when their warm orange sun rose the next morning, revealing the giant orb looming low over Kelejek's silent, blackened surface, there was no one left alive to see it.

1.5

Lydia – who was not called Lydia, but Terra – and it was fairly obvious WHICH Terra – was examining a small oval pod-like object. She'd removed it from her belt and was prodding at a button on its surface.

'Power cell's dead,' she muttered. 'Amazing it lasted as long as it did. No way to charge it up here. Only used it on very special occasions.'

'Huh,' replied Billy.

'The pod was calibrated for me back on Fnrr. Gravity's about ten per cent stronger on Earth, and I've got heavier in the last two years, AND it was lifting you as well. No offence, but I'm surprised it got us all the way up here.' She reattached the pod to her belt and took her phone from her rucksack.

'Huh,' said Billy.

'Now,' said Lydia who was Terra, 'let's see.' She held up her phone and peered at it, wanding it around.

Billy was sure he should say something but had no idea what. So many questions were stumbling over each other in the confined space of his mind that none could make its way to his mouth. He decided to pick one at random, a simple one, and start from there.

'Where … where are we?'

'We're on the roof of the Picturedrome.'

'How did we get up here?'

'Gravity pod. Weren't you listening?' Lydia/Terra was still scanning the rooftop with her phone.

'How… how did you know that Tracey was … that she wasn't … real?'

'Optical camouflage. I noticed a bit of phasing around

28

her face the other day when it rained. That sort of technology doesn't belong on this planet. So I knew she was an alien, and that meant she was here for me.'

'For you?'

'Yes. Not you. Sorry.'

Terra had not noticed any phasing around Tracey's face, nor did she have any idea if rain would cause optical camouflage to phase. Her suspicions had been aroused when the prettiest new girl in school had unaccountably found Billy irresistible, but she didn't think that was anything Billy needed to hear at that moment.

'So ... why did she ... what was she doing?' Billy sat down on the rooftop. The concrete was damp. He didn't care.

'She was draining your memory. I think she was going to become you.'

'Become me?'

'Yes. She could adjust the camouflage to look like you, and use your memories to convince me that she was you. Then she could get as close to me as she wanted. Ah! There you are,' said Terra with a triumphant smile. She strode across the roof. Billy stumbled to his feet and followed her.

'And once she'd become me, what would have happened to the actual me?' Terra did not reply but shot Billy a look that answered his question succinctly. He fell silent, his guts now in almost as much turmoil as his head.

Billy looked up to see Terra gesturing with her left hand. She moved it smoothly through the air, as if she were feeling something that wasn't there. Her fingers curled around an invisible shape, and she pulled on it.

A crack of bright light appeared in mid-air in front of her. Billy shielded his eyes. Terra turned to him. 'Are you coming?'

Billy stared at the light. Within it he could see walls, surfaces, controls? 'Is that ...?' he whispered.

'It's a spaceship, yes. An invisible spaceship, and I'm stealing it. Or trying to, anyway. Are you coming?'

1.6

Mr Bradbury – or Chris Clarke, as his current crop of friends and neighbours knew him – picked up the phone.

'Dad?' came the voice. Two years, and he still got a little jolt of happiness whenever she called him that.

'Are you okay, Lydia?' he asked.

'Actually' – a hesitant tone – 'I think it's Terra again, Dad.'

Mr Bradbury caught his breath. 'Has there been another one? Are you okay?'

'I'm fine, Dad, it's taken care of. But I can't stay here.'

Mr Bradbury sighed. He'd quite enjoyed being Chris Clarke. He liked the name, for starters. As his wife occasionally pointed out, 'Chris Clarke' sounded a bit like a super-hero's secret identity. Which it sort of was, except for the super-hero part.

They'd been living as quietly as possible, six months after Terra's return to Earth, when the first incident had occurred. One evening, with Terra asleep upstairs and his wife working on her laptop, he'd answered the door to find the house surrounded by black vans and a grim-faced government agent (whom Mr Bradbury had remembered from one of the many 'debriefings' he'd had to sit through shortly after Terra's return) informing him of 'credible intel' they'd received about an imminent attempt on Terra's life.

He'd had to scoop her, drowsy, from her bed and bundle her into her clothes. They were out of the house within twenty minutes. They never returned. From that moment on, for official purposes, the Bradbury family ceased to exist.

Just what the 'credible intel' had been, and how the authorities had intercepted it, Mr Bradbury did not know, nor did he expect he ever would. But from the haste of the evacuation – and the presence of white-coated scientists among the black-clad soldiers in the team that had evacuated them – Mr Bradbury suspected that whatever had been coming for Terra, had been coming from a very, very long way away.

They'd got even closer the next time.

Terra – or Susie Adams, as she'd been then – had just about settled into her new school, when a hooded figure had made his (its?) way into the grounds and detonated some sort of percussion device which had rendered everyone in the building unconscious.

The figure had zeroed in on Terra/Susie, picking her out from among the prone bodies littering the halls and classrooms. He had tossed her over his shoulder and was about to make off with her when he was apprehended by impressive numbers of exceedingly well-armed police officers (or similar) who'd turned up surprisingly quickly.

A quick bit of news management later, and the school had been the location of a dangerous, but non-lethal and swiftly contained, gas leak. No mention was ever made of any mysterious hooded figure. What had become of him, no one knew. Well, Mr Bradbury imagined SOMEONE knew, but they weren't about to let him know.

Something Mr Bradbury had figured out for himself was this: the use of the percussion device, the attempted abduction – whoever or WHATever wanted Terra, wanted her alive. Mr Bradbury wasn't sure if he found this thought encouraging or terrifying, so he tried not to think it too often.

Not that there had been much time to think. No sooner was Terra returned to the bosom of her family, than they were once again uprooted. A move of a good few thousand miles this time, and the Adamses became the Clarkes, and Terra became Lydia, who cut her hair, dyed it purple, went to Latimer Lane Comprehensive, and, in her attempts to keep a low profile, found herself gravitating towards the school's other principal misfit, a chubby sci-fi nerd called Billy.

Now, it seemed, they – whoever they were – had found Terra again. Time to move. 'Okay,' Mr Bradbury said grimly, 'I'll call the Agency.'

'No, Dad, not this time,' said Terra, with a maturity he'd never heard before.

Mr Bradbury got to his feet. 'What do you mean?' he asked.

'I've found its ship, Dad. I've found its ship, and I think I can fly it.'

* * *

Terra wriggled uncomfortably in the ship's command chair. It was designed for someone much taller and thinner (and with four arms, judging by the arrangement of the controls). She held her slate in one hand, waving it over the console and letting its optical translation program decipher the markings and readouts. Her other hand held her phone – or rather, her infralight comm, which while on Earth also worked as a phone – to her ear.

'What?' Terra's father's voice, though amplified only by the comm's tinny little speaker, was audible throughout the ship. Billy, who was sat on another equally uncomfortable chair across the poky cabin from Terra, flinched at the squeak of alarm.

'Listen, Dad. Those things are just going to keep coming unless I can figure out what they're after. We'll be running for the rest of our lives. You and Mum will never get any peace. And it's me they want. You'll be safer with me out of the way.'

'That's not the whole reason, though, is it?' Mr Bradbury's

voice was calm. 'It's not like I don't know where you're thinking of going.'

Terra paused, then said quietly, 'I'm sorry, Dad. But you understand. Of all people, you must understand. I have to find out what's happened. I have to see if he's all right.'

There was a pause. The only sound was the hum of the ship's gravity engines starting up.

'I'll come back,' said Terra at last. 'As soon as I know what's going on, I promise I'll come back.'

'It may not be up to you,' said Mr Bradbury quietly.

'Then we'll just be back where we started, won't we?' said Terra.

Another pause. The hum was building. Billy was pretending not to listen. Terra wasn't paying attention to him, anyway.

'I'll call,' said Terra.

'You'd better,' said Mr Bradbury.

'I love you,' said Terra.

'What am I going to tell your mother?'

'Tell her I love her too.'

Neither Terra nor her father said anything else. There was nothing else to say. After a few seconds Terra switched off the comm and exhaled heavily. She slumped back in the command chair and regretted it instantly as the ridged back support dug into her ribs.

Billy spoke at last. 'You didn't say goodbye.'

'And I never will,' said Terra.

Billy pointed at the comm. 'Can I call my dad before we leave?'

'We left about three minutes ago,' said Terra, turning to the control console.

'What?' yelped Billy. He scampered across to the only porthole he could see in the ship's walls. Earth, a half-lit crescent, was receding from view already.

'That's the thing about gravity engines,' mused Terra. 'You don't really notice you're moving.'

'But I wanted to call my dad,' muttered Billy.

Terra glanced at her comm. 'I've still got signal.'

'Up here? What sort of phone is that?'

Terra handed it to Billy, and he turned it over in his hands.

'An alien one, obviously. Make it quick, we'll be out of range soon.' Terra turned back to the console.

As Billy examined the comm, its screen configured itself into a keypad, with familiar Earth digits. He tapped in his home number, adding the international dialling prefix. (He thought this was probably a good idea.)

'Hello?' His mum's voice.

'It's Billy, Mum. Is Dad there? Could you put him on?'

Billy sank back into his chair. Terra noticed that Billy's chair, unlike her own, had sturdy-looking restraints built into the armrests and base. *Those will have been for me,* she thought.

After a few seconds. 'You all right, Bill? How was the movie?'

'Dad. You know you always told me to think of life as an adventure?'

'Yes?' A note of trepidation.

'Well, I think the adventure's starting, Dad. I can't quite explain, but I won't be home for a while.'

'Are you okay, Bill? You're not in trouble, are you?'

'No. No, I'm not in trouble, Dad. But I'm off on a journey, and I know you'd be okay about it if you knew where I was going.'

'You can't tell me? You can't tell me where you're going?' Not panic, just intense curiosity.

Billy swallowed hard. He stood up and went to the porthole. Earth was a tiny blue sliver of light. 'Look up, Dad. Just ... look up.'

Silence, except the gentle hum of the gravity engines.

'I'm losing signal, Dad. I love you.'

Billy wasn't sure he'd actually ever said that before.

'I love you too, Bill.'

The comm beeped. The keypad disappeared, replaced

by a jumble of strange symbols. Billy looked through the porthole. Earth was a blue dot.

'You'd better sit back down,' said Terra, as a high-pitched whirring sound started to come up through the floor. 'That's the neutrino shunt kicking in – we're about to go infra-light.'

'Like in *Star Wars*?'

'Bit of a confession, Billy – I still haven't seen *Star Wars*.'

Billy scrambled into his chair. 'Don't bother with the prequels,' he said.

I.7

Phil 'Sparky' Sparks was in pain, and annoyed. Annoyed with himself at forgetting one of his own golden rules (ALWAYS pay one last visit to the gents' before the pub closes; even if you don't feel like you need it now, you will the minute the door shuts behind you). Annoyed with the Duke's Arms for selling such weak lager so cheaply. Annoyed with his friends for having bought him quite so much of it, and just annoyed in general that there didn't seem to be any public toilets in this country any more.

With a mounting sense of urgency, Sparky surveyed his surroundings. His bleary eyes darted left and right, desperate to see an open late-night café, kebab shop, 24-hour garage, anywhere he might be able to empty his straining bladder in warmth and comfort and without fear of arrest. No such refuge was to be found. Sighing, and wincing, Sparky abandoned all thoughts of propriety and dignity and hobble-shuffle-scampered into the back entry behind the cinema.

Having looked over his shoulder to check that he had put enough distance and darkness between himself and the street, Sparky now peered into the gloom of the alley in order to pick the least appalling spot in which to perform the necessary. He spied a pile of bin bags, split, teetering, disgorging their fetid contents onto the concrete. Ah, well, he thought, that corner already stinks.

Sparky put one hand out to steady himself against the wall and set the other to work fiddling with his zip. His foot shifted, nudging the bin bags. The bin bags nudged back.

Sparky paused with his zip-fiddling, the pain in his

bladder suddenly overruled by curiosity. His eyes struggled to pierce the darkness. Was there someone under the bin bags?

He reached out. His hand touched cold plastic, searched below, found ... bone? ... shell?

The pile of bin bags exploded outwards. He saw something – alive, man-sized, but very definitely NOT human. He glimpsed claws, shiny, segmented limbs, eyes. A glimpse was all he needed. Sparky fled, wailing, into the street, having forgotten all about why he went into the alley in the first place, and only dimly aware of a spreading warmth that told him it was too late to worry about that now, anyway.

* * *

David Crew was a kindly but serious-minded individual. In particular, he took his responsibilities as a police officer extremely seriously. Even when off duty, he maintained an instinctive level of vigilance. He was 'never off', as Karen would remark to her friends, but then, she would remind them (and herself), that was one of the reasons she'd married him.

So when, on their way home from their favourite Indian restaurant, they heard the sound of a man screaming in pain and/or terror, and David immediately ran across the street to investigate, Karen felt neither alarmed nor abandoned, just proud. That's my Dave, she thought as she watched him go.

The man who emerged wild-eyed and babbling from the alley behind the cinema cannoned into David and yelled something which sounded like 'It's not human' before pushing past him and running away into the night. David Crew let him go; he wasn't making much sense and he smelled terrible. Besides, David now heard the screams of a young girl coming from the darkness. He ran, undaunted, towards the sound.

David's keen eyes adjusted to the gloom; there was

a teenage girl, maybe fourteen or fifteen years old, long blonde hair, standing next to a pile of bin bags. Her face was set with terror. 'What happened?' he asked.

The girl pointed upwards. 'Up there,' she said in a quavering voice. 'It climbed up there. It was like … Like a huge … I don't know what it was.'

David looked in the direction the girl was pointing. A blank wall; no signs of anyone or anything alive. 'It's okay,' he said to the girl, 'come with me and I'll get you some help.'

He turned. The girl was gone.

* * *

Throx of the Morbis Guild, once again wearing his human girl disguise, slipped quietly through the alley. The helpful human male hadn't seen him leave. His optical camouflage system had taken a second to reinitialise. The fool who'd glimpsed him undisguised had been intoxicated; he wouldn't be believed.

None of this altered the fact that this had NOT been a good evening.

Throx of the Morbis Guild had allowed his mark to escape. She'd incapacitated him and left him helpless on a potentially hostile world. And as he activated his gravity bubble and ascended to the roof of the building, Throx realised that his evening had just got worse.

She'd taken the ship.

Throx made a mental note to convey his displeasure to his clients with regard to the extent to which they'd under-estimated the Terra girl's intelligence and resourcefulness. Just a dumb Ymn, he'd been told. A simple job for a member of the esteemed Guild. He should have charged double what he had.

He'd had to purchase the extremely advanced optical camouflage system at his own expense, and spend many uncomfortable sessions with his cranium jammed into an ill-fitting interface in order to absorb enough of the Ymns' puerile culture to pass himself off as one of them. He'd thought of everything and yet somehow the Ymn girl had seen him coming.

Throx was the first Tastak – the first insectoid of any species – to gain entry to the Morbis Guild, the most feared and respected society of assassins, thieves and mercenaries in the galaxy. His own reputation – and that of the Guild – was at stake. He wasn't about to let it be tarnished by some nasty little pink mammal. This job was far from over.

His ship was gone and there was no way to procure a replacement on this primitive rock. Very well; if he couldn't go after her he'd have to persuade her to come back. What he needed was leverage.

Throx activated his mini-slate and accessed 'Lydia's' home address. 'Tracey' was going to call on her classmate's parents tomorrow.

1.8

'Where are we going?' asked Billy. 'And don't say "space". Way too vague.'

'The ship's navs were already set. We're going back to wherever its last stop was before it came to Earth,' said Terra, waving at a readout which looked to Billy like a crazed screed of pictograms. Billy had no idea if it meant anything; occasionally Terra would peer at it through that (extremely cool) translucent computer tablet-thing of hers, but all that this achieved was to translate one lot of weird alien symbols into another lot of weird alien symbols. Of course, thought Billy, that must be Fnrrn. The language of her adopted homeworld.

'Is that good?' Billy wondered.

Terra turned to face him. 'For the last two years I've been pestered by alien bounty hunters. Your little girlfriend back there was just the latest. I want to find out why, and at that rendezvous point' – she gestured towards the readout – 'there may be someone who knows.'

'And I suppose you have a plan for what to do when we get there?'

'We've got a few hours,' said Terra, getting as comfortable as possible in the command chair. 'I will have by the time we arrive.'

'Can I ask a question?' asked Billy.

'Why stop now?' Terra smiled.

'Why me?'

Terra frowned and wrinkled her nose.

'Why are you bringing me with you? I'm not going to be any use to you. I'm just going to slow you down, maybe even mess up and get us into trouble.' Billy crumpled a little at the thought of this, then recoiled when Terra stood up and loomed over him, as best a shortish girl in baggy clothes could.

'Now listen to me, Billy Dolphin. Ever since we met I've had to put up with you whining and moaning about how I ruined your life without you even knowing it was me you were moaning at. But,' she went on, sitting back down, 'you've been a good friend. Possibly the first human friend I've ever had. And tonight, being my friend nearly got you disintegrated. So I think I owe you.'

Billy had no idea how to respond. Fortunately Terra wasn't finished. 'Remember I said I thought you were just jealous? Jealous of me, 'cos I'd actually been to space and you hadn't?'

'Yes?'

Terra pointed out of the porthole. 'Well, there you go, then,' she said. 'No reason to feel jealous any more.'

Billy went to the porthole. Space. Your actual deep proper real genuine final frontier these are the voyages space. He beamed.

'Besides,' said Terra, putting her trainered feet up on the console, 'I'm starting to figure out that plan, and you're a big part of it. Now get some sleep, I'm going to.' She pulled her woolly hat down over her eyes.

1.9

Throx checked his reflection in the mirror of a parked car. Tracey looked as immaculate as ever. He adjusted his virtual hair and walked up to the front door of the house. He didn't need to check the address. He'd memorised it.

He'd used a depressingly simple Ymn communication device ('phones', they called them) to contact the girl's parents and get himself invited to their home. All too easy. He rang the doorbell.

An adult Ymn female opened the door. She held one of those rudimentary opaque metal slate-like devices that Ymns were all so impressed with.

'Yes?' asked the woman Throx recognised as Mrs Bradbury, although none of her current neighbours would be familiar with that name.

'Hello, I'm Tracey,' said Throx. 'I called earlier, remember? I'm a friend of Lydia's. I lent her some study notes, and I'm afraid I need them back. You said this would be a good time to come round.'

'Oh that's right, come in,' said the woman. 'I'll see if I can find them for you.' The Ymm seemed distracted but not particularly anxious; was it possible she didn't even know her child was gone?

Throx smiled gratefully – or at least his digitally gener-ated Ymn face did – and stepped into the house.

'Can I get you something? Tea?' asked the woman. Throx replied that that would be lovely, and looked around at the house's furnishings. Soft. These Ymns needed a lot of comfort. Weak.

Once he had the Terra girl's family hostage, he would send a signal to his ship. Terra would be given the choice;

return to Rrth, or he would employ all the many pain-giving techniques he had learned during his Guild training on first one, then the other of her parents. Throx didn't know how long a Ymn could survive his attentions. He was eager to find out.

He followed the woman into what appeared to be the food preparation chamber. She had picked up a sort of water jug from which a cable dangled, and was staring at it, seeming puzzled.

'Now,' said the woman, 'how do you suppose this thing works?' She smiled and put the jug-thing down on the counter. 'I really should have figured that out, shouldn't I?'

Throx stood in perplexed silence.

'So, I'm guessing … Morbis Guild?' asked the woman cheerfully.

'W-what?' stammered Tracey/Throx.

'It's the optical camouflage. It's quite convincing if you don't know what to look for. I do, of course. The hair pixel-lates when you turn quickly. Now, look at this—'

The Ymn female seemed to warp and shimmer. Suddenly Throx found himself addressing an adult female, but not a Ymn. The grey-blue skin, the black oval eyes, the smug presumption of intellectual superiority … He had always hated Fnrrns on sight; he saw one now, and hated it ac-cordingly.

'THAT's optical camouflage,' said the Fnrrn female cheerfully. 'Completely undetectable, either organically or mechanically. You won't have seen anything like it, of course. I've been monitoring the calls made to this house. I intercepted yours, and made sure you'd get here when these nice people were elsewhere. They've had a trying day and need some time to themselves.'

Throx had no idea what was going on and he didn't care. He just knew he'd had enough of this planet. He deacti-vated his own camouflage system and stood, glistening and black, in the suburban kitchen.

'There, that's much comfier isn't it.' The Fnrrn smiled.

'Now, you are NOT supposed to be on this planet, and neither am I, so why don't we try to sort this out in a civilised fashion? Of course, I'm not even supposed to be in this—'

Throx decided he'd also had enough of this prattling Fnrrn. She fell satisfyingly silent at the sight of the blast-tube he now brandished at her.

The silence didn't last.

'Is that a Frastik-Jalga blast-tube? I haven't seen one of those for AGES. I take it you've never seen this kind of body armour before, then?' She indicated the shiny metal plates dotted about her clothing. 'It's the latest thing and, I'm afraid, very effective against blast weapons. You see it doesn't just deflect blast energy, it actually refocuses it—'

Throx could stand it no longer. He set the blast-tube to 'obliterate' and fired.

'—back towards its point of origin. Oh dear,' continued the Fnrrn female, addressing the cloud of smoke which a second earlier had been Throx of the Morbis Guild.

She checked her chronoscope. The real Bradburys would be back in exactly six blips. A shame about the Tastak, but the galaxy still had plenty of thieves and assassins.

She heard the key in the door. Time to go. Lots to do, lots to do. With a faintly audible pop, the Fnrrn female vanished.

Mr and Mrs Bradbury helped each other in with the shopping. Mrs Bradbury dumped the bulging plastic bags on the kitchen table and sighed heavily.

'Are you okay?' asked her husband, placing an arm around her shoulder.

She sniffed. 'I will be.'

'I guess we always knew this would happen,' said Mr Bradbury, taking his coat off.

'I know, I know. I just hoped she'd be a bit more ... grown up.'

Mr Bradbury smiled. 'She'd changed the course of history on two planets by the age of twelve. Grown up is

44

a relative concept. She belongs out there as much as she belongs down here.'

'That's just it,' said Mrs Bradbury, her voice cracking, 'I'm not sure she belongs anywhere.'

A heavy silence; the kind that is best broken by putting the kettle on.

Mrs Bradbury picked up the kettle to fill it. She noticed it was unplugged for some reason. She was about to ask her husband if he had unplugged it, but he spoke first.

'You smell something?'

I.IO

Strannit Zek checked the clock. Thirteen gafgafs past shoob. The Tastak was late.

He heaved his bulk – considerable even by Kotari standards – off the couch and lumbered towards the communications console of his ship.

The ship was expensively furnished; finely upholstered couches, thick carpeting and art treasures from many worlds proudly displayed. It was Strannit's only home, and he liked his comforts.

The Kotari lived almost exclusively in space. There had been a Kotari homeworld once; no one even knew where it was now. Some said it had been polluted into uninhabitability; some said it had been devastated by an asteroid; others said (but never in the presence of a Kotari) that the race had been wandering the stars for so long that they had simply got hopelessly lost.

Some of Strannit Zek's people had settled on habitable worlds, but this was frowned upon by conventional Kotari. Most of them adhered to the nomadic tradition, speaking disapprovingly of the 'dirtfoots' as they called their planet-bound relatives.

The Kotari were traders. Whatever you might want, they would have it – or could get it for you. They would deal in any and all commodities, big and small, legal and illegal, live and inanimate.

At war with a neighbour who has you outgunned? The Kotari will ensure your enemies are stricken by a mysterious plague. For a price.

Planet stricken by a mysterious plague? The Kotari will get you the medicines you need. For a price.

Need to extract a lone female adolescent from her off-limits world? The Kotari will hire someone who will bring her to you alive. For a price.

Strannit had put a lot of work the way of the Morbis Guild over the course of his career. They'd never let him down before. He'd been somewhat taken aback when the operative they had assigned had turned out to be a Tastak – he didn't know that the Guild even admitted insectoids – but the Tastak had seemed extremely professional and focused. Strannit had gone ahead with the deal, in spite of his misgivings.

Now the Tastak was late and Strannit was reminding himself always to pay attention to his misgivings. He prodded at the communications console with a fat blue finger and spoke.

– Throx! Throx, are you in range? You're late, Throx! Another nine gafgafs and we'll be looking at deductions!

To his relief, the console lit up and a gravelly voice was heard.

– I'm inbound. Just come out of infra-light and with you shortly. I've got the item; it's intact as promised.

Item? Throx hadn't called the Ymn an 'item' when they'd discussed the job. He'd been content to call her a Ymn.

– 'Item', Throx? What's with the hard-being talk? If you've got the girl, just say so.

– I've got the girl. She's alive. Get ready to receive her.

The ship's proximity alert started beeping. Strannit checked the exterior visualiser; Throx's bug-eyed little ship was pulling alongside and extending a docking umbilical to connect with his own ship's cargo hatch. He dropped the ship's energy shields (an essential feature on any ship so laden with riches), deactivated the security protocols and opened the hatch. He hefted himself into a grav-chute and slid down to meet his visitors.

He emerged into the cargo hold just as the hatch swished shut. He was confused; standing before him was not a Tastak, but a Ymn. A youngish-looking male

(Strannit wasn't too familiar with the Ymn ageing process, but this one certainly didn't look very old). He was pushing a hovering stretcher, on which lay another Ymn, young again, possibly female, and unconscious.

- *Who the chak are you?* grunted Strannit.

- *It's me, you fool,* said the male Ymn. *Optical camouflage. I'm disguised as one of her little friends. That's how I bagged her. The system's on a timer, so I'm not exposed if I'm rendered unconscious. Stuck looking like this for a bit longer. Think you can handle it?*

Strannit made a gesture of benign disinterest, then waddled over to study the inert figure on the gurney. - *Is that it?* He frowned, his long snout quivering with distaste.

- *That's it. And it gave me a lot of trouble. A LOT of trouble.* A note of accusation in this last statement. Strannit felt the need to defend his professionalism.

- *I'm sorry if I gave you the impression this job would be easier than it was, but you must understand, I only have the information my clients supply me with. If they told me that the Ymn would be an easy mark I had no business telling you otherwise.*

The young Ymn's eyes narrowed. - *Perhaps I should take it up with them,* he hissed.

- *Out of the question, I'm afraid,* stated Strannit flatly. *I couldn't possibly divulge their identity. Confidentiality lies at the very heart of all Kotari transactions. As a member of the Morbis Guild, I'm sure you appreciate the importance of adhering to codes of professional conduct. Besides, if you'll pardon the vulgarity, should my clients and my contractors ever get talking to each other, they could decide to cut out the middle-being.* As a highly paid middle-being, Strannit wasn't about to let that happen.

- *In that case,* the young Ymn replied, *I might have to take my complaint back to the Morbis Guild. They may be able to think of some way of getting hold of that information. Bear in mind that when MY people decide to cut out the middle-being, they do it one piece at a time.*

Strannit paled from deep to royal blue. - *Oh come now,* he said. *It would never come to that. If the Morbis Guild found itself in dispute with the Walkers of the True Path,* he pronounced this with a knowing smile, *I'm sure it could be resolved entirely amicably.*

Naughty Strannit, he thought, giving away the name of your client. Still, it didn't sound like the Guild and the Walkers were likely to go into business together in the immediate future, quite the reverse in fact. A showdown between those two gangs of maniacs … Conflict always brought all sorts of lucrative opportunities for someone with contacts on both sides. Strannit silently congratulated himself on his own craftiness.

The young Ymn smiled coldly. - *That just leaves the matter of payment.*

Strannit got to his feet. - *Of course.* He waddled across to a decorated metal chest on the floor of the cabin. He flipped it open. It was full of silvery metallic strips.

- *Dolfric ingots, as agreed. Untraceable and good for trade in any system.* He shut the lid and went over to inspect the sleeping girl. Quite pretty in an alien way. Not for much longer, he suspected.

The Ymn bent to pick up the chest with one hand; he winced and dropped it the floor. The clang caused Strannit to wheel round in alarm.

The Ymn looked up at him. - *Could you help me get this to my ship? She managed to get a good wound in before I put her down.* He indicated one of his arms. *Like I said, trouble.*

- *Of course,* said Strannit, grunting with effort as he picked up the chest. Not the sort of work he relished, and he was glad that none of his fellow traders were there to see it (he'd never have heard the end of it at the next Traders' Association Hapto-Shan party), but the sooner he got this surly wokker off his ship, the better.

Strannit struggled through the umbilical, his feet sticking to the attraction strip running along its floor; at least the chest's weight was annulled in the umbilical, along with his own. Another being of Strannit's size might have relished a brief burst of weightlessness, but Strannit had worked hard to attain his bulk and was proud of it. He had to bend low to pass through the bug-eyed ship's hatch. He gasped as he entered the little ship's internal gravity field, and sighed gratefully as he lowered the chest to the floor of the poky flight cabin.

A sound came from behind him. A familiar sound. The sound of his own ship's hatch sliding shut. He spun around in alarm.

Strannit struggled out into the umbilical and looked at the closed hatch. There was a small triangular window set into it. Looking through this window was the smiling face of the perfectly conscious Ymn girl.

- *The Walkers of the True Path, is it? Be sure to give them my regards and tell them I'm sorry I couldn't make it,* said Terra.

- *Open that door!* shouted Strannit.

- *Now why would I want to do that?* Terra replied.

Strannit's mind raced. His powers of persuasion were legendary, if he did say so himself. He had urgent need of them now.

- *I'm sure we can come to some sort of arrangement.* He smiled.

- *We have come to an arrangement. I'm in here and you're out there,* said Terra. *I like this arrangement.*

- *Now be reasonable, young Ymn,* said Strannit with his most ingratiating simper. *What have I done to you?*

Terra's nose wrinkled and her eyebrows became horizontal. - *You mean other than hire a giant insect to abduct me so you can sell me to a bunch of savages?* she asked. *Is that a trick question?*

- *It was business!* squeaked Strannit. *A simple transaction! Nothing personal!*

- *I'm a person. Everything you do to a person is personal.* Terra frowned.

While Strannit struggled to think of a smooth rejoinder (and found none) he noticed that Terra's attention had moved from him to something on the other side of the hatch.

– *What are you doing?* gibbered Strannit, his face now sky-blue.

– *I'm trying to figure out these door controls. Is it the big orange pad that releases the umbilical?*

– *Y-yes*, stammered Strannit. *It's on a twelve–blip delay.*

– *Oh. Well, I'd get back into that little ship and shut the hatch if I were you, 'cos I pressed it about four blips ago.* Terra smiled.

– *No! No, look ...* Strannit pointed to the chest of ingots on the floor behind him. *I've got money!*

– *I don't want your money, I've got your ship. Bye now.* And Terra turned away.

Strannit scrambled into the Tastak ship and fumbled with the hatch controls. The umbilical started to make a high-pitched pinging sound. At the exact moment the little ship's hatch clicked shut, the umbilical disengaged. The whoosh of escaping gas sent the Tastak craft drifting away from his trading vessel; Strannit toppled over with the sudden movement.

Billy looked through the hatch window at the wasp-like Tastak ship as it drifted away. 'So that's what it looks like,' he said, reaching into his pocket and switching off the translation cube. Billy became aware that Terra was gazing at him in admiration.

'What?'

'That was ... AMAZING,' said Terra.

Billy shrugged. 'Did the trick.'

'What was that voice supposed to be? Clint Eastwood?'

'Bit of Clint, bit of Jason Statham, bit of all-purpose tough guy.' Billy grinned, then coughed and rubbed his neck. 'Glad we got rid of the fat blue bloke when we did, my throat's killing me.'

'It was YOU who got rid of him.' Terra beamed.

'It was your plan,' said Billy.

'Yes, but, you played it so ... How did you come up with all that?'

Billy smiled. 'Remember, I go to that improv workshop at the Youth Theatre on Saturdays? Kept trying to persuade you to come along but you wouldn't. And there's the Golden Rule.'

Terra's nose wrinkled. 'Golden Rule?'

'When in doubt, just ask yourself: what would James Bond do?'

Terra shook her head and smiled. 'It's amazing you've lived this long. Come on, we've got another spaceship to try to figure out.'

* * *

Strannit saw his ship drift out of sight and then gazed glumly at the interior of the Tastak vessel. On the navigation console lay the navigation computer, ripped from its housing, a mess of crystal circuits and bio-cabling. In a little while the Walkers would arrive to collect their prize. He doubted he'd have drifted far enough by then.

Strannit took a deep breath. It was fine, it was all right; he could explain everything. He had a chest of Dolfric ingots and the fastest tongue in the galaxy. They'd come to some sort of arrangement.

Probably.

Strannit climbed into the command chair and winced. It was the least comfortable chair he'd ever sat in.

I.II

'**N**ow THIS,' said Billy, 'is a spaceship!'

In contrast to the Tastak vessel's cramped cabin and knobbly chairs, the Kotari ship's flight deck was like a cross between the bridge of the Next Generation-era Starship *Enterprise* and the drawing room of a medium-sized stately home. Billy gazed in awe at the technology and opulence, and then sank happily into what, if asked, he would have had to describe as the command chaise longue.

'Get out of there, you,' admonished Terra, 'unless you fancy trying to pilot it.'

Billy pulled a face, got out of the chaise and slunk across the flight deck to another, equally luxurious couch. As he flopped onto it, a harsh voice barked out something alien and unintelligible. Billy leapt to his feet, startled. Terra rolled her eyes in annoyance and took the translation cube out of her pocket.

'Computer,' she said, 'this is your new captain speaking.'

- MY CAPTAIN IS ALL-MONGER STRANNIT ZEK. I ACKNOWLEDGE THE AUTHORITY OF NO OTHER.

'Strannit Zek is no longer aboard this vessel. So either you can start taking orders from me, or we can drift in space until I die of old age and your reactors fail.'

There was a pause, and then the room was dominated by a holographic star-chart. Terra smiled. 'Seems like the Kotari program their computers to be just as self-centred as they are. Had a feeling they might,' she said to Billy.

- PLEASE STATE DESIRED DESTINATION, said the voice.

'Tftk system, fourth satellite,' said Terra simply. The

holographic star-chart started zooming in on a particular constellation. Terra leaned back in the command chaise and exhaled heavily.

'So now what?' asked Billy. 'Who are the Walkers of the … whatever it was?'

'The True Path,' said Terra. She sighed. 'They're a rumour. A nasty rumour.'

Billy sat up, his confusion and keen interest obvious. Terra went on.

'The planet where I grew up …' she said.

'Fmrrm?' ventured Billy.

'Fnrr,' corrected Terra. 'There was a war. A nation called the G'grk invaded my island, Mlml. They were going to enslave the adults and conscript the young as child soldiers. I … managed to stop it.'

Billy had read something about this, about how a human child had stopped a war with a song, of all things. He was sure there was more to it than that but didn't want to interrupt.

'There was a peace treaty. The G'grk leader, Grand Marshal K'zsht, renounced war and retired. He was the first Grand Marshal ever to retire alive. That freaked them all out a bit back in the G'grk homeland, but they respected K'zsht enough to go along with it. He nominated his grandson Zst'kh to succeed him. His grandson said he was going to carry on with the peace process. This disappointed some of the G'grk, who thought the young Grand Marshal would go back to their old warrior ways. There were reports that a hardline G'grk faction, the Walkers of the True Path, had broken off from the nation and left the planet. They were supposed to be plotting to return to Fnrr, overthrow the Grand Marshal and start the war up again. With Sk'shk as the new leader.'

'Sk'shk?' asked Billy.

'The old Grand Marshal's deputy,' said Terra with a shiver that Billy felt from across the room. She remembered being on her knees on the cold, quartz floor of the council dome … The harsh, ranting voice … The gleaming, curved, bronze blade of that sword, that sword … Being more afraid than she – surely than ANYONE – had ever been.

'Where is Sk'shk?' asked Billy.

Terra took a deep breath and composed herself. 'Nobody knows. Banished somewhere. The Walkers were supposed to be looking for him. And me. They haven't forgiven me for embarrassing them so much.'

Billy sensed Terra's fear. He steered the conversation towards a more general take on the topic. 'So the Walkers are planning to attack Fnrr?'

Terra's face fell. 'If they haven't already,' she said quietly.

'What?'

Terra looked at Billy. There were tears in her eyes. 'I haven't heard anything from Fnrr in months, Billy. My last visit from my stepfather was well over a year ago. My last message came shortly after. Then nothing. I've been calling and calling on that alien phone-thing and no reply. And if any of the human politicians or scientists have heard anything, they haven't told me. I'm afraid something terrible has happened.'

Terra got up and stared at the holographic display. Stars rushed past her as the star-chart zoomed in on their destination. She went on: 'My human parents – they love me, they love me so much, and they suffered so terribly for so long, but they don't … GET me. No one on Earth really gets me. There's only one person in the galaxy who gets me, and I don't know whether he's alive, dead, or—' Her voice cracked. Billy got up and placed what he hoped were comforting hands on her shoulders.

'That's why I stole the bounty hunter's ship. I've got to find out what's happened. I've got to go—'

Go on, Terra, she thought. Say the word. The word you never say. The name you've never allowed yourself to call that place.

'I've got to go home,' said Terra. She looked at the little

orange-green holographic globe with its six holographic moons. Tears streamed down her face, and she found that she was smiling.

INTERLUDE

Perfect Day

The planet had been known by many names throughout its history.

Many civilisations had risen and fallen on its surface over the aeons, all coining their own names for their homeworld in their respective languages. But now the planet was home to a single culture, and was known by a single name.

Perfection.

Because it was.

The planet was inhabited by a unified, homogenised culture not as a result of war or conquest but as the product of a centuries-long process of peaceful unification. The philosophy of Sha'ha-las, the simple principle of equality and forbearance, had arisen on the island of La'Shul and spread from nation to nation, continent to continent, through sheer force of moral example. Sha'ha-las was simply, self-evidently, a better way to live.

The tenets of Sha'ha-las, as codified by the ancient philosopher-priests of La'Shul, were poetically phrased and eloquently succinct. They boiled down to three things: don't take what you don't need, help those who require it, and (most importantly) no whining.

Adherence to these three 'laws' (although 'law' was almost a forgotten concept on Perfection) had brought the planet to a state of universal peace and contentment.

There was no war on Perfection. What purpose would it serve?

There was no crime; no one wanted for anything.

There was no hunger, and little disease; with no misery to relieve, the citizens of Perfection's dietary habits were the healthiest in all the known worlds, and with few competing social or economic priorities, the planet's medical facilities were the best equipped in the galaxy.

There had not even been a natural disaster on Perfection within living memory. While this was, of course, nothing more than a bizarre coincidence, it was hard for the people of Perfection (and indeed others) to avoid the suspicion that Fate itself could not bear to mar such serenity with anything so vulgar as a flood or quake.

Life on Perfection could not be improved upon in any way.

And that, its people came to realise, was the problem.

PART TWO

Bring it on Home

2.1

'When I was a little boy,' said Billy, 'I went on holiday to Wales. We were supposed to set off on the Saturday, but Dad had a work thing, so we had to go on the Sunday instead. We were staying in this self-catering caravan and we didn't have room in the car to take any shopping with us. We decided to drop all our stuff off in the caravan, then go and stock up at a shop near the site. But could we find anywhere open? Not a thing. No big supermarkets anywhere in sight, just little local shops, all closed and shuttered up. We drove to the next town; it was completely silent and deserted. Same with the town after that. If we hadn't found a garage selling Pot Noodles we'd have starved until Monday. Nobody had warned us that Wales on a Sunday is like that bit at the beginning of *Day of the Triffids*. But compared to THIS' – he gestured around himself – 'Wales on a Sunday is like the Westfield Shopping Centre on Christmas Eve. What's HAPPENED here, Terra?'

'I have no idea,' said Terra. 'No idea at all.'

They stood on one of the main streets of Terra's home city of Hrrng. The familiar glass and steel spires glinted in the orange afternoon sun. Clouds drifted through the calm pink sky. It was the middle of what, by Terra's reckoning, should have been a busy day, but there was not a soul to be seen. Anywhere.

'I, er, take it it's not usually like this?' ventured Billy.

Terra shook her head.

Images and scenes from all sorts of movies that Billy was still too young to have seen legally began to flash through his mind. He shuddered and cast a look at Terra. He hoped she hadn't seen them. Instinctively, he took Terra's hand. She was trembling but trying not to let it show.

Billy was still running through the movie scenes in his head; finding himself unable to stop the procession of disturbing images, he decided to mine them for possible explanations. 'Disease?' he suggested, nervously.

Terra shook her head. 'The ship's scanners would have detected it and warned us.'

'What about some sort of infection that rips through the population, then burns itself out?' Billy went on. He had a feeling he'd read about such things. 'There wouldn't be anything left for the ship to detect.'

'Fnrr had a quarantine beacon, like most civilised planets,' said Terra. Billy chose to overlook the implied criticism of Earth and let her continue. 'If there were some sort of plague, they would have activated the beacon. We'd have been warned not to approach.'

'What if it were some sort of virus – or something – that wiped everyone out in seconds? What if there wasn't time to activate the beacon?' Billy was aware of the horror of what he was suggesting, and was reluctant to do so, but it was a possibility he felt they needed to consider. Fortunately it wasn't a possibility which seemed to trouble Terra. She shook her head emphatically.

'There'd be bodies everywhere.'

It was true. The streets were devoid of Fnrrns, living, dead or otherwise. There was no sign of catastrophe at all, in fact; no bodies, no burned-out buildings, no abandoned machinery. Whatever had happened, it appeared to have happened in an orderly fashion.

'Well, that's one thing,' said Billy encouragingly.

'What is?' asked Terra.

'Your angry warriors – the Walkers? They didn't sound like the kind of people who'd invade your city and leave it quite this ... tidy.'

Terra pondered Billy's words. It was true; whatever had happened here, her worst nightmare – the vengeance of the Walkers of the True Path – did not appear to have come true. That at least was encouraging. But it still didn't explain this.

They'd left the Kotari ship in stationary orbit over Mlml (Billy was beginning to wish they'd raided its considerable larders beforehand) and set off for the surface in Strannit's landing dinghy, still a far more comfortable ride than the Tastak vessel had been.

All the way down, Terra had been calling Hrrng traffic control, the Preceptorate – anyone on the surface – to try to tell them of their approach, but she hadn't managed to raise anyone. She was speaking a language that seemed to consist entirely of consonants; Billy couldn't understand a word, but he sensed her mounting concern and panic as they descended.

Terra's distress had only increased as they left the dinghy (parked invisibly in a well-maintained city park, its landing struts making dents in the tidy purple lawn) and walked into town, finding it silent and deserted. Now, as their eyes and ears searched in vain for any sign of life (or similar), Billy decided to take charge. Terra's breathing was quickening, he noticed, and her eyes were misting. If she were to succumb to panic, Billy realised, then they really would be in trouble, for however bewildered Terra might be, she had at least been here before.

'So,' said Billy with a lot more calm and focus than he was actually feeling, 'where to now?'

It did the trick. Terra blinked, swallowed and reached into her bag. From it, she produced her translucent tablet computer (her 'slate' he thought he'd heard her call it) and gazed at it. Her eyebrows knitted crossly. 'The Source is on,' she said. 'It's still active but it's locking me out. I can't connect, but at least there's still something to connect to. That's a start, I suppose.'

'What's the Source?' asked Billy. 'Is it like the Internet?'

Terra smiled. 'Yes, in the same way a jet fighter is like a

steam train. Come on.' She stuffed the slate back into her bag and strode purposefully off.

'We're going to the Preceptorate,' she announced over her shoulder. (Billy had so obviously been about to ask 'Where are we going?' that she thought she'd save him the trouble.) 'If there are any answers anywhere, that's where they'll be.'

Terra had set off at such a vigorous pace that she'd gone quite a distance before she realised Billy wasn't with her. She turned to see where he was.

Billy was sat slumped on the ground where she'd left him. 'Billy?' she called, concerned for his well-being (and her own – was there some sort of disease lingering after all?). He did not reply; she hurried back towards him. 'Billy!' she said again, more urgently.

He looked up at her. His eyes were moist and bleary. 'I'm sorry,' he sniffed, 'but it just hit me – I'm on an alien planet.' Billy smiled tearfully.

Terra gave him a very understanding smile. 'Alien to you, maybe,' she said, extending a hand. 'Come on.'

* * *

They pressed on through streets as strange to Billy as they were familiar to Terra, though their quietness and emptiness continued to disturb her. While he knew better than to say so, Billy found the solitude reassuring. Thus far he'd met aliens one at a time. The thought of suddenly being surrounded by them – on their planet, moreover – was unnerving, even if (as Terra assured him) these aliens would be by some margin the nicest he'd met thus far.

As they walked, Terra reminisced about her childhood in the city – pointing out a park where she'd played with her adoptive father, a building where her friend had lived. Billy suspected that this narration was less for his benefit than to keep Terra's mind occupied, to block the various nightmare scenarios he knew would pass through if she

66

allowed them to. He felt desperately sorry for her, and wretchedly powerless to help.

At last they arrived at the Preceptorate, which Billy recognised as some sort of college, except it seemed to be the size of a small town in its own right. They passed between towers and through open plazas, and still found no one. Then, rounding a corner, the first clue.

Terra flinched and gripped Billy's hand tight (he'd quite forgotten she was holding it). She was looking at what appeared to be a pile of rubbish, heaped up in the middle of a little five-sided courtyard. On closer inspection, Billy saw that rather than a jumble of objects, it was in fact a pile of many examples of the same object, a sort of desk lamp affair, with a glass shade and curved metal stem. All had been smashed.

'What are they?' he asked.

'Interfaces,' said Terra quietly. 'Someone's destroyed all the interfaces. Why would anyone do that?'

Terra had never been fond of the telemnemonic information transfer devices; her first experience with one had left her with singed hair and a blinding headache, but to see them smashed – deliberately smashed – chilled her to the bone. Billy did not recognise the shattered objects, but something about the pile of debris put him in mind of scratchy black and white films showing stacks of burning books.

Terra shuddered and led Billy away. They passed between a white-domed building and a curious twisting horn-shaped tower. Suddenly Terra let out an excited yelp. 'They fixed it!' she said.

Billy was greatly relieved to hear Terra sounding happy; he looked to see what had delighted her so. It was a statue; a blue metallic statue, some ten metres high. As they approached, Billy saw that the statue wasn't actually on the ground; rather it hovered a metre or so above its stone plinth, rotating slowly. He was interested to notice that this didn't surprise him in the slightest.

Terra danced happily over to the statue. 'It was smashed!' she said. 'The G'grk blew it up in the invasion! It's Tnk, the inventor of GravTech! All this, the whole Preceptorate, was down to him! I'm so glad that—'

Terra froze. She was looking up at the statue as it rotated. Her smile evaporated.

'Who IS that?' she said.

Billy looked up at the statue. He hadn't seen many Fnrrns – just TV pictures of Terra's stepfather in fact – and couldn't imagine he'd be able to tell them apart very easily. They didn't seem to have enough in the way of facial features. But he could tell, as the statue turned to face them, that something about its face had struck Terra as being terribly wrong.

'That's – that's not Tnk. Who is it?' Terra ran over to the plinth. She stared at the symbols carved into it.

'Gfjk-Hhh,' she said. She looked at Billy, her eyes full of tears and anger. 'WHAT is a Gfjk-Hhh?'

2.2

Terra and Billy stood beneath the turning statue that was not of Tnk, but of someone or something called Gfjk-Hhh. Billy sensed waves of sadness and anger coming from Terra and decided that who or whatever this Gfjk-Hhh was, he would be in serious trouble when Terra got hold of him.

Terra breathed deeply, then paused. 'Do you hear that?' she whispered.

'What?'

'That – listen,' said Terra quietly. Billy closed his eyes and listened. He heard nothing except the wind whistling between the buildings. After a second, it dawned on him that there was no wind. He opened his eyes.

'What IS that?' he asked Terra.

'It sounds like … cheering,' she said thoughtfully.

'That sounds like cheering? It's just a sort of faint hiss,' protested Billy.

Terra shrugged. 'That's how they cheer here. I think it's coming from the Gshkth Pit,' and she set off.

'Gesundheit,' said Billy, and set off after her.

* * *

The Gshkth Pit turned out to be a sports stadium, with a large circular stand. The streets surrounding the stadium were as deserted as everywhere else, but as they approached, the hissing cheers became identifiable even to Billy's ears. He remembered the translation cube in his pocket. He touched it to activate it and was startled when the sound became a full-throated bellow, such as might greet a goal in a sold-out football ground. Evidently the cube translated sounds as well as words.

'Terra,' he said over the noise. Terra jumped (she was still listening to the hiss, so Billy's shout rather came out of nowhere as far as she was concerned). 'Aren't we going to be a bit, well, conspicuous in there?'

Terra thought this over. 'It sounds like they're focused on other things,' she said. 'If we don't draw attention to ourselves we could be okay.'

Billy wasn't convinced, but he knew there would be no way to dissuade Terra from finding out what was going on inside that stadium.

They found a side entrance. It was unlocked and unguarded. They crept inside, climbing white stone steps. Emerging into the light, they crouched at the top of the steps, remaining as hidden as possible. This was what they saw.

The stadium was full to capacity, every seat occupied and yet more Fnrrns standing in the aisles. Billy's hair stood on end; to find himself literally surrounded by aliens was every bit as disturbing as he'd feared, except, as he reminded himself, he was the alien here. There were, by his estimation, at least ten thousand of them; taller, on average, than humans, grey-skinned, domed heads, black oval eyes. He'd seen TV pictures of Terra's stepfather soon after her arrival on Earth; he'd seemed harmless enough, on his own, surrounded by humans. This was different. This was VERY different. Billy felt horribly exposed and vulnerable. He tried to shrink into himself. He was under little illusion that it was making any difference.

Fortunately, the attention of all present was focused on the central pit. Terra noticed that while many of the Fnrrns were cheering with unfeigned enthusiasm, others seemed less sure, glancing around themselves nervously and occasionally letting out a half-hearted hiss.

At the front of the stand there was an enclosed area, which reminded Billy of the royal box, from which the

Queen (or nearest offer) would pretend to watch the FA Cup final. The enclosure was occupied by what looked like cowled monks, clad in white robes with hoods over their heads. Seated in the middle of this enclosure was a young Fnrrn in a resplendent green and gold robe, and an oddly shaped brass-coloured helmet. Terra tensed up.

'That's him,' she whispered to Billy, 'the statue; that's him.'

Billy peered at the robed Fnrrn; he was going to have to take her word for it. While he wouldn't have gone so far as to say that Fnrrns all looked the same to him, thus far they did all look pretty similar.

The green-and-gold-robed Fnrrn got to his feet. Behind him, an orange-clad guard stood up and bellowed, - *Love and glory to the Gfjk-Hhh!* and the crowd repeated this, some (Terra noticed again) more vigorously than others.

Terra saw that some among the crowd were clad in the same hooded, monkish robes as the Fnrrns surrounding the Gfjk-Hhh in his enclosure. They might be the 'party faithful', Terra thought. Was everyone else here under compulsion? If everyone had indeed been rounded up and forced to attend this event, whatever it was, that did at least explain the emptiness of the streets. Of course, even at full capacity, the stadium couldn't hold more than a fraction of the city's population. Perhaps those who couldn't attend in person had been ordered to stay at home and watch on the visualiser? It was a theory, and one that Terra found vaguely reassuring, but she still didn't like the look of this Gfjk-Hhh character one bit.

This Gfjk-Hhh character spoke.

- *Beloved children! Are you ready for some GSHKTH?*

The crowd cheered with varying degrees of commitment. Is that all we're here for? thought Terra. To watch some gshkth? She'd played gshkth herself at the Lyceum. It had never been regarded as a big deal. The Gfjk-Hhh continued:

- *Captain, who do we have to entertain us today?*

The guard (Guard Captain, evidently) produced a paper-like scroll (paper – here? thought Terra) and read aloud:

– *We have Crkl-sh-Gkh-sh-Lfft of Jfd-Jfd, Luminescence.*

A scared-looking Fnrrn was pushed out in front of the 'royal box' by two more guards.

– *Ah yes, there he is,* said the Gfjk-Hhh cheerfully. *What's he been up to, then?*

– *Sedition, Luminescence,* said the Captain. The Gfjk-Hhh flopped into his seat, looking comically bored.

– *Sedition AGAIN?* he asked. *Is that the only thing anybody ever gets arrested for these days?* He stood up and bellowed, *Doesn't anyone just STEAL anything any more?*

There was a tense silence. The Gfjk-Hhh's face split into an expectant smile. Realising that he'd made a joke, the crowd began to laugh. At first nervously, then loudly, eventually hysterically, as if everyone present was afraid to be seen to be finding the Gfjk-Hhh's pleasantry less hilarious than their neighbour.

The Gfjk-Hhh sighed theatrically. – *Fine, sedition, whatever. In he goes.* The guards holding the scared-looking Fnrrn shoved him into the pit. He landed with a painful-sounding thud, then stood up, evidently unhurt, but terrified.

– *Next player!* barked the Gfjk-Hhh, rubbing his hands together as another Fnrrn was dragged before him.

The Captain read from his scroll. – *Pfftl-sh-Bknp-sh-Thrk of Fzkl, Luminescence. Arrested for—*

The Gfjk-Hhh interrupted him. – *Altogether now!* he shouted.

– *SEDITION!* shouted the crowd.

– *Erm … no, tax evasion, actually, Luminescence,* said the Captain a little nervously.

– *Really? Almost as bad. In he goes.* The Gfjk-Hhh smiled, and the second Fnrrn was pushed into the pit alongside the first. The two prisoners eyed each other nervously.

This was repeated twice more; two more prisoners were paraded, two more charges were read out, two more scared Fnrrns were pushed into the pit.

- *Right! If we're all here, let's play!* declaimed the Gfjk-Hhh, to more cheers.

The Gfjk-Hhh approached the pit. In each hand he brandished two gfrgs, the curved sticks with which one played gshkth. - *Now then*, he said, *everyone knows the rules of gshkth. Last one standing wins a reprieve; the other three ... don't.*

Terra noticed something odd about the gfrgs. They seemed to glint in the afternoon sun in a way she'd never seen gfrgs shine before. Edging forward, apparently willing to risk being seen, she stared at the objects being held aloft by the Gfjk-Hhh. As he tossed them into the pit, she gasped in horror.

The gfrgs had blades. Long, sharp metal blades.

This was not gshkth. This was some hideous perversion of gshkth. This Gfjk-Hhh had taken a harmless – if rigorous – game, and turned it into a method of execution. Anger and disgust welled up inside her, in a way she simply couldn't contain.

- *NO!* screamed Terra.

Thousands of grey heads, thousands of pairs of oval black eyes, turned to look at her.

'Nice not attracting attention to yourself there,' hissed Billy.

The Gfjk-Hhh, startled by the sound and by the hushed reaction it provoked, got to his feet and stared right at Terra. A succession of emotions passed across his face; confusion, surprise, perhaps a little revulsion. Finally, a broad smile.

- *Well now*, he said, *look who came home. GET HER!*

2.3

Terra felt a hand tugging violently at the back of her hoodie.

'Come ON!' shouted Billy.

Terra took one last horrified glance at the Gshkth Pit and then hurtled back down the white stone steps into the dark interior of the building.

The assembled spectators had taken a moment to respond to the Gfjk-Hhh's command, and indeed, not all of them had responded at all, but within moments there was a crowd surging down the steps after them. Two figures clad in the white hooded robes pushed their way to the front of the throng. As Billy fled, he stole a glance over his shoulder. He could have sworn that one of the hooded figures deliberately tripped the taller Fnrrn that was following, causing him to fall, which in turn caused the three or four Fnrrns behind HIM to fall. Soon there was a pile of grey bodies at the foot of the steps, while the hooded figure who had started the pile-up stole away unharmed. 'Did you see that?' Billy shouted, but Terra was too intent on running to hear him.

They came to a length of corridor. They were somewhere underneath the stands. Terra was racking her memory, trying to get an image in her mind of the layout of the place, when a door popped open. A voice, one Terra knew from somewhere, said, - *In here!*, and in desperate want of any better ideas, Terra rushed through the door, dragging a bewildered Billy with her.

Terra – and especially Billy – jumped with fright when the door closed behind them, and they found themselves alone in a tiny room with one of the hooded figures. Terra turned and began to struggle with the door catch when the voice said, - *It's okay! It's me! Terra! It's okay! And what have you done with the stuff on your head?*

The figure lowered its hood. It was Shnst. Or possibly Thnst.

Despite their many years together in the same class at the Pre-Academy, and later at the Lyceum, Terra had never been able to tell the twin sisters apart. At that moment she didn't care which one it was. She was so happy to see a friendly face that she nearly flattened Shnst (or Thnst) with her hug.

- *It's gone all short and spiky and it's a weird colour! Seriously, Terra, what have you done with it?*

- *Never* (Terra thumped Shnst or Thnst in exasperation) *MIND my hair, what's happened here? And what's with the costume?*

- *It's the uniform. The New Believers. We all have to wear them. He makes us.*

The door burst open and another hooded figure limped in. It was Thnst (or Shnst). - *Nice idea, of yours, sis, they all fell everywhere,* she said. *Hurt my leg a bit tripping that big f'zft up, though. Oh, there she is. What's she done with the stuff on her head?* she asked her sister.

Terra ignored this and continued with her questions. - *He MAKES you? How does he make you? And who IS he?*

- *He's the Gfik-Hhh,* said Shnst/Thnst. *He's in charge now.*

- *Yes, because of the prophecy,* said Thnst/Shnst.

The sound of the crowd rushing around the stadium in search of the humans rumbled through the walls and ceiling. Billy looked nervously at the door. Was it locked?

Terra was flabbergasted. - *Prophecy? What prophecy? This is Fnrr! This is Mlml! You don't do prophecies!*

Shnst and Thnst looked at each other. - *But it's true. He's the Gfik-Hhh and he's come back, like the prophecy said, so he's in charge now. There's nothing we can do.*

- *Come back? When was he here the last time?* The more

75

information Terra gleaned, the more confused she got. *When did all this happen?*

– *An orbit or so ago.*

– *That might explain why you haven't heard anything for so long,* said Billy, who then wondered why his mouth and throat felt so odd. Wait, am I speaking Fnrrn now? he thought. He took the translation cube out of his pocket and glowered at it suspiciously. He wasn't sure he liked the idea of it getting inside his brain like this, but as long as he could make himself understood ...

– *Who's this?* asked Shnst (Terra was fairly sure this one was Shnst).

– *It's another one,* said Thnst (probably).

– *Another one?* asked Shnst.

– *Another Ymn,* said Thnst. *Looks like a boy one.*

– *Is it a boy one?* asked Shnst. She turned to Terra. *Why have you brought a boy one?*

– *He's my friend Billy,* said Terra, *but he's not important right now.*

– *Oh, cheers,* said Billy.

– *What's important,* said Terra, ignoring him, *is where the others are.*

– *They ran away,* said Thnst. *Soon after the Gfjk-Hhh took over, Preceptor Shm and all the others went ... somewhere else.*

Terra breathed hard. Did that mean he was safe?

The sound of the crowd died away. Either the search had migrated to outside the building or they'd given up looking, Billy thought.

– *We don't all follow him,* insisted Shnst. *We have to wear these stupid robes and everything, but we don't all do what he—*

There came a thunderous knock at the door. – *Open up in there!*

They exchanged horrified glances.

2.4

Custodians Bktg and Slgf were annoyed. They'd been looking forward to the gshkth – they were fans of the Gfjk-Hhh's new improved version of gshkth – and it had been ruined by the arrival of the little alien interloper. They had no idea what His Luminescence had in mind for the Ymn when they caught her, but they hoped it was something nasty. Maybe something they'd get to watch.

They'd found a locked storeroom (which evidently no one had checked) and heard voices coming from inside. Now they were hammering on the door, and contemplating what rewards might await custodians who pleased the Gfjk-Hhh. They'd heard tantalising rumours.

The door opened. Bktg and Slgf saw four youngsters; two in everyday garments and two in the white robes of the New Believers.

- *Thank you!* said one of the youngsters. *They locked us in here!*

- *They're monsters! Aliens! Horrible!* said another one, who looked and sounded remarkably similar to the first.

- *They said they were going to the Forum to attack His Luminescence when he arrives! Quickly, you need to get there before they do!*

With thoughts of reward still fresh in their minds, the two custodians hurried away, with a shouted - *Love and glory to the Gfjk-Hhh!* as they left.

Shnst and Thnst looked at each other, and then at Terra and Billy. - *Well, THEY were stupid,* said Shnst.

- *If that's the average intelligence of the Gfjk-Hhh's followers, we should be okay,* said Terra, lowering the hood of her white robe. *Do you mind if we keep these? We won't last a blip out in the open without them.*

- *Listen, Terra,* said Thnst. *About what you said – about his followers being stupid. Take care. They're not all stupid. Some of them are very clever.*

- *And not all of us are resisting,* said Shnst sadly. *A lot of people were really happy when he took over. They said the government was useless and Mlml needed some real leadership, especially after nearly getting invaded. And what with the prophecy ...*

Terra snorted.

- *Don't laugh!* said Thnst. *They believe it. They really do. They think this is what's supposed to be happening. They believe he's meant to rule us. And when people really believe something ...*

- *There's no end to what they'll do,* said Shnst quietly.

There was a leaden pause.

- *Where to now?* asked Billy.

Terra looked hopefully at the sisters, but Shnst lowered her eyes. - *No,* she said, *not our place. You see, our parents ... they'd ... They wouldn't ...*

- *They're his,* said Thnst simply.

- *I see,* said Terra.

- *We'd better get home,* said Shnst. *Good luck.*

- *You too,* said Terra, and she hugged them both.

2.5

The Forum building in the centre of Hrrng was still known by that name, although the Forum hadn't been in session for a long time now.

On the benches where once had sat rows of sombre, robed delegates, now lounged a curious collection of characters. Bizarrely dressed courtiers, off-duty Retinue custodians merry on too much zft-zft, others sleeping this off, panicking servants cleaning up the mess. This was the Gfjk-Hhh's inner circle. Some he kept around because they amused him, some because they had some exploitable talent or other, many just because he enjoyed watching them trying to compete for his favours.

Busying through the crowd was Wffk. He'd been a lowly scrivener in the old Forum; recording the details of debates and meetings. Of course, every word spoken on the Forum floor had been electronically recorded since orbits past, but the post of Forum Scrivener had been preserved for reasons of ceremony and tradition. Upon his rise to power, the Gfjk-Hhh had kept Wffk on, since he possessed an almost extinct skill. He could write with a stylus on paper. The Gfjk-Hhh had employed Wffk as his personal scribe and clerk, mainly because he admired Wffk's immaculate handwriting.

Wffk peered disapprovingly at the jumble of bodies littering the Forum benches. His Luminescence demanded high standards in all things except the company he kept, reflected Wffk.

With a blare of trumpets, the doors to the chamber burst open and the Gfjk-Hhh swept in. The conscious ones leapt to attention as best they could; some of the others merely slid off the benches and onto the floor. The Gfjk-Hhh didn't seem to notice.

– *Is all well, Luminescence?* enquired Wffk.

The Gfjk-Hhh removed his brass-coloured helmet, handed it to Wffk and looked about himself in a distracted fashion. – *It has been … an interesting morning, Wffk. Most interesting. I think I need to speak to the Deceiver again.*

– *So early in the day, Luminescence? But you know it tires you so,* said Wffk with genuine concern.

– *Not today, Wffk. I think both he and I will find the conversation very stimulating indeed. I will speak with him now.*

Wffk, wary but acquiescent, stepped over a couple of prone bodies and led the Gfjk-Hhh through a small door behind what had once been the Chancellor's seat. This led to a short corridor, at the end of which a staircase – this part of the building predated GravTech by many eras – spiralled down through the floor.

Wffk and his master descended the staircase. At the bottom lay one of the Forum building's guilty secrets. A dungeon, an actual subterranean prison in which enemies of the state – or at least, enemies of whoever had been in charge of the state – had once been confined, in secret, in perpetuity. It had lain empty for eras. Until a few cycles ago.

The Gfjk-Hhh had been delighted to learn of the dungeon's existence shortly after taking up residence in the Forum building. It would be just the thing to contain the most treacherous criminal in the nation. The most dangerous mind he'd ever encountered. The Deceiver.

The Deceiver had been held there in isolation since the Gfjk-Hhh's earliest days in power. Few beside the Gfjk-Hhh knew of the Deceiver's presence below the Forum, and no one beside the Gfjk-Hhh was allowed to speak to him.

Wffk opened the door to the cell with a large black metal key and stepped aside to let the Gfjk-Hhh pass through it.

– *That'll be all, Wffk. I'll lock up after myself. Leave us.*

- Very good, Luminescence. Wffk handed the key over and stepped away silently.

Looking through the unbreakable crystal barrier (that he'd had installed especially), the Gfjk-Hhh could see the Deceiver slumped in a corner. He tapped on the crystal. No response. He tapped more heavily. He thumped on the crystal with his fist. The Deceiver stirred.

- That's better. Now come here! I need to talk to you.

The Deceiver did not get to his feet but swivelled round on the floor. He raised his eyes and fixed the Gfjk-Hhh with a look of pure hatred.

- What do you want? asked Lbbp.

2.6

T he Gfjk-Hhh smiled. - *Same as always – to talk. I mean, we could try playing dfsh, but I think this might get in the way.* He tapped on the crystal. Lbbp did not respond to the joke.

- *I've got nothing to say to you,* Lbbp said quietly, and turned away, leaning against the crystal.

- *Oh, but you have!* said the Gfjk-Hhh. *You still have so much to teach me! I couldn't have done any of this without you.*

Lbbp spun around to face him. - *YOU did this, whatever your name is. You did it all by yourself. Don't try to blame anyone else for what you're turning into.*

The Gfjk-Hhh's expression became one of hurt and astonishment. - *Blame? Blame for what? There's no blame to be shared here, Deceiver. I'm trying to share the credit for my achievements with you. Of course, strictly speaking, it isn't really you I should be thanking, is it?*

Lbbp's fists clenched a little tighter. The Gfjk-Hhh noticed this, and it pleased him. He went on, - *I mean, you're a tricky old f'zft and no mistake, but where did you learn it? You were just the same as the rest of us, weren't you? Truthful, literal ... boring. And then you found her.*

Lbbp screwed up his eyes tight, as if by shutting out the image of the Gfjk-Hhh he could shut out his words as well. But the words continued.

- *All those sneaky little Ymn tricks she taught you! Made quite the storyteller out of you, didn't she? But you were too timid, too ordinary, too SMALL to understand what you had! If you hadn't met me, we might never have achieved anything.*

Lbbp said nothing, just waited for it to be over, waited for the Gfjk-Hhh to get bored and go away, as he always did – eventually. But the Gfjk-Hhh wasn't finished.

- *But it really is all down to the little Ymn, when you think about it. What a shame I never got to meet her.* The Gfjk-Hhh crouched down to study Lbbp's face closely. *I know what you're thinking, Deceiver. You're relieved. Relieved she's so far away. Relieved she'll never know of your disgrace. Relieved she isn't here to witness my rule, that I'll never meet her ...*

The Gfjk-Hhh stood up and reached inside his robe. - *I have something to show you, Deceiver.* In spite of his better judgement, Lbbp opened his eyes and turned to see.

The Gfjk-Hhh held a slate.

- *I thought you were trying to ban those,* said Lbbp.

The Gfjk-Hhh smiled airily. - *You can still get hold of them if you know the right people. And I know ALL the right people, Deceiver. Everyone comes to visit me, sooner or later. For example ...* He held up the slate for Lbbp to inspect. *Just LOOK who turned up to the gshkth this morning.*

Lbbp's eyes, weary from so long in darkness, struggled to focus. The slate showed a crowd of Fnrrns, some robed, others in more normal garments ... and in the middle of them, what? Another figure, clad in ill-fitting, multi-coloured clothes, some sort of headgear ... hair? Oddly coloured hair? Pink skin? It couldn't be!

- *NO!* Lbbp hurled himself at the barrier.

- *And here I was, thinking you'd be pleased to see her,* said the Gfjk-Hhh. *I'M pleased. I've always wanted to thank her in person.*

- *If you hurt her,* rasped Lbbp. *If you TOUCH her ...*

- *You'll what? Beat yourself to death against the crystal? Be my guest. Although please,* the Gfjk-Hhh added imploringly, *don't do that while I'm not here. I'd hate to miss it.*

The Gfjk-Hhh turned to leave. He half-closed the cell door, then paused and said, - *I'll tell her you said hello.*

The Gfjk-Hhh locked the cell door and strode away. Even at the top of the staircase, he could still hear Lbbp pounding on the crystal and howling with rage and anguish.

2.7

The small door behind the Chancellor's chair burst open and the Gfjk-Hhh emerged into the Forum. His courtiers (at least those who were able) leapt to their feet at his approach.

- *Good session with the Deceiver, Luminescence?* asked Wffk.

- *He's feisty today!* The Gfjk-Hhh smiled. *Maybe a little too feisty. Reduce his rations by an eighth.*

- *Of course, Luminescence.* Wffk made a note on his scroll.

- *You were right, though. It has left me quite drained. I must retire for a while. I'll call if I need anything,* said the Gfjk-Hhh, proceeding towards his private apartments.

- *We'll be here,* said Wffk, following him along the corridor.

- *I know,* said the Gfjk-Hhh, and stepped through the door to his chambers.

The door swished quietly shut behind him. The Gfjk-Hhh exhaled heavily. He was alone. He could relax.

There was a large mirror covering one wall of the room. The Gfjk-Hhh had ordered it installed upon moving in. The chambers' previous occupant, the erstwhile Chancellor, had not felt the need to inspect her own appearance quite so frequently (or in quite so ostentatious a manner) as the Gfjk-Hhh. But then, she'd been a lot more secure in her own identity.

Until a couple of orbits previously, until the brief war with the G'grk, the Gfjk-Hhh had gone by the rather less prepossessing name of Bfgsh. Bfgsh had lived an unremarkable life, performing unremarkable tasks in an unremarkable fashion. He'd shown promise as a young

Fnrrn; his Lyceum reports would routinely acknowledge his keen intelligence but bemoan his lack of application. He was smart, very smart ... but he was lazy.

By the time the war started, Bfgsh had attained the most prestigious job he'd ever had; he was a cleaner, scrubbing and tending the hallowed halls of Hrrng Preceptorate.

The war and Bfgsh had rather passed each other by; he'd stayed hidden inside his cupboard on the morning of the G'grk assault, and hadn't even ventured outside later that same day when the cries of celebration had echoed through the streets. He took the sounds for G'grk victory chants; it was only when he heard familiar voices among the jubilation that the truth dawned.

Over the next few days, Bfgsh, along with everyone else on Fnrr, discovered what had happened; how the Ymn child had softened the heart of the fearsome Grand Marshal K'zsht with a 'snng', whatever that was, and how her guardian, a Postulator named Lbbp, had heroically risked his own life to protect the Grand Marshal from the fury of his own deputy, Sk'shk.

The relief and euphoria of the 'victory' (if that was indeed what it was; opinion was divided on this) soon palled in Bfgsh's case when two facts had dawned on him: firstly, that this meant he was still a cleaner at Hrrng Preceptorate, and secondly, that there was more cleaning up to be done at the Preceptorate than ever.

So it was an especially glum Bfgsh who, a few days after the brief war, now found himself tasked with sweeping up bits of debris in the Preceptorate's domed council chamber. His cleaning trolley's little GravTech motor had failed; he had to drag the thing over the quartz floor to get it into place. He didn't bother to check whether he was damaging the floor; repairing damage was someone else's department. He had only to concern himself with mess, and as he surveyed the chamber, he decided that there was more than enough mess to keep him occupied.

- Here, let me help you with that.

Bfgsh started. He'd thought himself alone in the chamber. A tall thin Fnrrn, a little older than himself, was extending a hand to him, offering assistance. Just the one hand, Bfgsh noticed; the other arm he held close to his body, as if it were injured.

Bfgsh smiled gratefully as the stranger helped him haul his trolley into position. He looked familiar, thought Bfgsh. Where had he seen him before?

It came to him. This was Lbbp! This was Postulator Lbbp himself, the hero whose bravery and selflessness had brought G'grk and Mlmln together and averted destruction. Bfgsh couldn't help himself. He turned to the stranger, - *I'm sorry,* he said, *but are you Postulator Lbbp?*

The stranger looked momentarily pained and weary, as if Bfgsh's question – honestly meant and humbly put – was a great burden to him. He made as if to reply to Bfgsh, then paused, a curious look on his face. As Bfgsh pondered the meaning of this, the stranger answered him.

- *No,* said the stranger. *A lot of people have asked me that. I think I must look like him.*

- *Oh,* said Bfgsh, disappointed. Odd, this tall Fnrrn did look a lot like Postulator Lbbp, he was standing in the very place where Lbbp had performed his now famous feat of bravery, he even (Bfgsh now noticed) seemed to have a sore shoulder much as Lbbp would certainly have, but he'd said he wasn't Lbbp, so he obviously wasn't. He wouldn't say it if it weren't true, would he? Why would anyone do something like that?

Bfgsh resumed his duties with even less enthusiasm as the stranger walked away.

* * *

It was a couple of days later that Bfgsh hovered through the window of his shabby apartment after a rather gruelling day's scrubbing and scraping (his sonic broom had packed in and there was no sign of the maintenance co-ordinator; he'd probably got himself killed in the invasion, the selfish f'zft), deactivated his gravity bubble and wandered into the servery to fix himself some configuration 8. The visualiser activated itself at his approach and began to show the local Hrrng news.

The main story was the departure of the Rrth-child. She'd been offered passage home as a reward for whatever it was she'd done to avert the war (Bfgsh was still a bit hazy as to how she'd managed that) and was being seen off with some sort of ceremony at the Forum square. There she was, a funny-looking little pink thing, with the Preceptor (Bfgsh thought that was him, anyway – the purple robe was the Preceptor's official garb, wasn't it?), the Chancellor, and—

It HAD been Lbbp!

Definitely definitely! That absolutely WAS the Fnrrn he'd spoken to in the council dome. There he was with his arm round the little alien, proud as Pfzk. And yes! The announcer had named him! He was Postulator Lbbp! Stepfather of the Ymn child Terra and hero of the moment.

Bfgsh's mind turned the facts over and over but couldn't get them to fit together. He'd said he wasn't Lbbp, but he WAS Lbbp. He'd said he wasn't, but he was.

What Lbbp had said – it wasn't true. Like the st'rss the Rrth child had got everyone telling each other. It was made up.

But it wasn't the same thing, was it?

St'rss, f'k-shnn, the books and plays, the imaginary histories which were now so popular on Fnrr – they weren't true, but they weren't MEANT to be true. You weren't supposed to believe them, you just pretended to believe them for as long as they lasted.

What Lbbp had said to him – Lbbp had intended Bfgsh to believe. He'd taken an untruth and presented it as a truth, in order to benefit himself. This wasn't f'k-shnn, this wasn't st'rss, this was …

There wasn't a word for it in the Mlmln language.

Bfgsh had a lot of trouble getting to sleep that night, his

mind buzzing with contradictions, paradoxes ... and just the faintest glimmer of possibility.

* * *

Bfgsh awoke the next morning with a start. He was lying on his sleep-room floor. His sleep-well had deactivated at the proper time, lowering him to the floor, but he'd been so exhausted it hadn't woken him up. He'd carried on slumbering, curled up in a heap.

Bfgsh leapt to his feet and checked the clock. Fifth spectrum-blue. He was late, very late.

He struggled into his work clothes and hurtled out of the window, just activating his gravity bubble in time to avoid a nasty, jolting drop.

He hovered frantically towards the Preceptorate, through deserted skies. Everyone else was already at work. He was in serious trouble.

He landed awkwardly on the street in front of the temporary cabin that his overseer, Dff, was using as an office while the building which had housed his old office was being repaired. (The G'grk had managed to destroy Dff's place of work while leaving Dff himself completely unscathed. Just one more thing Bfgsh would never be able to forgive them for.)

Bfgsh tiptoed around to the rear of the cabin, where his trolley was stashed, in the hope that he could collect it and set off about his tasks without Dff noticing his tardiness. But his trolley was nowhere to be seen.

– *I gave it to Hshk,* came Dff's voice from behind him. *We got tired of waiting for you so I sent him off to do your rounds.*

Bfgsh turned to face his overseer, his mouth moving silently in search of something to say.

– *I suppose there's a reason you're this late?* Dff went on. *A reason I shouldn't just fire you right now?*

Bfgsh's mind raced, and suddenly it was as if the top of his head had been prised open and glorious sunlight streamed into his brain.

- *Of course there is,* he said. *My apartment was burgled during the night.*

- *Burgled?* said Dff in alarm.

- *You know, when someone sneaks into your place and steals all your stuff.*

- *I know what it MEANS,* said Dff testily, but in fairness, not much of that sort of petty crime went on in Hrrng; not everyone would be familiar with the term.

- *Yes, they just sneaked in while I was asleep; cleaned the whole place out without even waking me,* said Bfgsh with what he thought was a most convincing shudder of horror. *So obviously when I woke up I had to call the Retinue, and THEY had to call the Municipal Investigators' office. I've been giving statements and making lists of missing items all morning. Wasn't allowed to leave until I was done. I would have called to tell you, but of course one of the missing items was . . .*

- *Your comm?* ventured Dff.

- *Yes, my comm,* smiled Bfgsh apologetically. His comm was of course in his pocket at that moment. He really hoped it didn't beep. It almost certainly wouldn't; at that moment Bfgsh was quite glad he didn't have many friends.

Dff grunted. - *Fair enough. Anyway Hshk's off doing your rounds, like I said, so today, you'll have to—*

- *Actually,* said Bfgsh, having another flash of inspiration, *before they let me leave, they sent for an Emotional Well-Being Specialist from the Brain Science Hub. Standard procedure, apparently. Anyway, she says I'm having a . . .* (take your time, Bfgsh, get this right) *a Severe Post-Traumatic Reaction, and I'm not to come into work until I've recovered.*

Dff's eyes widened. - *What, for the rest of the rotation?*

Bfgsh tried to look sorry. - *I think she said for the rest of the cycle, actually.* I am REALLY good at this, he thought.

- *The CYCLE?* spat Dff.

Bfgsh made a what-can-you-do-about-it face. - *Standard procedure, like I said. I wasn't even supposed to come in to tell you, but . . . you know . . . didn't have my comm.* Bfgsh smiled.

Dff gave a heavy sigh. It wasn't his place to question

'standard procedure', and now he thought about it, a whole cycle without having to look at Bfgsh's face was immensely appealing. - *Go on, then,* he said with a dismissive wave.

- *Thanks.* Bfgsh smiled. *I'll pop in once a phase to get my payment.*

- *Whatever,* said Dff, going back into his cabin.

* * *

Bfgsh spent most of the early part of his leave of absence asleep. He would wake in the morning, yawn, stretch, remember he had no work to go to, congratulate himself on his cleverness, reset his sleep-well and doze off again.

After a few days, boredom began to set in.

Bfgsh decided to test out some other applications of deliberate untruth. He crashed private parties, helped himself to goods and services free of charge, assuring the suppliers that payment would be forthcoming, then when some of these suppliers began to get impatient, he discovered ways of obtaining funds through duplicitous means; forging payment documents in the name of non-existent co-workers, going into the Mlmln National Repositorium and making hefty withdrawals from other people's accounts ...

By the time the cycle was over and his leave of absence was up, Bfgsh was, by his own standards, comfortably off. He never returned to his cleaning job and they never came looking for him to find out where he'd gone. They didn't check. That was something Bfgsh was beginning to realise. Nobody checks, he thought. Nobody ever checks.

Life went on in this happy, dishonest fashion for a few more cycles. Bfgsh, though sated and pampered, grew dissatisfied. There was more to it than this, he was sure. He was only barely tapping the potential of this way of life. The possibilities were, he was beginning to see, literally endless. What he needed was a plan.

Bfgsh decided to devote some of his limitless free time to a pursuit he'd never tried before. Bfgsh started reading.

He unpacked his new slate (- *Hello? I bought a slate from you last phase, and it didn't work properly. I've handed it in to the service department, but they said because it's a new one I should just come to you for a free replacement. Thank you, that's very kind*) and started to do some research.

The first thing he decided to find out was what the Ymns called what he was doing. LYING, they called it in one of their main languages, which, confusingly, seemed to be the same word they used in that language for how they went to sleep; Bfgsh couldn't tell whether there was a connection between the different uses of the word, but it didn't matter. He wasn't interested in the vagaries of Ymn linguistics. He was interested in how they USED these lies.

There was no end to the Ymn race's dishonest ingenuity. Life on Rrth must be very confusing, he thought. How would you ever know whether you were hearing the truth?

In particular, Ymns seemed very adept at lying their way into positions of power. The list of false kings, duplicitous ministers and crooked presidents went on and on – and those were just the ones who'd ultimately been found out.

Had that ever happened here?

Eagerly, Bfgsh looked into the question of whether anyone had ever deceived their way into a position of power or status on Mlml.

No one had, in the whole recorded history of the nation. What a sickeningly honest race he belonged to.

All right then, he thought, let's approach this from a different angle. Even if no one had deliberately used falsehood to advance themselves, surely not every claim to greatness had been genuine? There would never have been any conflict on the island at all if every leader had been unopposed, every transition from one regime to the next calm and orderly. Bfgsh knew from what little history he remembered from his time at the Lyceum that there had indeed been wars and conflict on Mlml, just not since eras past.

If there had been no fraudulent claims to greatness, had

there not at least been some sincere but mistaken ones?

Bfgsh changed his search parameters and tried again.

There he was.

The Gfjk-Hhh.

Back in the pre-rational epoch, in the eleventh era, a great tribal chieftain known as the Gfjk-Hhh had been the first to unite all the noble houses of Mlml under his leadership. The nation had been unified for the first time, after eras of squabbles and skirmishes between competing warlords and robber-shgfts. The Gfjk-Hhh had repelled foreign invasions, instituted law and order, founded the Hrrng Forum and established rights and freedoms for the people which Mlmlns enjoyed to this day.

All fine, honourable stuff, no deception or error there. But it was the second half of the entry on the Gfjk-Hhh which caught Bfgsh's eye.

The prophecy of his return.

After many orbits of wise and benevolent rule, death had come to the Gfjk-Hhh, as it must come to us all. But, so legend had it, with his dying breath, he had promised one day to come back, to rise from the dead to lead his people once more, in their time of direst need.

Whether the Gfjk-Hhh had actually said this, or whether (as was far more likely) this was something his surviving acolytes had made up to soothe the people's anguish at his passing, was of course anyone's guess. And back in those days, in the pre-rational epoch, when superstition and myth still had quite a grip on the minds of the populace, it wasn't uncommon for such predictions to be made. This was before science and reason became the foundations of Mlmln society, and people understood that it was impossible to foretell the future (until they built the Extrapolator, anyway).

As it was, the prophecy went unfulfilled, history moved on and the Gfjk-Hhh's name faded from general consciousness, to be replaced by those of more recent leaders and luminaries; Rspgh, Admiral Knssf, Tnk.

But it was a compelling story, thought Bfgsh. A great and benevolent leader, beloved and feared in equal measure, and a people awaiting his return ...

Bfgsh smiled. Their wait was almost over.

* * *

A cycle or so later, the Mlml Forum was mired in a particularly unproductive debate.

The Chancellor yawned and stretched in her chair as Delegate Bfftm's speech on the importance of drawing up a final and definitive phrasing for the peace treaty with the G'grk entered what, to her, felt like its third or fourth spectrum. If this was indeed such an urgent matter, why was he being so long-winded about it? As far as she could recall, the war itself hadn't lasted as long as Bfftm's summation of it. She pitied the Forum Scrivener, whose presence she barely registered in a chair just beside her own, having to note down every word of this drivel.

The Chancellor stretched again and looked up at the Forum ceiling. The repairs were complete now, but it didn't have the grandeur of the old one. She shuddered at the recollection of that dreadful morning, and tried to refocus her attention on Bfftm's dronings.

- *And furthermore,* said Bfftm as the Chancellor felt another drop of her remaining will to live ebb away, *if a lasting peace is to be maintained, it is vital – indeed, it is ESSENTIAL – that we ...*

She was jolted out of her reverie by a loud noise. Delegate Bfftm had fallen silent. For a sweet moment the Chancellor wondered if perhaps he'd been struck dead by some mysterious ailment, but, opening her eyes, she saw him still standing, looking around himself in bewilderment. The Chancellor heard that noise again, blaring, and realised that it was this that had stopped Bfftm.

A wave of panic passed through the Forum; memories of the G'grk assault sprang to everyone's mind and horrified glances were exchanged. The blaring sound was heard again.

But when the ornate (and immaculately restored) debating chamber doors flew open, what came through them into the room was NOT the G'grk. It was something else entirely.

Proceeding into the chamber there came the most curious parade. First, a column of some six Retinue custodians, clad in their accustomed orange overalls but with the addition of a green sash. Then, two Fnrrns bearing long metal trumpets. (These had been the source of the blaring, though since it was many orbits since a trumpet had sounded in Hrrng, the delegates stared at the long flared metallic tubes with mystified horror. Were they weapons of some kind?) Next, two standard bearers carrying long green banners. Then, borne aloft on a litter carried by four more bearers, a young Fnrrn wearing a long green and gold robe and an ornate brass-coloured helmet. He glared imperiously at the delegates as he passed between them down the chamber's centre aisle. Behind him, four more armed Retinue custodians completed the party.

The Chancellor shook her head, rubbed her eyes and leapt to her feet.

- *What is the meaning of—?*

The front column of custodians turned to face her. Their hands went to their holstered pulse-orbs.

- *You will address the Gfjk-Hhh only when spoken to!* barked one of the custodians.

- *The what?* said the Chancellor, who fell silent when another of the custodians drew his pulse-orb and levelled it right at her.

- *Outrageous!* shouted Bfftm, finding his voice again. *This is sedition! This is treason!*

- *No, sir,* came a loud but measured voice. *This is RESTORATION.*

Bewildered silence. The helmeted Fnrrn – the one who had spoken – descended from his litter and approached the Chancellor's chair. He held a cylinder in his hand, from which he now produced a scroll of a yellowed, paper-like substance.

- You recognise this, Honoured Chancellor? It's one of the six copies of the Scroll of Shnf-Shngst, the foundational document of this Forum.

- W-what does this h-have to—? stammered the Chancellor. The helmeted newcomer interrupted her.

- If you'll permit me – and you WILL permit me, the stranger said with a cold smile, *I'd like to draw your attention to the clause pertaining to the Laws of Succession.* He unfurled the scroll and pointed to a section of text. The script was ancient but clearly legible. The Chancellor peered at it.

- 'This Forum, being the creation of His Luminescence the Gfjk-Hhh, is endowed with all his powers and authorities and therefore licensed to exercise governance in his stead.' The Chancellor blinked and looked up at the stranger. *So?* she asked.

- You notice that final clause? 'In his stead?' What do you think that refers to, Honoured Chancellor?

The Chancellor paused, then replied, *- This Forum was founded in the eleventh era by the Gfjk-Hhh shortly before his death so that it could govern in his absence.*

The stranger smiled triumphantly. *- In his absence, yes. The Forum's authority is entirely contingent upon the ABSENCE of the Gfjk-Hhh. So if the Gfjk-Hhh were to return, all its powers, according to this document, would revert to him, isn't that correct?*

Snorts of derisive laughter were heard from all corners of the chamber. The guards glowered around at the delegates and the laughter subsided. Nonetheless, the Chancellor felt obliged to point out, *- The Gfjk-Hhh has been dead for over twenty eras!*

- But his return was prophesied, was it not? said the stranger.

- That's an absurd old legend, said the Chancellor dismissively.

- Old, certainly, said the stranger. *Legend, perhaps. But*

absurd? No, Honoured Chancellor. For you see, the stranger stood as erect as possible, *I AM the Gfjk-Hhh.*

- *Love and glory to the Gfjk-Hhh!* shouted the custodians. Whether they expected the delegates to join in, the Chancellor couldn't tell, but she was pleased to note that none of them did.

But before the Chancellor could even formulate any objections, let alone give voice to them, the stranger pulled another scroll from the cylinder. - *This,* he proclaimed, *is the transcript of the Gfjk-Hhh's final message to his people.*

- *That's been missing for eras!* cried one of the delegates.

- *It has recently been rediscovered,* announced the stranger.

Someone shouted - *Where?* but he ignored them and went on.

- *You will notice that it goes into far greater detail about the circumstances of the Gfjk-Hhh's return than has ever been known before. It gives the date of his rebirth — my own birth date. It gives the place — my own birthplace. It gives the EXACT TIME of the birth — my own. It states that the revenant will be known by a star-shaped mark on his upper arm — see!*

The stranger lifted his sleeve to show a dark blue birth-mark in the shape of a five-pointed star above the elbow of his right arm. This provoked a satisfyingly awe-struck gasp from the delegates. Good. It had hurt a LOT getting that birthmark done. The stranger continued.

- *And there is one final detail I trust you will find most ... illuminating.* He allowed himself a smirk at his clever pun-ning, then held up the scroll with a flourish.

The scroll was, in fact, illuminated. It bore a large, detailed, full colour portrait of the Gfjk-Hhh. None had ever been seen before. As the stranger turned slowly, displaying the portrait to all corners of the room, the delegates' doubts dissipated. It was him. The face on the ancient scroll was, without a shadow of a doubt, the face of this helmeted stranger.

There was a breathless silence.

The stranger noticed the Forum Scrivener, frantically making notes on his slate.

– *You there,* he said, *what's your name?*

– *My name?* The Scrivener couldn't remember ever being asked his name before. *It's Wffk.*

– *Wffk, eh?* The stranger produced a sheet of paper from his robe and handed it to the Scrivener. *Read that out, Wffk. Nice and loud.*

Wffk peered at the paper, coughed and then recited:

– *Love and glory to His Luminesence the Gfjk-Hhh, Champion and Defender of Mlml, Commander of the Platinum Legions, the Past and Future, the First and Last and Always. Love and glory to the Gfjk-Hhh.*

There was an icy silence. The stranger looked around expectantly at the delegates.

– *Just that last bit will do,* said the stranger, a smile of anticipation on his face.

The first response came – halting, hesitant, but audible.
– *Love and glory to the Gfjk-Hhh,* said one of the delegates.

– *Love and glory to the Gfjk-Hhh,* echoed another. And another. The words got louder, and louder, until it became a chant. – *LOVE AND GLORY TO THE GFJK-HHH!* The Chancellor, despairing, slumped back into her seat. The stranger closed his eyes and wallowed in it.

The chanting subsided. The stranger smiled at the Scrivener. – *I like you, Wffk, you can stay.* He turned to the Chancellor. *Honoured Chancellor . . . ?* his smile was reproving.

The Chancellor looked up. – *Yes?* she replied feebly.

– *You're in my chair.*

The Chancellor rose unsteadily to her feet. The Gfjk-Hhh – for, by whatever measure, that was who he was – flopped happily into the seat she had vacated. He gestured to one of the guards. – *Tell the others they can come in now.*

All the doors to the chamber flew open and many more custodians – all with green sashes over their orange uniforms – burst in. That's okay, thought Bfgsh (he would have to stop thinking of himself by that name). It's already over. They've already conceded. It's not a coup.

– *Honoured delegates!* the Gfjk-Hhh announced. *Thank you for your orbits of devoted service. You have the gratitude of the people of Mlml. And now, go away.*

Confusion. The delegates looked at each other, bewildered.

– *This Forum is dissolved. It no longer serves any function. I have returned. Enjoy your retirement, honoured delegates. Get out.*

The delegates hesitated. The custodians began to bustle them out of the chamber. A few protested; none resisted. The Chancellor was last to leave. She turned in the doorway.

– *You won't win, you know.*

The Gfjk-Hhh leaned back in the chair and threw a jaunty leg over one armrest. – *I already have. But I find I am a magnanimous ruler. So far. Don't push your luck, Honoured Used To Be Chancellor.*

With a tug from one of the custodians, the Chancellor was gone. The Gfjk-Hhh smiled at his loyal Retinue guards. It had been a very clever idea to work on securing their loyalty first – getting to know them, buying them drinks, promising to triple their pay with the savings he would make by dismissing all the delegates ...

The Gfjk-Hhh examined the two scrolls. One genuine; one a very expensive forgery. He didn't think there'd ever been a forged historical document passed off as authentic before. He was the first to think of it. He was the first to think of so many things.

The Gfjk-Hhh (he'd already half-forgotten the name Bfgsh) drummed his fingers excitedly on the arms of the chair. Now to have some real fun ...

But there was one thing he had to take care of first.

* * *

- There's nothing we can do about it from here, said Preceptor Shm. *If the members of the Forum have taken leave of their collective senses, we can hardly restore them.*

- We can challenge the legitimacy of his claim! said Lbbp. *It all hinges on these scrolls of his. I bet you anything you like at least one of them is a forgery.*

- A what? asked Pktk.

- Forgery. A fake. Not real. Made to look real but not real, explained Lbbp. He'd had to look up the word himself.

- Wow. Who would make such a thing? mused Pktk.

- Oh, I don't know, said Fthfth impatiently, *maybe someone who wanted to overthrow the Forum and take over Mlml?* She shot Pktk an exasperated look (he returned it) and turned to the Preceptor. *It doesn't really matter, though, does it? The Forum's always been less important to the well-being of the nation than the Preceptorate, anyway. And we're not going to be fooled by some magically reincarnated long-dead emperor, are we?*

They were at a hastily convened crisis meeting in the recently renamed Vstj Memorial Hub (formerly the Leisure Hub). Preceptor Shm, Lbbp (SENIOR Postulator Lbbp, lately elevated to the position of head of the Life Science Hub) and the heads of various other departments. Fthfth and Pktk were attending in their capacity as representatives of the student body, but Lbbp suspected that Shm just liked having them around in a crisis. As did he. And being surrounded by Terra's dearest friends made it easier for him to forget that she wasn't there any more, although at that moment Lbbp was quite glad that Terra was far away.

He hadn't seen her for nearly half an orbit. On his last visit to Rrth, he'd been surprised to find her living in hiding, under a false name, and alarmed to hear about the foiled attempt to abduct her. He'd offered to bring her back to Fnrr but understood when she told him of her desire to stay, to 'have a proper go at this whole being human thing', as she'd put it. Nonetheless, he'd been sure to leave behind a well-stocked 'goody bag' of Fnrrn technology to supplement the infra-light comm he'd secretly given her when he

99

first returned her to Rrth. She'd rummaged eagerly through the bag, finding the slate, the translation cube, even the not-entirely-legal unregistered pulse-orb which Lbbp may or may not have found lying around after the war …

He'd been due to pay her another visit within a cycle or so, but with the nation suddenly mired in constitutional upheaval it looked as if his travel plans might have to change. Sadly, he put thoughts of Terra from his mind and turned his attention back to the meeting.

- *It's not as simple as that, Fthfth,* said Shm grimly. *The precedence of the Preceptorate over the government is a matter of convention, not law. If a state of conflict were to arise between the two institutions, the government would have the upper hand. They're empowered to abolish us, not the other way around.*

- *ABOLISH! Yes, that's the word. I was trying to think of it on the way over here.*

The voice had come from the Hub's main entrance. They all turned to look. The Gfjk-Hhh, surrounded by his loyal custodians, stood framed in the doorway.

- *I was going to go with 'dissolve', but I already used that when I got rid of the Forum. Yes, you're right,* the Gfjk-Hhh said, *'abolish' is a far better word. Sounds much more … final.*

Preceptor Shm stood up and strode towards the Gfjk-Hhh. His custodians' hands instinctively went to their pulse-orbs, but they hesitated at a gesture from their leader.

- *The people may have tolerated the dissolution of the Forum,* said Shm calmly, *they may even thank you for it, but if you touch the Preceptorate, they will rise against you, prophecy or no prophecy. You don't have enough loyal acolytes yet* – he waved dismissively at the handful of guards – *to stop them.*

The Gfjk-Hhh smiled. - *You're probably right, Preceptor. But relax, that's not why I'm here. The Preceptorate may continue in its useful service to our nation, on one condition.*

A heavy pause.

- *And what might that be?* enquired Shm.

The Gfjk-Hhh raised his hand and pointed a long, grey finger at Lbbp.

- *Him.*

Shock. The department heads glanced at each other in horror. Fthfth screeched in alarm. - *No!*

The Gfjk-Hhh went on undaunted. - *Postulator Lbbp is wanted for crimes against the state. If he comes quietly, the rest of you can stay here and continue to conspire feebly against me. If not, then I will ... what was that word again? Abolish?*

Pktk and Fthfth leapt to their feet and stood in front of Lbbp. - *You'll have to come through us first, and we've faced scarier things than you,* declared Pktk. And it was true.

Lbbp placed his hands on their shoulders. - *Not this time, children.* Pktk turned, horrified.

- *But you can't go with them!*

Lbbp smiled and spoke quietly. - *It'll be okay. You have work to do here. I can look after myself. I faced the scary things too, remember?*

Fthfth managed a quiet - *But* ... Pktk remained silent. Lbbp looked over his shoulder at Preceptor Shm.

- *Look after them,* he said, and walked towards the custodians.

The Gfjk-Hhh smiled as Lbbp approached. Lbbp held his gaze impassively, then as he got close ... - *Don't I know you from—?*

- *Bind him! Gag him!* cried the Gfjk-Hhh. *Don't let his filthy slanders be heard any longer!* The custodians grabbed Lbbp and dragged him away, one clamping a gloved hand over his mouth. Pktk howled in outrage and would have launched himself at the custodians had Shm not restrained him.

The Gfjk-Hhh watched Lbbp's struggling form vanish through the Hub doors, then turned and smiled at Shm.

- *Goodbye, Preceptor. Happy ... precepting.* And he was gone.

A bewildered, stunned silence, which Fthfth broke, of course.

- *Now what?*

Pktk's jaw flexed. - *We can't stay here,* he said.

The philosopher-priests of La'Shul had been on retreat for almost a generation.

The people of Perfection had turned to them, the descendants and successors of the very founders of Sha'ha-las, to find a solution to their problem.

Decay was inevitable. Decline was inevitable. Entropy, collapse, fall, all these things were inevitable.

Nothing lasted for ever, but this had never mattered before, because nothing had ever been truly perfect before. For most things, decline and decay were simply a matter of change, shifting from one flawed state to another. But Perfection was different. It had to be preserved.

For season upon season, year upon year, the philosopher-priests had pondered and cogitated in the quiet of their Monasterium on La'Shul, walking the cloisters and gardens, heads bowed in concentration.

And then, at last, they announced to a breathless population that a solution had been found.

They emerged from the Monasterium and explained their plan.

It was perfect.

2.8

'And this was your favourite? What do the others taste like?'

Billy was chewing disconsolately on a slice of configuration 6.

'Well, similar-ish, I suppose. You want to try number nine? Or five?'

Billy pondered this. 'No, you're all right,' he said, and took another bite of 6.

They were in an empty apartment in a building a short walk from Terra's childhood home. Terra decided against trying to go back to her old apartment; if the Gfjk-Hhh knew anything about her, it was more than possible he'd be having her childhood home watched. But what little she'd seen of the new regime led her to suspect that quite a few people would have 'disappeared', having fallen foul of the leader's caprices, and as such there might be plenty of vacant properties. She was equally relieved and depressed to discover that she was right.

Sneaking along the corridor, they'd found a locked apartment door with a crude message daubed across it: THIS DOMICILE SEALED BY ORDER OF THE GFJK-HHH (LOVE AND GLORY TO HIM). Terra chose not to dwell upon what might have happened to the occupants and chose instead to concentrate on their own good fortune in finding the place.

They'd placed the apartment door back in its frame – from the outside it wasn't immediately obvious that it had been pulse-orbed open – and gone to raid the servery. Terra was hungry. Billy was starving.

The walk through the city streets had been interesting,

to say the least. Fortunately they were by no means the only ones wearing white hooded robes, and Terra noticed as they went that people walked differently in Hrrng now. For a start, they WALKED – when Terra had lived here, any journey of more than a few hundred steps had been taken by gravity bubble, but, stealing a glance upwards, Terra noticed that the skies were deserted. Why? Had gravity pods been outlawed? Confiscated?

Meanwhile, the pedestrian population shuffled along, their gazes determinedly downwards. Eye contact seemed to be regarded as something best avoided, as if it didn't do to let your neighbours see what you were thinking. What a wretched state of affairs, thought Terra, although it suited her purposes at that moment.

Now, in the vacant apartment, she looked out over the city skyline. Three of the six moons shone silver over the spires and cones. There weren't as many lights as Terra was used to. Whole sections of the city seemed to be in darkness. The sight disturbed her profoundly. She turned away from the window.

'We'll stay here tonight,' she said, 'and in the morning we'll try to find the others.'

By 'the others', Billy understood Terra meant her stepfather and her schoolfriends. From what he'd heard about her previous adventures here on Fnrr, they promised to be invaluable company. Billy was keen to have them around, and Terra would obviously draw a lot of strength from their presence. It sounded like a plan, or at least would have if they'd had any idea where to start looking.

Billy got up, stretched, and went off to explore the apartment. Terra looked through her rucksack. She retrieved her slate and activated it; still no access to the Source itself, but the official news feed was loading easily enough. Oh, look at that, she thought, I'm Mlml's most wanted.

Billy reappeared, confused. 'Erm … there aren't any beds,' he said.

'Oh, yes – about that …'

2.9

Terra dreamed.

In her dream she was small, maybe two or three orbits old.

She was with Lbbp and they were at the nature reserves at Rfk. Towering blooms, pink sky, orange sun.

She was happier than she'd ever remembered being. She ran to Lbbp, who scooped her up in his long thin arms, and she held him tight.

She wanted to be there for ever, small, safe, protected.

But she knew, even in the dream she knew that she would have to leave.

Fthfth was calling to her.

- *Terra?*

It was definitely Fthfth's voice but Terra couldn't see her.

- *Terra?* Fthfth's voice again. Then Pktk's.

- *She's not getting you. Boost the signal.*

- *I AM boosting the signal. You haven't got it tuned in properly. Let me have a go.*

- *Don't touch that, you'll lose her completely—*

Terra was confused. She looked to Lbbp in her dream, and he shook his head. He didn't understand either.

- *I'll try again. TERRA!*

Terra wondered if she could answer. She walked through the trees to the rainbow beach. - *Yes?* she said.

- *THERE you are. Listen, Terra,* said Fthfth, *you're NOT dreaming.*

- *Yes she IS dreaming, that's the whole point,* said Pktk testily.

- Shush! I mean you ARE dreaming, but you're not dream-ing us.

Terra gazed out across the sea. - *I don't understand,* she said.

- This is a transmission, said Pktk, *a long-range telepathic transmission. While you're awake your conscious mind drowns it out, but we can contact you while you're asleep. Do you understand?*

Terra found herself on top of Mount Hddf, looking down at the clouds. - *I think so,* she said.

- Good, said Fthfth, *now listen. You have to get out of Hrrng. Leave Mlml and come and find us in Lsh-Lff. Did you hear that? Lsh-Lff! Get here and we'll find you.*

Terra found herself waiting for the bus in front of Latimer Lane Comprehensive. It was raining.- *Lsh-Lff?* she said.

- That's right, said Pktk. *Now listen, when you get here, don't be surprised if—*

'Terra! Wake up!' Billy was shaking her. She was upside down, a metre and a half off the floor, suspended in a sleep-well, and Billy had grabbed her by the shoulders and shaken her awake.

'Billy!' she shouted. 'I was in the middle of something important!'

Billy couldn't even begin to guess what Terra was on about, and dismissed it as the kind of half-asleep thing people say when you wake them up unexpectedly.

'Switch this thing off and get your boots on. We have to move. They're in the building. They're checking all the flats. They'll be here in a minute.'

Terra flipped forward and landed two-footed on the floor. She hadn't been able to resist the sleep-well; she hadn't had a go in one for two years, and while she was perfectly okay in a bed these days, it just wasn't the same.

Billy had baulked at the idea of sleeping in a well of artificial weightlessness and had opted for the sort of sofa-thing. It had not been especially comfortable, and he'd had a restless night. This was lucky, since, just as the sun was coming up, a party of custodians had started barging into people's apartments on the floor below in search of the Ymn fugitives, and Billy had been awake to hear them.

'I think they're on this floor now,' said Billy. 'What do we do?'

Groggily, Terra scanned the room. Where did people keep them? Hers had always been in its charger beside the sleep-well, but there was no sign of one there.

'Terra?' said Billy, his fear mounting.

'Quiet, I'm thinking,' said Terra, still looking left and right. Some people kept spares for emergencies, she remembered. Probably somewhere near the window.

Terra scampered into the main room, Billy following. The custodians were hammering on the door of the next apartment. There was a small, white chest tucked discreetly next to the window. Terra ran to it and wrenched it open.

'Yes!' she shouted. She produced two gravity pods from the chest and tossed one to Billy. 'Put this on,' she said, clipping hers to her belt and opening the window. A blast of cold morning air.

Billy felt glumly around his waistband. 'I don't have anything to attach it to,' he said.

Terra rolled her eyes. 'Well, whatever you do, don't let go of it.' She pulled Billy across to the window, tapped the button on his pod and shoved him out.

A voice came from the lobby. - *This one's door's smashed in!* Terra hit the button on her pod and leapt out after Billy, who was hurtling away and howling in alarm.

'Try to steady yourself and follow me!' she shouted.

'What do I do? What do I do?' cried Billy.

'It's hard to explain,' called Terra. 'There's kind of a knack to it.'

'NO TIME FOR KNACKS!' shouted Billy.

Two custodians had appeared in the open window and were levelling pulse-orbs in their direction.

Terra tugged her hoodie off (being careful not to drop

her rucksack) and, keeping hold of one sleeve, flung it towards Billy. 'Grab this!'

Billy caught the other sleeve and was suddenly yanked downwards as Terra went into a precipitous dive. He felt the shock-waves of pulse blasts as they passed close by.

They rushed towards the ground at almost terminal velocity before levelling out with a few metres to spare. Terra called across, 'Are you getting the hang of it? Want to let go?'

'DON'T YOU DARE LET GO OF THAT HOODIE!' yelled Billy, wide-eyed and white-faced.

They sped along horizontally. It was still too early for most Fnrrns; a few shift workers were on their way home. Some spotted the two hurtling Ymns; most of them gazed in bemusement, but a few smiled and waved, and at least one cheered. You don't own all of them yet, thought Terra.

'Where are we going?' asked Billy.

'Back to the dinghy,' said Terra. 'The good news is I know where we're going, and the better news is it's a long way from this place.'

2.10

- *So what EXACTLY happened? asked the Gfjk-Hhh.*

The Guard Captain barked, *-Answer His Luminescence!*

Two custodians knelt in front of the Gfjk-Hhh as he sat on what had become his throne, the old Chancellor's seat in the Forum. To one side of the Gfjk-Hhh stood his loyal Guard Captain; to the other stood Wffk, taking notes. On the benches, the usual collection of courtiers and hangers-on paid varying levels of attention to the impromptu disciplinary hearing which was unfolding in front of them.

- *We were checking apartments in Upper Blue District,* murmured one of the custodians.

-*Speak up!* said the Gfjk-Hhh impatiently. The custodian knelt up a little straighter and began again in a clearer voice.

- *We were checking apartments in Upper Blue District, Luminescence, as per the Captain's orders.*

- *Your orders, Captain?* interrupted the Gfjk-Hhh. *You assigned these idiots, then?*

- *Yes, Luminescence,* said the Captain. *Simple and clear tasks which they couldn't carry out without—*

- *Yes, all right, Captain, I get the idea. You.* He pointed to the custodian. *Continue.*

The custodian avoided the Gfjk-Hhh's gaze and went on. - *We found an apartment with a broken-down door. We investigated and found the Ymn fugitives—*

- *You did? How exciting!* The Gfjk-Hhh clapped his hands delightedly.

-*Yes, Luminescence, but—*

- *BUT? Hmm. I don't like buts.* The Gfjk-Hhh frowned.

- *But the Ymns escaped using stolen gravity pods, Luminescence.*

- *Gravity pods? Like the ones I declared illegal and ordered rounded up? Dear me. I must find out who was in charge of getting that done. Wffk, make a note of it*, said the Gfjk-Hhh. Wffk duly made a note on his scroll. *Right, you two, stand up.*

The two custodians scrambled to their feet, keeping their eyes fixed on the ground.

- *Pulse-orb, please, Captain,* said the Gfjk-Hhh. The Captain unholstered his weapon, handed it over and turned back to glower at his two disgraced inferiors.

- *The Captain's right you know. You are idiots. Utter idiots. Buffoons. Abject g'fbbts, the pair of you.*

The two custodians trembled.

- *BUT,* the Gfjk-Hhh said with a broad grin, *I can't very well start punishing people for being idiots, can I? The nation's full of them! I wouldn't have time to do anything else! All day, every day, punishing idiots! Imagine! No, no, my friends, it's no crime to be an idiot.*

The Gfjk-Hhh laughed. The custodians laughed nervously. The Guard Captain guffawed. Even Wffk allowed himself a discreet chuckle. Still hooting with mirth, the Gfjk-Hhh examined the Captain's pulse-orb. It was already on its maximum setting. Of course it was.

The Gfjk-Hhh raised the pulse-orb and shot the Guard Captain square in the back. His shattered body flew across the chamber and slid to a halt between the Forum benches. All laughter ceased, followed by a few horrified gasps, then silence. The Gfjk-Hhh got to his feet.

- *EMPLOYING idiots, now that's another matter.* The Gfjk-Hhh peered at the Captain's body with distaste. *Wffk, get that cleaned up, will you?*

The Gfjk-Hhh turned to the two trembling custodians. - *Right, my foolish friends, you're free to go! Go on, be off with you.* He smiled.

The two custodians managed nervous smiles of terror and gratitude, then turned to go.

- *Ahem . . .*

They paused at the sound of the Gfjk-Hhh's voice.

- *You'll have to leave the weapons, obviously.*

The custodians unfastened their holster belts and placed them on the floor. They walked on. The Gfjk-Hhh spoke again. - *And the boots.*

The custodians exchanged confused glances, then dutifully removed their boots.

- *And the clothes. All of them.*

As the two custodians struggled out of their garments, the Gfjk-Hhh rose to his full height and announced, - *If anyone in the city offers either of these two food, shelter or clothing, they will find themselves in the Gshkth Pit tomorrow.* He turned to the two nude Fnrrns. *Get out.*

They scampered, grey and naked, out of the Forum.

The Gfjk-Hhh slumped back into his chair. For a moment he seemed lost in thought. Then he addressed the assembled courtiers.

- *Who's hungry?* he asked. *I'm hungry.*

2.11

We could just go home, thought Billy.

We're in a little space-dinghy, high above this loony planet where Terra used to live. But at the end of the day, it's not OUR planet, and just a short ride away, there's an enormous comfy starship full of food and sofas which could whisk us away back to Earth in luxury within a couple of days. We could just go home.

But looking at Terra's face, he knew he didn't dare suggest this.

She WAS home, he thought. That was her home back there and somehow, while she's been away, it's become a nightmare, and now there's no way she's going back to Earth until she finds a way to fix it, or gets herself killed trying.

And all I can do is help or stay out of her way, he concluded.

Terra had decided to take the dinghy straight upwards into orbit, make one circle of the planet (if nothing else this gave them a few hours to collect themselves after the terrifying day they'd spent on Mlml), then redescend to Dskt. That way, if anyone had been tracking their escape from Hrrng, they might assume they'd left the planet. The dinghy was perfectly capable of flying to Dskt aeroplane-style, but Terra was afraid they'd be followed, maybe even shot down.

They'd deactivated their gravity bubbles and landed in a heap in the park where they'd left the dinghy. No one saw them arrive except a little Fnrrn playing with a bdkt. She'd made an excited squeak when Terra and Billy crashed onto the purple lawn and another when Terra, having opened the invisible ship's hatch, shot her a friendly wink and then disappeared. The little Fnrrn called excitedly to her mother, who was on the other side of a patch of nx-nx bushes, and had missed everything.

'So where are we going?' Billy asked.

'Dskt,' said Terra. 'Just across the sea from Mlml. Specifically, the ancient walled city of Lsh-Lff.'

'Right ... Lsh-Lff.'

'One of the oldest cities on Fnrr. It's right by the coast. I went there on a Lyceum trip once.'

'Okay ...'

'Dskt was invaded just before Mlml. The G'grk overran the place and used it as a base to attack us from. That was a couple of orbits – I mean years – ago. Should have had time to rebuild itself by now.'

'Uh huh. Terra, can I ask you a question?' said Billy tentatively.

'Go ahead.' Terra's attention was focused on the dinghy's navigational readouts.

'WHY are we going there?'

'Because that's where my friends are. They told me in a dream.'

'Of course they did.' It made about as much sense as anything else Billy had heard in the last few days. He decided not to query it.

The dinghy had begun its descent, bumping through Fnrr's atmosphere. Lsh-Lff made sense as a hiding place, thought Terra. The eras-old city walls (Lsh-Lff had been founded before Dskt was unified as a nation; its walls were a souvenir from the days when it had consisted of many individual city-states) would make for a good defence if the Gfjk-Hhh were foolish enough to attack. As mad and evil as her brief experience of him led her to believe he was, Terra didn't imagine the Gfjk-Hhh would be so crazed as to try to invade Dsktn territory. Would he?

The dinghy's retro-gravs kicked in and it slowed into its final approach. Terra noticed that there was a lot of low cloud over Lsh-Lff; she wasn't sure if the city even had artificial climate control like Hrrng, but if so, it didn't appear to be working today. Maybe it had been damaged during the G'grk invasion?

The dinghy bumped downwards through grey cloud. Billy looked for some means of strapping himself in but saw none; he clung to the edges of his seat and smiled nervously at Terra. Terra returned the smile, then turned back to the ship's readouts.

Her face fell. She went pale. 'No! NO!' she wailed. Billy let go of his seat and rushed to her side.

The readout had switched to a front visual display; it showed Lsh-Lff ahead of them. Or rather, it showed what was left of Lsh-Lff.

The walls still stood, but that was about it.

As the dinghy circled the city, Terra rushed to the large side porthole and gazed out desperately. She saw blackened, burned-out buildings, shattered towers, fallen spires, deserted streets, ash, dust, debris. No signs of life anywhere.

'We're too late,' she said quietly. 'We're too late.' She clutched Billy and wept into his shoulder. He stared at the devastation. There was nothing he could do but hold her.

The dinghy completed its automatic descent and set down in front of Lsh-Lff's coastward gates.

'Come on,' said Billy.

'No,' said Terra quietly.

'They might be hiding in there,' said Billy. 'There might be a message, or—'

'They're dead,' said Terra, her voice emptied of emotion. 'There's nothing here.'

'Wait, wait,' said Billy. 'This message, the one you dreamed – it was last night, wasn't it? Look at those ruins. No smoke, no embers – everything's cold. Whatever happened here, it happened WEEKS ago at least.'

'So?' asked Terra tearfully.

'If your friends were alive last night, then they're still alive today! They didn't die when the city was destroyed because it was destroyed ages ago! Either they're hiding out in there somewhere, or they're somewhere else entirely, or ...' Billy decided against finishing the thought.

'Or what...?' probed Terra.

'Or ... it really was a dream.' Billy shrugged.

Terra leapt to her feet. 'Right,' she said. 'Come on,' and she stomped towards the hatch.

That's more like it, thought Billy, and followed her.

By the time Billy descended the ladder, Terra was standing in front of the coastward gates. They were shattered and scorched, hanging off their huge metal hinges. There was no sound but the lapping of waves against the shore, a few hundred metres behind them.

Billy stood beside Terra and took her hand. 'Shall we?' he said. She looked at him with friendship, gratitude and the last traces of tearfulness. They marched through the gates.

And everything changed.

2.12

Terra and Billy stood, amazed, on a busy city street. Fnrrns, dressed in typical Dsktn smock-like garments, walked to and fro. Above them, others went about their business borne aloft by gravity bubbles. In front of them, a line of stores and kiosks.

They exchanged astonished glances, and then Terra's face lit up with understanding.

'They hid it. They hid the whole thing. Incredible.'

'Who hid what?' asked Billy.

'They hid the whole city,' said Terra. 'The people of Lsh-Lff, they threw up a massive camouflage field around THE WHOLE CITY. I've never heard of anything like it.'

Billy didn't think it was worth pointing out that he hadn't either. So he confined himself to asking, 'Why?'

Terra shrugged. 'I don't know, to fool the G'grk, maybe? The country was being invaded – if you convince a marauding army that your city's already a burned-out ruin, they might just assume they'd been beaten to it and keep moving.'

Billy whistled. 'Ingenious.'

By now, their presence had been remarked upon. Some passers-by had spotted them and exchanged concerned mutterings, and soon they were approached by a uniformed officer.

– *Who are you? What are you doing here?*

Terra was about to respond, but Billy put his hand on her arm. 'Wait, I've got this.' He touched the translation cube in his pocket, and said to the officer:

– *We come in peace. Take us to your leader.*

Terra rolled her eyes.

2.13

*- Y*ou're wrong, you know. *About why I keep you here.*
The Gfjk-Hhh was visiting Lbbp in his cell. He
was sitting on one side of the crystal barrier, Lbbp on the
other. Lbbp did not look at his captor or answer him. The
Gfjk-Hhh went on regardless.

*- You think you're here because I'm afraid you can expose me.
'That's not the Gfjk-Hhh,' you'd say, 'he's a cleaner, that's all. A
cleaner I once told a pointless lie to because I couldn't be bothered
to show a moment's civility to a stranger, and that's why you're
all suffering now.' Wouldn't you love everyone to hear that?*

Lbbp did not react.

*- Well, you're wrong, Deceiver. That's not why you're here.
You're here because I enjoy reminding you of the fact that this is
all your fault. Do you understand?*

No reaction.

*- I have so many toys these days, Deceiver. All the toys I could
ever want. And you're still my favourite. Does that make you
feel good?*

Still nothing. The Gfjk-Hhh leapt to his feet.

*- Perhaps I'll let you tell them. Take you out onto the roof of
the Forum, and let you scream it to the whole city. 'He's not the
Gfjk-Hhh! He made it all up! He's nobody!' Because you know
what would happen? NOTHING. They didn't believe me
because I had them at the point of a weapon. They CHOSE to
believe me. They WANT me to be the Gfjk-Hhh. They LOVE
ME.*

The Gfjk-Hhh still addressed the back of Lbbp's head.
He paused a moment, then went on.

*- If I decide you're no fun any more, you die, you realise that?
Think about it.*

The Gfjk-Hhh swept out, slamming the cell door.

What the Gfjk-Hhh hadn't been able to see was that Lbbp had been smiling throughout their encounter.

Not a word about Terra. Not a gloat, not a boast, not so much as a mention.

Which meant she'd got away.

Alone in his dungeon, Lbbp's face was one radiant smile.

2.14

Kssh-Thll was not having a good day.

He'd been Steward Intendent of Lsh-Lff for three orbits, since before the Concealment. He'd had a vote, as one of the Civic Trustees, when the decision was made to hide the city. Not an easy decision; much anguish would be caused in the rest of Dskt when the news of Lsh-Lff's 'destruction' got out. And within the walls, many who had family in other regions had protested against the necessity of allowing their relatives to believe them lost, to mourn and grieve while all the time their loved ones lived on, hidden beneath the optical shield.

When the invasion of Mlml had failed, or been repulsed, or whatever it was that had happened across the narrow strip of ocean (no one in Lsh-Lff was entirely sure how the G'grk's campaign had been stalled; some bizarre rumours flew around involving aliens and strange tonal chanting, but no one believed a word of that) and the G'grk began to withdraw their troops back to the Central Plains, another dilemma had arisen: should the city reveal itself, safe and intact? Was the G'grk retreat a ploy? Would Lsh-Lff, having spent all that time hidden, be overrun as soon as it was exposed?

Surely, the Trustees thought, if the ceasefire held, if the truce were genuine, help would come. Wouldn't Dskt's national government, once reinstalled in the great capital city Hff, send troops and engineers to rebuild the city? They would come, with their tools and machines, ready to demolish the ruins and start again – only to find the city and its people safe and sound! The joy of that reunion! The relief! The jubilation!

No help came.

The G'grk withdrawal MUST have been a ploy. The country was NOT free and safe.

In fact, the government in Hff had decided not to rebuild Lsh-Lff, but to leave the ruins standing as a permanent, sombre memorial to those who had fallen during the war. Of course, no one told the people of Lsh-Lff about this; as far as anyone knew, there was nobody to tell.

The city remained hidden. No one was allowed to go beyond the city walls. No transmissions to the lands outside the city walls were allowed. No one had ever found them. No one was ever supposed to find them.

Especially not a pair of aliens.

- *I don't suppose there's a British consulate, is there?* Billy smiled weakly. Terra glowered at him.

Kssh-Thll rubbed his temples. He had one of those headaches that only Fnrrns get coming on. He looked across his desk at the two bizarre creatures who had been brought to his bureau. Even once he had got used to the garish, ruddy skin colouring and the horrid fibrous excrescences on their heads, there remained the ridiculous attire and the clanging accents (although to be fair, everyone from Mlml sounded like that to Kssh-Thll). He decided to try again.

- *So, you say that you have come here looking for some friends – friends who have fled the tyranny in Mlml. You have walked into a city that the whole of Fnrr thinks is a dead ruin, and you think your friends are here. Why?*

Terra stared at the floor. Billy nudged her. - *Tell him,* he said.

- *It sounds stupid when you say it out loud,* she muttered.

- *Please, young Ymn,* said Kssh-Thll, *indulge me.*

Terra sighed. - *We came here because ... because ...*

- *Because it came to her in a dream!* said a familiar ebullient voice.

Terra and Billy wheeled round. Terra's face lit up like a supernova. She didn't care if she was under arrest – she didn't even know if she was under arrest – she'd never been so pleased to see anyone in her life.

- *FTHFTH!* she shouted, and ran to her friend.

Terra flung her arms around the young Fnrrn so hard that for a moment she was worried she'd injured her.

- *You look weird,* said Fthfth when she'd got her breath back.

- *You look bigger!* replied Terra.

- *I AM bigger. And so are you. MUCH bigger.*

- *Not THAT much bigger,* protested Terra with a smile.

- *Yes, you are. MUCH MUCH bigger. You're ENOR-MOUS. What have you been eating?*

- *Almost nothing since I got back,* said Terra.

- *Erm ...* came a quiet voice, *I'm here too you know.*

Terra turned. - *PKTK!* she said, and gave him almost as fierce a hug as the one she'd given Fthfth. That done, she turned straight back to Fthfth. - *How's Lyceum?*

- *If I might beg your pardon,* said Kssh-Thll stiffly, suspecting that they'd quite forgotten that he was there, never mind that they were still in his bureau.

- *Oh yes!* said Fthfth, who had quite forgotten that Kssh-Thll was still there and that they were still in his bureau. *Thank you, Steward Intendent. I have here* – she handed him a shard of crystal on which was engraved an insignia – *the crest of the ArchRector of Lsh-Lff Polynasium. These Ymns are members of Preceptor Shm's party and are to be treated as guests of the ArchRector.*

Kssh-Thll studied the shard.

- *I think you'll find it's quite in order,* said Fthfth.

Kssh-Thll had no idea if this was indeed the crest of the ArchRector of Lsh-Lff Polynasium, or if crystal shards were considered a proper form of documentation; he wasn't even entirely sure he'd ever HEARD of Lsh-Lff Polynasium. But it looked like these two Ymn interlopers were about to become officially someone else's responsibility, and that was good enough for him.

- *Of course it is.* Kssh-Thll smiled. *Have a pleasant stay.*

He handed the shard back to Fthfth, sat back at his desk and tried to look busy. As they turned to go, Terra and Fthfth's conversation resumed without missing a beat.

- *I'm nearly in orbit four now! Actually they said I might skip orbit four altogether and go straight to five. Of course that was before all this Gfjk-Whatsit nonsense started. But never mind that, tell me all about Rrth.*

Billy and Pktk caught each other's eye.

- *I'm Billy,* said Billy. He extended a hand for Pktk to shake.

Pktk stared at the hand for a moment, then said, - *I'm Pktk.*

- *Right,* said Billy, withdrawing the hand.

For a moment, they stood wordlessly as their female counterparts chatted excitedly. Then, as Terra and Fthfth trotted away happily, the two young males shared a knowing look and followed them. Interesting, thought Billy, that the 'let's leave the girls to get on with it' face was truly universally understood.

* * *

- *So why here? Why Lsh-Lff?* asked Terra, as they passed out into the street.

- *Safest place to hide is a place that no one even thinks is a place.* Fthfth smiled.

- *But how did YOU find it?* Terra persisted.

- *Er, that was me actually,* said Pktk, shuffling up behind them. *I found Lsh-Lff. Or rather I figured out that it was still here.*

Terra could tell that Pktk was dying to say how he'd done this but was far too modest – even now, after all he'd done to save his friends during the invasion – to volunteer the information. So she asked him.

- *Well,* said Pktk happily, *I've been writing an account of the invasion for the Preceptorate archives.* Terra nodded; she remembered Pktk's fondness for military history. No doubt the opportunity to record some military history that he'd actually played a part in himself had been irresistible.

Pktk went on. - *I'd been interviewing refugees from Dskt who'd ended up in Mlml about their experiences of the G'grk occupation – pretty heavy stuff actually. You can read it if you like, but I'll warn you it's not very … Erm. Yes, so anyway, I made lists of where all the refugees had come from, and when I sorted them all out, there weren't ANY from Lsh-Lff. Not one. It just didn't seem possible. There's never been a city attacked and NOBODY got away. I've been reading the histories of wars on other planets and it's NEVER happened. Even when a city's been wiped out with one of those massive bomb-things like they have on Rrth* (at this Terra and Billy exchanged sheepish glances), *SOMEBODY'S got out in time. It just struck me as odd.*

While Billy was listening, he was trying to make sense of it in his head. So Terra's home country was Mlml, this was Dskt, the previous bad guys were the G'grk. The new bad guy is the Gfjk-something. If only I had an idea how to spell any of this, Billy thought sadly, it'd be so much easier to understand.

- *So, anyway,* Pktk continued, *I looked at images of the city taken from orbit, and sure enough, it was burned out and deserted, but when I looked at ENERGY readings taken from space, there's a MASSIVE energy field being generated, right in the centre of the city. The fusion stations here are working permanently at full capacity to maintain the camouflage field. I don't think they'll be able to keep it up for ever.*

- *Why ARE they keeping it up?* asked Terra. *They do know the war is over, right?*

- *They do since we got here,* said Fthfth importantly, *but now that the Gfjk-Stupid-Thingy-Face has taken over back home, they're as scared of him as they were of the G'grk. I don't think they'll be switching the field off just yet.*

Pktk coughed. He hadn't quite finished his story. - *So after I told Preceptor Shm that Lsh-Lff was probably not destroyed after all, he managed to get a message to ArchRector Qss-Jff at the Polynasium. They're old friends.*

- *Used to play gshkth together apparently,* said Fthfth matter-of-factly. Terra boggled at the idea of stiff old Preceptor Shm playing gshkth, and shuddered at the memory of what gshkth had become back in Hrrng. She looked around at the blithe, bustling streets of Lsh-Lff and felt envious on Hrrng's behalf.

- *The ArchRector invited Preceptor Shm and his closest advisers—* began Pktk.

- *Which these days includes US,* interjected Fthfth proudly.

- *To stay here, at the Polynasium, so we can work on ways to beat the Gffk-Hhh and take Mlml back,* said Pktk. *And there it is!* He pointed to a grand, colonnaded temple-like structure a few hundred metres ahead of them.

- *Impressive,* said Terra. *So what's Lbbp been doing all this time?*

A leaden silence. Fthfth and Pktk stopped walking, glanced sorrowfully at each other and then lowered their eyes. Billy sensed Terra's sudden alarm and panic.

- *Fthfth? Pktk?* Terra said, with just the faintest tremor in her voice. *Where's Lbbp?*

2.15

Lbbp looked through the doorway.
       He looked into the main room of his apartment in Hrrng.

Someone was there.

Sitting on the bench seat, gazing out of the window as the orange evening sun streamed into the room.

- *Bsht?*

She turned and smiled.

- *Bsht,* said Lbbp. *Oh, Bsht, I'm so sorry. I looked everywhere for you – the refugee centres, the nosocomia ... I checked the casualty lists; I even looked through pictures of the unidentified dead ... Where have you been?*

She raised a hand and touched his face.

- *Where are you now, Lbbp?*

- *I'm ... what do you mean, where am—? I'm here, aren't I?*

Lbbp looked around the room.

- *I can't be here. I'm not here, am I?* He looked sadly at Bsht. *And neither are you.*

He slumped onto the seat beside her and plunged his face into his hands.

- *He's won. He's won, hasn't he? He's finally driven me out of my mind.*

She put an arm gently across his shoulder.

- *No, silly,* she said, *he hasn't won. He hasn't won at all. And you'll see why. But first you have to go.*

He turned to her imploringly.

- *No, not yet, please ...*

Bsht smiled in that exasperated, understanding way she used to smile at him.

- *It's time, Lbbp. It's time to—*

- WAKE UP!

Lbbp sat up with a nerve-jangling start. He felt hard stone beneath him.

A custodian – one he'd not seen before – was hammering on the crystal.

- Breakfast, the custodian said simply. He opened a tiny flap at the bottom of the crystal barrier and pushed the hexagonal dish of grey slop through the open slot. He then closed the transparent flap, and the slot sealed itself.

- Might as well eat it, said the custodian. *He's in a weird mood. You'll need your strength.*

Lbbp stared at the dish of slop. He would probably eat it in due course, but it didn't interest him. He had too much to think about.

I was dreaming, wasn't I? he thought. Like a baby ... Like a Ymn.

He got up and stretched. Had the Gfjk-Hhh finally driven him insane?

No, he was certain that wasn't it. Lbbp began to pace, and think.

Prolonged isolation ... sensory deprivation ... Fnrrns don't dream past infancy, but I haven't been LIVING like a Fnrrn. Sleeping on a hard floor instead of weightless in a sleep-well ... darkness and silence instead of the constant bombardment of information ...

My brain isn't broken, concluded Lbbp, it's restarting itself. Those parts of the mind that years of comfort and convenience have rendered inert and silent, they're all coming back to life because I need them now – I need them like no Fnrrn has needed them for eras.

Lbbp smiled.

He began to eat the slop. It was disgusting, but he needed some fuel. Fuel for his starving body and his racing mind.

Come on then, he thought. Come and play with your favourite toy. Because your favourite toy has just figured out how he's going to beat you. Even from inside this box, thought Lbbp, I can beat you.

2.16

*B*ut I can't stay here! I've got to go back! I've got to get him out of there!

Terra was pacing frantically round and round the Polynasium committee room. The ArchRector had allocated it to Preceptor Shm and his friends for meetings and general conspiracy purposes.

- *Get him out of where?* asked Shm wearily. *No one knows where Lbbp, is, or even if he's still alive.*

Fthfth looked at Terra with great sadness. Sadness at her friend's distress and sadness at what she felt obliged to say.

- *Terra. The Gfjk has executed HUNDREDS of dissidents since he took over. Lbbp was the very first one he had arrested. It seems INCREDIBLY unlikely he's kept him alive all this time.*

- *But we'd know!* cried Terra. *We'd know if he'd killed him! That's how he does things! He doesn't just quietly do away with people, he makes a show of them!* Terra stopped pacing, turned and screamed at Fthfth right in the face. *He's got people HACKING EACH OTHER TO DEATH IN THE GSHKTH PIT!*

There was a moment's silence, and then Terra collapsed, weeping piteously, into the nearest chair. Billy rushed over and threw his arms around her. He tried to imagine her anguish, but failed. To have travelled across so much space, braved so much danger to find the person dearest to her in the whole galaxy – only to find that, at best, he was being tormented by a crazed tyrant. Billy could only guess how distressed she must be. So he did the only thing he could, and held her tight.

After a few moments, Terra's sobs stopped. Billy felt her

tensing up, as if she were hardening herself both mentally and physically. Terra looked up at her friends, and spoke in a level tone.

- *This has to stop. We have to stop this and we can't do it alone. What are we? A bunch of dusty old professors and scared schoolchildren, hiding out across the sea. We need help. We need an army.*

She stared at Preceptor Shm. Her jaw clenched and unclenched, as if reluctant to open, to allow her mouth to say the words she knew she had to say.

- *We need the G'grk,* said Terra.

2.17

When James Hardison had joined the Air Force as a young man, he'd imagined many of the places his career might end up taking him to. This, he thought as he looked around him, had not been one of them.

-Ymn! Ymn! Drink! You play hard! You play well! Like G'grk!

The slap on the back felt more like a punch in the ribs. If James Hardison – COLONEL James Hardison, as he now was – hadn't spent enough time among the G'grk to acquire an appreciation of just how boisterous they could be in their expressions of comradeship, he might have felt threatened, or at least challenged. As it was, he winced, grunted, took the d'kff and drank long and deep.

His companions set up a roaring hiss of approval. It resounded through the stone hall of the H'dksh Tribe's Winter Fortress, and their celebrations continued.

The game had been hard fought. Literally; since the ceasefire between the G'grk and their neighbouring peoples had been in effect, their reserves of aggression had been channelled in other directions, and one of these directions had been sport. Kkh-St'grrss, a sort of full-contact cross between polo, lacrosse and medieval jousting, was particularly popular at the moment among fit young G'grk males, combining as it did skill, vigour, bravery, and the very real possibility of serious injury.

It was still only a little over two years since Colonel Hardison – or Major Hardison, as he had been back then – had received the phone call that had changed his life. He'd been asleep when the phone rang and still half asleep as he answered, but upon hearing General Wyndham say the words '... the real thing this time, James,' he'd woken up sharply.

The scientists at the Hat Creek SETI (Search for Extra-Terrestrial Intelligence) lab had greeted him with bleary terseness – none of them had slept enough either, and the lab guys always got nervous and defensive around uniforms, however hard you tried to convince them you were all on the same side – but as he studied their readings, and they all got some hot coffee inside them, the atmosphere eased and a mutual excitement took over. This was, after all, what they had been waiting for their whole professional lives, and as Air Force/SETI liaison officer he'd met most of them before. In particular he recognised Dave Steinberg, a highly distinguished but extremely talkative and excitable Canadian scientist with whom he'd had a number of 'conversations' over the years. Thus far he'd managed to get about six words in.

That morning. The morning of the signals, the numbers, the coffee, the map-reading, more coffee, and finally the helicopter ride with the giggling Professor Steinberg, to what was being referred to, in that specific-but-vague way the military have of naming things, as the Location.

It was only when the ship materialised above the heads of the expectant onlookers that Major Hardison realised he had indeed been expecting it to be lemon-shaped, but he couldn't, for the moment, remember why.

When the beam of light burst from the underside of the vessel and revealed a human child standing beneath it, Major Hardison felt a faint twinge of memory in a neglected corner of his, by and large, unusually well-organised mind. Something on the news, years ago now, about a couple whose baby had disappeared, a story no one had believed, a story about a deserted road and a lemon-shaped UFO (had there maybe even been a court case?). When the child enquired (in English!) about the whereabouts of her parents, everything suddenly made a glorious sense. Major Hardison found himself blinking back extremely uncharacteristic tears of joy as he realised that for him, this adventure had only just begun.

Major Hardison spent the next few days in a state of riveted fascination as he sat in on – and occasionally conducted – interviews with the returned child (Terra, she was called; even the name was perfect) and her alien ... well, stepfather, it appeared. Their planet sounded both surprisingly similar to and unimaginably different from Earth. He was disappointed to hear that the planet had been at war until recently. He'd hoped that armed professions such as his own might be obsolete on other worlds – but was astonished and delighted at the story of how the war had been ended by the bravery of these two remarkable individuals, who – for want of a better word – were a family from two worlds. This had led to her nation's leaders (the planet – Fnrr, it was called – was divided into nation states, much like Earth) granting her request to be returned to her own people, breaking a century-old moratorium on contact with the human race. The aliens had always believed humans to be too primitive and brutal to be exposed to advanced technology. Major Hardison couldn't honestly say he blamed them, although it sounded like Fnrr wasn't exactly free from brutality itself (Terra's descriptions of the G'grk invasion had been vivid and compelling; he hoped that the peace accord they'd managed to bring about would endure).

Then the time came for Terra to be reunited with her original family, her human family. Major Hardison reflected that there had been nothing in any Air Force training manual on how to deal with the deluge of conflicting emotions he'd felt standing in that little house. As the girl's decision to stay was greeted with tearful jubilation by her parents (and Professor Steinberg – Hardison was still unsure as to how he'd managed to get himself invited), the Major caught a glimpse of the alien – Lbbp, he was called – sitting alone and in silence. The alien's smooth grey face had hardly any features to read, but Major Hardison knew a broken heart when he saw one.

As soon as it became apparent that some sort of envoy was to be appointed and sent to Fnrr to formalise relations with Earth, James Hardison volunteered immediately. The chance to spend a year on this alien planet was just irresistible. He'd accompanied Lbbp (and, inevitably, Dave Steinberg) in the little spaceship and was pleased to see that the alien had rallied a little morale-wise. He saw Terra and her parents waving them off and felt a fleeting twinge of regret that he couldn't stay to see how she turned out. But he already had a feeling their paths would cross again one day.

As the ship containing himself, Lbbp and Professor Steinberg had ascended silently into deep space, the newly promoted Colonel Hardison finally got over his disappointment at having joined the Air Force just too late to sign up for the space shuttle programme.

Colonel Hardison took his role as the first Senior Earth Attaché to Fnrr seriously – Colonel Hardison took EVERYTHING seriously – and so when, a few months after his arrival, his assignment working with the Mlml government ended and the time came for him to take up temporary residence in T'krr, the G'grk capital city in the heart of the Central Plains, he had immersed himself in study of G'grk culture, suspecting it to be more complex and less brutal than his Mlmln hosts had described it.

He'd been right about the more complex part.

Colonel Hardison had been invited to his first Kkh-St'grrss match (battle?) as a spectator shortly after arriving in T'krr, and later, during conversation with the conscious members of the winning team, he got the distinct impression that he was being goaded into saddling up and having a try himself. He'd learned to ride at his uncle's farm as a boy; looking at the way the G'grk riders handled their saddled gnth-sh'gsts, he felt confident that he could at least give it a shot.

After meeting with varying degrees of success on his first couple of attempts (he was very glad that the G'grk's post-ceasefire softening of their attitude towards modern Fnrrn technology had at last allowed the use of bone-regenerators) Colonel Hardison had now progressed as a Kkh-St'grrss player (combatant?) to the point at which he was, if he did say so himself, pretty darn good at it.

A contributing factor was that his stay in T'krr had become rather less temporary than had been intended. The Gfjk-Hhh's sudden takeover on Mlml had caught him out along with everyone else; his return to Hrrng had been delayed indefinitely, and moreover, he discovered that his attempts to contact his superiors back on Earth were being thwarted. Some sort of jamming signal set up by the Gfjk-Hhh's people, that was the theory. Apparently the dictator was convinced that his opponents had been trying to contact a powerful race of aliens (called the FerZing, or something) in an attempt to enlist their aid in overthrowing him, and so he'd sabotaged all extra-planetary communications.

Without new orders, and without any way of requesting new orders, Colonel Hardison acted like the good officer he was, and stayed put. And got better at playing Kkh-St'grrss and drinking d'kff from hollowed-out gnth-sh'gst horns.

As it happened, subtle differences in body chemistry between humans and Fnrrns meant that while the d'kff had a highly intoxicating effect on the G'grk, Colonel Hardison found that he could knock it back and feel none the worse for wear until the fourth or fifth hornful. He hadn't shared this with his hosts; he suspected that a reputation as some-one who could hold his d'kff was probably worth having.

One end of the long hall was dominated by a huge stone hearth, in which blazed a great open fire. Above this was set a blackened metal grate, onto which a large animal carcass was now tossed by a party of happily hissing G'grk. As the smell and sizzle filled the hall, Colonel Hardison recalled an earlier conversation with a G'grk chieftain in which he explained that while there was an Rrth game called 'polo' which bore a superficial similarity to Kkh-St'grrss, it dif-fered in a couple of major respects. Firstly, polo was an altogether less egalitarian affair than Kkh-St'grrss, being very much the preserve of wealthy Ymn elites. Secondly, after a polo match, the victorious team did not, as a rule, get to eat the losers' horses.

A clanging chime was heard throughout the stone hall. With varying degrees of grogginess, the G'grk registered that their party was being interrupted and peered around for the source of the noise.

Two drones, bearing the blue standard of the Grand Marshal, strode through the double doors at the other end of the hall. Behind them came a Drone Major in gleaming armour. The assembled Kkh-St'grrss players and their assorted friends and supporters struggled unsteadily to their feet and saluted.

- *The Grand Marshal commands the presence of the Rrth warrior!* barked the Drone Major.

- *That's me, boys,* said Colonel Hardison in heavily accented but grammatically perfect G'grk. He rose from his seat, grunting as he felt that day's fresh bruises blooming, and marched stiffly out of the hall, behind the Drone Major and flanked by the two standard bearers.

As he went, he heard one of his erstwhile drinking companions call out, - *Ymn! Ymn! Careful you don't leave bootprints on your own back!* followed by hisses of raucous laughter.

Colonel Hardison walked on. He was learning the G'grk language and mastering G'grk sports. G'grk humour, he suspected, would always be a mystery.

2.18

Grand Marshal Zst'kh felt his blue blood pumping. At last. At last, something to do.

From birth, he'd been trained by his grandfather, the wise and mighty K'zsht, in the arts of leadership, of strategy, of battle. Preparing him for the day he would grasp the sacred lance of office and take his grandfather's place.

There had always been a tension between ambition and loyalty within G'grk culture, between the ruthlessness necessary to achieve victory, and the fealty necessary to maintain order. But not for Zst'kh, not as far as his grandfather was concerned. His devotion to the old warrior had been absolute.

When Zst'kh had learned that his father, the Grand Marshal's eldest son, had grown impatient waiting for his own turn as leader, and had been plotting against K'zsht, he'd had no hesitation in exposing the subterfuge. And when sentence had been passed, Zst'kh had volunteered to carry it out himself.

He remembered that cold morning, on the plains outside T'krr – his father's pleading voice, the weight of the ks'trg in his hand, the dawning sun glinting off the blade, the hissing cheer of the assembled Drone Lords as the blade fell … He had never lost a moment's sleep over it. His father had been weak, devious, duplicitous. An unworthy successor to the Grand Marshal. He would be better.

Zst'kh had been in Dskt that morning, establishing his prefecture over the city of Bssq-Fmm, when the order had arrived to withdraw back to the Central Plains. His grandfather's order. He had been confused, surprised, he might even have experienced a moment's doubt, but he had not hesitated. He marshalled his drones and the retreat began. Doubtless he would hear his grandfather's explanation in due course.

The explanation had not pleased him.

The war had been neither won nor lost, but abandoned. His grandfather had ordered the withdrawal and then, also, announced his intention to retire. Alive.

He'd even decreed clemency for his deputy, Sk'shk, even though he'd tried to kill the Grand Marshal with his own sacred lance. G'grk justice demanded Sk'shk's head, but this was not to be. Another punishment would have to be found for him. Meanwhile, the lance itself, the eras-old emblem of office, broken. Unthinkable.

Zst'kh was inaugurated Grand Marshal in a subdued ceremony in the First Temple of the Occluded Ones in T'krr. He had been the first Grand Marshal NOT to be handed the sacred lance at the end of the ceremony. Once broken, its symbolic power was destroyed for ever, and to forge a replacement would have been a pointless sham. Even now, Zst'kh would sometimes catch himself flexing the fingers of his right hand; it felt curiously empty, sorely lacking a thing it had never held. It was not how he'd anticipated coming to power, nor, he now pondered, was this the sort of power he'd hoped to come to.

That's not to say that he wasn't in a position of considerable authority. In many respects, as commander-in-chief of extra-planetary defences for the whole planet Fnrr (as per the terms of the peace treaty) he found himself with a more onerous responsibility than any previous Grand Marshal. But it wasn't the same – he'd been trained to lead armies, command divisions, draw up invasion strategies, not read reports of diplomatic conferences or peruse star-charts. It did not get his blue blood pumping.

Until today.

- Again, St'nn-brkh, and slower this time.

Professor Steinberg did not attempt to correct Zst'kh's pronunciation of his name. He'd got used to it, and besides, his own command of the G'grk tongue left a great deal to be desired.

This command centre, the station from which the G'grk monitored extra-planetary activity, had been built under his direction and largely to his design (albeit with the inclusion of some exciting Fnrrn technology); it had almost begun to feel like home, but every now and again Professor Steinberg remembered just how far away from home he was. He took a deep breath, racked his brain for G'grk words and grammar, and spoke.

– *Is big maybe badness but is not tell now. Too long away. Not see goodness still.*

– *The cube, St'nn-brkh, the cube! Or we'll be here all cycle.*

Professor Steinberg muttered an apology, reached into his pocket and switched on the translation cube. Now was not the time to practise his G'grk.

– *It's a possible threat, but it's too far away to tell. It doesn't respond to any signals, and it hardly even shows up on the long-range scans at all. But it's—*

– *Yes, yes, St'nn-brkh, but it is definitely … what is the word, inbound?*

Professor Steinberg nodded. – *It's on an inbound trajectory, yes. It will pass through Fnrr's orbital path in just over three days – um, I mean rotations.*

Zst'kh smiled. A threat from space. Definitely his jurisdiction. And since all communication with the other nations of Fnrr was being blocked (apparently the work of that clownish amateur tyrant who had overthrown the weakling government of Mlml), his SOLE jurisdiction. Excellent.

The door of the command centre opened and the Rrth warrior entered. He saluted the Grand Marshal in the Rrth manner, touching his fingers to his brow (a curious custom, thought Zst'kh) and went to speak with his fellow Ymn.

'What do we have, Prof?'

'Man, am I glad to see you, James – look at this.' Professor Steinberg touched a panel and a holographic star-chart appeared in front of him.

'Here,' said Professor Steinberg, pointing at what, to Colonel Hardison, seemed to be blank space.

'What?'

'Exactly. It hardly shows up on the scan at all. If it hadn't created a gravity ripple as it passed through that asteroid field I probably wouldn't have spotted it.'

Colonel Hardison peered at the chart. 'Comet?' he asked. Professor Steinberg shook his head.

'Would be much more visible. And if it's an asteroid I haven't seen anything like it. And there's something else.' Steinberg touched another couple of controls and a thin line appeared, tracing through the chart.

'Look at this, James – it's not drifting. It looks like it is, but it isn't. This kind of course correction doesn't come about just from moving between gravitational fields, it's being steered towards us.'

Colonel Hardison, brows knitted, stood deep in thought for a moment. 'So what do we do?'

Professor Steinberg shrugged. 'Keep watching it. If it changed course once, it could do it again.'

Hardison gave a sideways nod towards Zst'kh. 'And what will HE do?'

Steinberg gave a heavy sigh. 'That, my friend, is a whole 'nother question. I yield to your superior experience of the workings of the military mind.'

Hardison smiled grimly. 'The HUMAN military mind,' he said quietly. 'I wouldn't even begin to guess what's going on inside that big grey skull.' He stretched, shook his head and flexed his limbs. Good thing he'd only had the one d'kff, he thought. 'Looks like it's gonna be a long night, anyway. I need to get cleaned up. I'll be back in an hour.'

Professor Steinberg watched Hardison walk stiffly towards the door. 'You've been playing that stupid game again, haven't you?' he said in an admonishing tone.

Hardison turned and smiled. 'Cultural immersion, Prof. It's all part of the mission.' He strode out.

Professor Steinberg shook his head. Some guys, you

could take them out of high school, but you could never quite take high school out of them …

* * *

Colonel Hardison's quarters in the command centre barracks were a great deal more comfortable than when he'd moved in, and they were still pretty sparse and spartan.

Thankfully he'd been tipped off as to the G'grk's preference for sleeping on hard metal surfaces; the Bradbury girl had mentioned it when she recounted the story of how she'd discovered – and ultimately averted – the G'grk invasion of her homeland. Remarkable young lady, thought Colonel Hardison; he wondered how she was doing back on Earth. So he'd known to bring his own bedding from his previous lodgings on Mlml. (Although that hadn't exactly been easy to come by in the first place, on an island where everyone slept in zero-gravity wells. He'd tried that just once. Never again.)

Apart from that, he had few personal effects (years in the Air Force had taught him the art of travelling light); spare uniform, dress uniform (even the G'grk had to acknowledge that he looked pretty damn sharp in that), and a few photos of his parents, and of Sarah, probably the most patient and understanding fiancée in the ENTIRE galaxy.

The one item of Earth gadgetry to be seen in his room was an old field radio, and even that had been augmented with Fnrrn technology. The young student whose name he really COULDN'T pronounce (Pgtf? Pkkt?) had been a frequent visitor – a VERY frequent visitor – during his stay on Mlml, bombarding him with questions about his own career and the history of the Air Force, and Earth military history in general. He'd spotted the radio in Hardison's quarters and been so fascinated by its simplicity and elegance that Hardison had offered to let him borrow it, saying that he should feel free to take it apart and have a good poke around inside. Hardison had figured that, if nothing else, this should keep the kid out of his hair for a while.

After about two weeks (or phases, as the Fnrrns called them) the kid had returned the radio, announcing happily that he'd stripped it down, figured out the circuitry and built one of his own. He added that since he couldn't help but notice that the radio's battery had long since gone flat, and since alkaline nine-volts were in short supply on Fnrr, he'd taken the liberty of installing a mini-fusion cell, so that now the radio would work, well, for ever. Impressed, and charmed, Hardison had taken the kid's bet, and left the radio permanently switched on.

So far the fusion cell had lasted nearly two Earth years, and showed no signs of failing. Hardison noticed the radio's little red light glowing away as he examined his new bruises in the mirror (another thing he'd had to import; the G'grk military regarded mirrors as effete and vain, which occasionally led to the bizarre – and, Hardison thought, oddly touching – sight of armoured G'grk warriors applying each other's war paint).

Hardison was just frowning at a livid purple blemish running the whole length of his upper arm, and reflecting that *that* was going to hurt in the morning, when he heard a sound he hadn't ever expected to hear again. Not on this planet, anyway.

A human voice. A female human voice.

In the same moment he worked out where it was coming from, he also figured out where he'd heard it before.

He picked up the radio, and the words came again.

'Major Hardison? Are you there, Major Hardison?'

He smiled and pressed the talk button.

'It's COLONEL Hardison now, and it's good to hear from you again, Miss Bradbury.'

* * *

Terra had not been particularly surprised to discover that Pktk had built his own Rrth-style radio. He and Fthfth had, after all, managed to create a telepathic transmitter using an old interface, a signal booster and a gene-scanner; he'd tuned it in on Terra's genetic profile using skin cells they'd found stuck to the end of Fthfth's gshkth gfrg – Fthfth had been desperately sorry about accidentally thwacking Terra with it all those orbits ago, but now she was very glad she had, and even MORE glad that she'd insisted, over the protests of her companions, on bringing her gfrg with her into exile. (– *They play gshkth in Dskt*, she'd pointed out, *and I might not have anything to do over there*.)

Pktk had brought the radio with him from Mlml when it became apparent that the Gfjk-Hhh was jamming all extra-planetary transmissions; he'd figured (correctly) that no one would think of blocking an old Rrth-type analogue radio signal.

But for all the ingenuity that had made this conversation possible, the conversation itself was not going as Terra had hoped.

'The young Grand Marshal isn't going to start a war with Mlml, not after the promise he made to his grandpa,' said Colonel Hardison. 'The old guy made him swear not to pre-emptively attack any nation.'

'But he wouldn't be attacking Mlml, he'd be attacking the Gfjk!' protested Terra.

'Hey, I get the difference, Miss Bradbury, but it's not a distinction the Grand Marshal is going to make. He's not about to take it upon himself to invade Mlml just because it would make SOME of the population happy.'

'So what do we do?' Terra said quietly. She was aware of all the expectant eyes upon her in the committee room. Pktk was fiddling with his radio to keep the signal strong, Fthfth was making herself useful (and keeping herself busy) handing out bowls of zff to Preceptor Shm and ArchRector Qss-Jff. But everyone was listening keenly.

'Listen, Zst'kh isn't particularly thrilled about the Gfjk – he'd prefer to have a happy democratic Mlml than a potential rival warlord rising just off the coast. And the whole reincarnation thing is making him kind of twitchy as well – his belief in the Occluded Ones is pretty strong.

The idea that the Gfjk has come to power on the back of an ancient prophecy is basically blasphemous as far as he's concerned …'

- *Nothing worse than having your own ancient prophecy upstaged by somebody else's,* muttered Pktk.

'… but I'm afraid you won't get Zst'kh to attack your Gfjk- … whatever he calls himself, unless the Gfjk attacks HIM,' said Colonel Hardison, before asking, 'Just how crazy is this guy?'

Terra looked around the room. 'Probably not crazy enough,' she concluded.

Billy, meanwhile, was quite glad to be listening to a conversation in English. He still had his doubts about the translation cube. Pondering how it did what it did made the inside of his skull itchy. The cube itself now sat on the long meeting table, next to the radio, translating Terra and Hardison's words for the Fnrrn listeners.

'Well, right now I'd have difficulty getting Zst'kh's attention away from this rogue planet he's spotted,' mused Hardison. 'I've never seen him so happy. Steinberg thinks it may be nothing, but Zst'kh's convinced we're under attack. He's got his own war at last. I don't think he'd be interested in yours.'

- *Rogue planet?* asked Pktk, intrigued.

'What rogue planet?' asked Terra.

'Steinberg spotted it a few hours ago. Big black thing, about the same size as Fnrr. Hardly shows up at all on the scans – it's like a hole in space. And it's headed this way.'

There was a sharp, clattering sound. Terra and the others looked round to see what had happened.

Preceptor Shm, his black oval eyes wide, had dropped his bowl of zff.

- *What … what did he say?*

* * *

Colonel Hardison wasn't using a translation cube; he didn't have to in order to speak to Terra and was quite enjoying having an old-style human non-psychic conversation.

The cube that was sitting next to Pktk's radio in Lsh-Lff had been translating Terra and Hardison's conversation for the benefit of the Fnrrns listening in, but it couldn't work the other way. When Shm spoke up, Hardison heard his words through the radio in the original Mlmln. The Colonel had only picked up a smattering of the clipped, clickety tongue during his stay in Hrrng, but out of respect for the old Preceptor, he decided to try to answer him in his language.

- *Black planet*, said Hardison in faltering, basic Mlmln. *Black planet coming.*

Preceptor Shm shuddered as if Hardison's words had struck him in the chest. Terra gazed at him in confusion. She'd never seen such fear in the old Fnrrn's eyes, not even during the invasion.

- *Preceptor?* she asked.

- *Oh no*, said Preceptor Shm, almost inaudibly. *Oh no . . .*

PART THREE

The Final Countdown

The day had arrived, the day of joy, the day of bliss, the day of perfection.

In the time that had elapsed between the philosopher-priests' announcement and today, the day their plan would be enacted upon, the scientists of Perfection had laboured upon the instruments of deliverance.

Crowds gathered on the steps of the Temple-Palace of Sha'ha-las at dawn. The philosopher-priests and the scientists emerged together to rapturous cheers.

They carried before them a great golden urn, a sealed vessel within which the Deliverers, as they had come to call them, were contained.

At the appointed hour, the urn was opened and the Deliverers were released to carry out their task. To preserve. To perfect.

The Deliverers sprang forth, and began to unweave Perfection. Cell by cell, molecule by molecule, they took the planet apart.

The people of Perfection sang songs of joy as they and their world were reduced to fine, black dust.

It was over within moments. The Deliverers reproduced at an astonishing rate, and soon they had swarmed across the planet's surface, leaving it silent. Black. Dead.

And so, the story of the planet Perfection came to an end.

Except it didn't.

The Deliverers had been endowed with just enough conscious-ness to carry out their task. Find life, and perfect it through dissolution at the molecular level.

Now the planet was dead. But the Deliverers' task had not yet been fulfilled.

As they swarmed, communicating through a low-level psychic field, they began to combine their meagre, insect-like intelligence and learned to think as one.

The Deliverers understood the concept of 'planet'. It had been vital to their programming.

Knowing that they were on a planet – and knowing what a planet was, and how such things were formed, from the accretion disc of a cooling star – they deduced that theirs was not the only such planet. There were billions. And logic dictated that of billions of worlds, at the very least hundreds, if not thousands, would support life.

Their programme was not complete.

The Deliverers devised a solution, a way to fulfil their task.

They ate away at the planet itself, multiplying by the billion, until the rock, mantel and core consisted entirely of black dust. Of themselves.

Then, using gravitational vibrations, they pushed the planet out of orbit and out into space. Drifting, steering, surging, riding the winds of gravity and spatial flux, the Black Planet began its quest in search of life to perfect.

The Coshrai people of the planet Sagaska were the first to see it.

3.1

It has to be here somewhere … Honestly, Qss, can't you keep your scrolls in orthographical order?

Preceptor Shm was rummaging through the contents of Lsh-Lff Polynasium's antiquities library. ArchRector Qss-Jff winced and flinched as his old friend manhandled and shuffled the ancient scrolls, many older than the Polynasium, some older than the city itself.

- They ARE in orthographical order, Shm, you just don't know your Dsktn spellings as well as you think you do. Look, get out of the way.

ArchRector Qss-Jff elbowed Shm aside and peered at the shelves. He'd recently had his eyes replaced and wasn't convinced that this new genetically optimised pair were half as good as his old ones.

- Now, what is it we're looking for again?

- The Zfft-Zkks Testimonial, said Shm. *It's the most complete account of the legend of the Black Planet. It's nine eras old.* He sighed. *I know EXACTLY where my copy is back at the Preceptorate.*

- But we're not there, are we, Shm? muttered Qss-Jff. His gaze fell upon a scroll bound with a black band. On a hunch he took it down.

- Ah! Here we are! Zfft-Zkks. I found it right away. He smiled. Shm took the scroll and frowned.

- It's a twenty-sixth era reprint, he grumbled. *My copy is one of the originals.*

- Does this one have all the same words? enquired Qss-Jff.

- Yes, murmured Shm.

- Well then, said Qss-Jff, *stop being such an ossified old fss-sft and let's have a look at it.*

With a disgruntled mumble, Shm took the scroll. The little gravity platform on which the two old academics were standing gently descended the thirty metres or so to the floor of the library.

Below them, Terra, Billy, Fthfth and Pktk watched them coming down.

- For a moment I thought they were going to shove each other off, whispered Fthfth to Terra.

The platform reached the floor and Shm strode along the aisle, through a door and into a reading room, the others hurrying along behind him. Billy shuffled up alongside Terra.

'What's he got there?' he asked.

'This black planet thing that's approaching – there's a legend told about it on many worlds. I think I may even have heard about it when I was little,' said Terra, suppressing the sharp pang of grief and worry that any flash of memory involving Lbbp always caused her. She composed herself and went on. 'The legend says it drifts through space and any planet it comes near to ... well, everything there dies and there's nothing left but black dust.'

'A cursed planet. Sounds like a pirate legend to me, like a ghost ship or something,' reflected Billy.

'Well, on a much bigger scale, that's more or less exactly what it is,' replied Terra. She was impressed at how many things Billy was able to take in his stride, and made a mental note to tell him so.

Shm was now unfurling the scroll across a dark stone table, and reading it intently.

'But what makes the Preceptor think that the legend is true?' asked Billy. And is he sure that this planet that's approaching now is the same one?'

'I don't know,' whispered Terra. 'I'm dying to ask what this scroll he's found is, but I don't want to disturb him.'

- So what's this scroll you've found, Preceptor? asked Fthfth loudly.

Shm grunted and looked up. - *The Testimonial of*

Zfft-Zkks gives details of all the recorded sightings of the Black Planet. I'm trying to find the last one.

- *Why the last one in particular?* asked Pktk.

- *Because the planet hasn't been seen for eras,* explained Shm. *It spent a whole epoch rampaging through space, wiping out entire species and cultures and then suddenly it vanished. Which suggests that the last race to encounter it—*

- *Found a way to beat it,* suggested Pktk, smiling.

- *Exactly,* said Shm. *And if they did beat it, or at least repel it, maybe we can too.*

Shm read on, pleased that the others were permitting him to do so without interruption.

Finally, he broke the silence, - *Here, this seems to be the last entry.* He gave a cough and read aloud:

- *'In the ninth cycle of the ninety-ninth orbit of the Age of Lamentation'* – odd calendric system, never mind – *'In the ninth cycle of the ninety-ninth orbit of the Age of Lamentation, the Hosheen people of the planet Despair'* – hmm, cheerful bunch – *'saw the Black Planet from a great distance. It approached Despair from such an angle that it was visible for many days as a black dot against their sun, which they called Hope'* – oh I see, Hope and Despair, quite poetic I suppose. Shm coughed and read on. *'The Hosheen appealed to their neighbours, the GoGorigols of the nearby planet Osfal, for help, and a plan was hatched. Despair was abandoned, the Hosheen crowding into any vessel fit for space travel. The GoGorigols helped, sending many ships. The Black Planet came on, arriving just as the last refugees fled. And the Hosheen made the ultimate sacrifice...'*

The listeners exchanged worried glances. That didn't sound encouraging. Shm went on.

- *As the Black Planet bore down upon Despair, scouring its surface, the Hosheen fired a massive anti-matter probe into the heart of their star Hope and detonated it.*

Pktk gave a quiet yelp of alarm. Shm either didn't hear or ignored it.

- *The star imploded, becoming a black hole. As the Hosheen watched, their dead sun consumed their homeworld and the*

Black Planet, dragging it out of space and time, never to return.

Shm rolled up the scroll. There was a moment's heavy silence. At last, Shm spoke.

- *Hm. That's not really an option, is it?* he said.

3.2

- Can I ask you a question?
The Gfjk-Hhh paused mid rant.

He'd been boasting to Lbbp of having thwarted yet another conspiracy against him. At least, it had looked like a
conspiracy to him. Lots of things looked like conspiracies.
He'd read something about how whenever an absolute ruler
is assassinated, it's very often his own bodyguards who finish
him off, so he'd had his personal protection squad arrested
and cast into the gshkth pit to be on the safe side. When
the victor had emerged, exhausted and bleeding, he'd had
him shot by his NEW personal protection squad. Good
for the new boys to get some proper on-the-job training.

The Gfjk-Hhh had been in the middle of explaining
how he was going to ensure the unswerving loyalty of his
new bodyguards (he'd had a few ideas and was currently
favouring one involving getting them to spy on each other
during their brief periods of free time) when Lbbp spoke.

The Gfjk was stunned into momentary speechlessness.
Lbbp hadn't said a word for days, not since the Gfjk had
had the pleasure of telling him of Terra's return to Fnrr.
(And yes, what was going on with the effort to capture
her? Heads would roll! Well, maybe not heads, but body
parts of some description. What else rolls?) The Gfjk had
more or less resigned himself to using Lbbp as a sort of
silent stress toy. It was less fun tormenting someone who
didn't react to the torment, but it was still more fun than
not tormenting him at all.

The Gfjk took a moment to formulate his reply, then
spoke.

- Yes? he said.

- Isn't this all a bit disappointing?

The Gfjk had no idea what Lbbp could possibly mean. Disappointing? What could be disappointing about wielding absolute power? - *Disappointing?* he replied.

- *You know,* said Lbbp, turning to face the Gfjk-Hhh, *after last time.*

The Gfjk really was confused now. - *Last time? What last time?*

Lbbp smiled. - *The last time you were here.*

- *I was here yesterday, don't you remember? You didn't say a word, of course … Wait, were you asleep? Because if you're going to start sleeping through my visits, I shall have to—*

- *No, no,* said Lbbp calmly. *The last time YOU were here, among us.*

The Gfjk peered at him in bewilderment for a moment, then burst into hissing laughter. - *Hkh hkh hkh! The last time I … you mean the last time the Gfjk-Hhh was … all those eras ago? Hkh hkh hkh hkh! Surely, Deceiver, you of all people, you should—*

Lbbp stood up. The very sight of this startled the Gfjk into silence. Lbbp leaned right up against the crystal and spoke in a conspiratorial whisper. - *Hey – it's just us, just you and me. We don't have to pretend.*

- *But I AM pretending!* said the Gfjk, who suddenly wondered if he'd said this a bit too loud.

- *Are you?* said Lbbp, fixing the Gfjk with a stare. *Are you sure?*

The Gfjk-Hhh had no immediate reply, so Lbbp went on. - *You've fulfilled the prophecy. Whether you meant to or not. There IS a Gfjk-Hhh reigning over Mlml, just like it said there would be. What makes you think it isn't supposed to be you?*

- *But …* the Gfjk struggled to put his thoughts in order, *but you – you gave me the idea to …*

- *Well, that's the thing about prophecies,* said Lbbp, *they work in strange ways. What if meeting me was all part of the plan? Why would you assume the new Gfjk would be born knowing who he was? What sort of newborn comes into the world knowing its own fate? It'd be singled out from birth as an anomaly, a sort of hyper-intelligent freak of nature. They'd spot him, they'd see him coming – the Gfjk-Hhh's enemies would have carried him off and killed him in infancy long before he'd had a chance to fulfil his destiny.*

The Gfjk considered all this. It was making sense. A glorious, radiant sense.

Lbbp went on, - *Wouldn't it be better if the child were born in innocence, in humble surroundings, and only discovered his true identity – perhaps met someone who would inspire him to go and discover it himself – when he was of age? When he was READY?*

I was ready, thought the Gfjk-Hhh. I was so ready. He smiled to himself. Lbbp saw the smile but did not react.

- *But like I said, it's all a bit disappointing. Last time round, you united a nation. You built a whole society out of nothing. You gave the people rights and freedoms. This time, all you've done is play petty, cruel games with them, toy with them. Hardly the actions of a great and noble leader.* Lbbp sat down and turned his back on the Gfjk. *Maybe you're right,* he said. *Maybe you are a fake after all.*

- *How DARE you!* shouted the Gfjk, rising up to his full height.

Got you, thought Lbbp.

3·3

- *T*erra! Wake up!

Terra's eyes popped open. Fthfth was standing by her sleep-well. Or rather, Fthfth was hopping up and down excitedly by her sleep-well. Terra groaned.

- *What time is it?*

- *Time to wake up!* said Fthfth happily. *Well, actually, no it isn't, that's not for ages, but wake up anyway!* She deactivated Terra's sleep-well.

Terra descended gently to the floor. The evening had been spent in fruitless discussion of how to address the twin problems of the Gfjk-Hhh and the Black Planet, and everyone had turned in for the night tense and anxious. Terra's sleep had been pretty restless, but she still felt like she needed more of it. - *What's going on, Fthfth?* she asked testily.

- *I couldn't sleep!* said Fthfth.

Terra was about to say, - *I could*, and switch her sleep-well back on, but Fthfth continued.

- *I've been running these problems round and round in my head, and I know what to do! Or at least I know who to ask what to do. Actually I know WHAT to ask what to do.*

Before Fthfth had woken her, Terra had been having a dream in which she'd been feeding slices of configuration 9 to a massive robot hippopotamus which kept saying, 'Where's Keith?' That dream had made a lot more sense to her than anything Fthfth had just said.

- *Start again*, said Terra. *You're babbling.* She shuffled off to the ArchRector's servery to get some zff and a couple of slices of configuration 6. There was something slightly odd-tasting about the protein configurations here in Dskt,

156

Terra thought. Like Dsktn protein manipulators didn't quite manipulate proteins the same way the ones back home did. Fthfth followed her.

- *The Extrapolator!* announced Fthfth, beaming. *Before we left Mlml, we tried to ask it what to do about the Gfjk-Hhh, but we couldn't seem to get it interested.*

Terra wasn't surprised. The Hrrng Preceptorate's super-computer, known as the Extrapolator because of its ability to collate and cross-reference all known data about the past and present to predict the future with a fair degree of accuracy, was notoriously uncooperative. Probably with good reason; were it to start granting any and all requests for knowledge of things to come, the laws of cause and effect would cease to apply and reality itself would be in serious trouble. Occasionally, the Extrapolator would take it upon itself to steer the course of events – such as the day it intervened in Lbbp's disciplinary hearing and insisted that the baby Terra be allowed to stay with him – but by and large, requests for help – even for the slightest hint about the future – went ignored.

- *The Extrapolator only gets involved when it suits the Extrapolator,* said Terra, chewing on a slice of what the protein manipulator insisted was configuration 6 but didn't taste like it to her.

- *Exactly!* beamed Fthfth. *And while it might not regard the Gfjk-Hhh as its problem – it doesn't really matter to the Extrapolator who's in charge, as long as he doesn't switch it off, and I don't think anyone even knows how – the Black Planet is DEFINITELY the Extrapolator's problem. If it destroys the planet, the Extrapolator will be gone, same as everything else. We know it has the power of reason, or it wouldn't keep doing things on its own initiative. So it MUST have the will to survive, the instinct to preserve its own existence. It HAS to take an interest.*

Terra's nose wrinkled. - *The Extrapolator's processor centre and data banks are a long way underground in a massive bunker* (she remembered this from a Lyceum trip);

and, thinking about those Black Planet legends, it only seems to be the surface of the planets that gets blackened. Maybe the Extrapolator reckons it can just sit it out.

Fthfth disagreed. - *The Extrapolator might be all-knowing, but it needs to be maintained, serviced, rebuilt occasionally. With no one to take care of it, it wouldn't last more than a few orbits.*

Terra pondered this as she finished her configuration 6 and made a mental note to try a different configuration next time. - *So why isn't it doing anything?*

Fthfth thought this over for a moment, then her eyes lit up. - *It doesn't know!* she said. *All communications between the nations are down, apart from Pktk's little radio-thing! We only know about the Black Planet because the Rrth soldier told us. If the information hasn't passed through any system connected to the Source ...*

- *... then the Extrapolator wouldn't have seen it. It doesn't know,* mused Terra. *Wow,* she went on, *we know something the Extrapolator doesn't! How cool is that?*

Fthfth was lost in thought, for a moment. Then she fixed Terra with a determined stare.

- *We have to go back,* she said. *We have to go back to Hrrng. Run all the information about the Black Planet through a slate, an interface, a visualiser, anything, then get the Extrapolator to run a long-range scan in the direction the Black Planet's coming from. Then it'll know how much trouble it's in!*

Terra went pale. - *You haven't been there for ages!* she said. *You don't know how bad things have got over there. We'll be lucky if we last a couple of days!*

Fthfth's stare became even more determined. - *Terra,* she said, *if we don't go back, this PLANET won't last more than a couple of days.*

3·4

- *So what do you suggest, Deceiver?*

SEven as the Gfjk-Hhh had swept out in fury at Lbbp's suggestion that he might not be the real thing (despite moments earlier acknowledging that he wasn't), Lbbp had known he'd be back soon enough.

And though the Gfjk's displeasure was obvious (Lbbp noticed that his pitiful rations had shrunk even further) Lbbp knew that his curiosity, his fascination at the possibility that he might, in fact, BE the person he'd been claiming to be, would overrule his anger. He'd be back, and he'd want to talk.

And here he was.

- *Well, Luminescence,* began Lbbp, using the 'proper' form of address for the first time, *what you need is ... some sort of quest, a challenge, a mission, if you will. Some way to carve your OWN place in history. You don't want to end up as nothing more than a footnote, an appendix to the accounts of the deeds of your former self.*

The Gfjk smiled. - *You forget, Deceiver. I know your ways. I see through your tricks. You're trying to get me to leave, aren't you? To set out on some foolish adventure, abandoning my people, my homeland ... Perhaps you think you might undo all I've done while I'm away, is that the idea?*

Lbbp pulled as innocent a face as he could manage. - *Not at all, Luminescence. I'm just talking about the scale, the SIZE of the task you need to undertake. It wouldn't have to involve going on a journey — who knows, the thing you seek could be right here, right at home. It only matters that it's something BIG, something heroic, something WORTHY of the Gfjk-Hhh.*

You'll work it out, Luminescence. Of course you will. I have ...
faith in you.

Lbbp watched a rapturous haze fall across the Gfjk's eyes and laughed inwardly. Yes, he thought. That's it. You're starting to dream. Dream big, as big as you can.

Because unlike you, thought Lbbp, I actually paid attention at the Lyceum. I read about the rise and fall of tyrants and emperors, on this world and others. And every time one falls, it's because the same thing happens.

He starts to believe his own legend, believe he's invincible, that there's nothing he can't do, no one who can stop him. So one day he pushes his luck just that little bit too far. He invades a country that he can't possibly hold, he extends the bounds of his empire further than he can maintain, he starves and humiliates his people while believing his own lie that they love him, and ends up looking on in astonishment as they storm his palace and burn it to the ground.

The Gfjk rose and turned to go. - *We will speak further on this, Deceiver.*

Lbbp watched him leave. Off you go and dream some more, he thought. You're going to – what was the Rrth expression? That was it – bite off more than you can chew. Because I'm going to feed it to you.

3·5

If it weren't for the fact that we're probably all going to be dead soon anyway, I'd say my parents were going to kill me, complained Pktk.

They had stolen through the quiet streets of Lsh-Lff before dawn, the two young Fnrrns and two young humans, and now passed through the broken coastward gates. Looking behind them, they saw the highly convincing – and disturbing – sight of the burned-out, ruined city.

- *Where are your parents, anyway?* asked Terra.

- *Back there in Lsh-Lff,* muttered Pktk.

- *They came with you?* said Terra, surprised. Fthfth grinned at this.

- *You don't think Pktk's parents would let a little thing like exile in the face of tyranny and insurrection make them let him out of their sight, do you?* Pktk glowered at her, but Terra smiled. She'd known Pktk's parents well. War hero he might be, but Pktk would always be their baby.

- *Mine are okay, so far . . . probably,* Fthfth went on. *They've got a little house in the forest in Mntp. No one knows where it is but them. They're hiding out there . . . I think.* Fthfth's smile faded.

Billy interrupted the conversation. - *Erm . . . it's not there, guys.*

Strannit Zek's dinghy, the luxurious well-appointed landing craft in which they'd escaped from Hrrng, and which they'd left parked outside the gates, was nowhere to be seen.

- *Invisibility shield?* asked Pktk.

Terra frowned. - *Well, it has one, but it wasn't switched on when we left it here.* She produced her comm from her rucksack and waved it towards where the dinghy wasn't. *No*, she said, *it's gone.*

– *They'll have moved it inside,* said Billy. *Look closely and you can see the tracks in the grass. They've pulled it through the gates. I suppose if you want everyone to think that there's no one alive in the city, having a spaceship parked right outside the gates is a bit of a giveaway. They've hidden it.*

– *So now what?* asked Terra, exhausted and discouraged.

– *Come with me.* Pktk smiled. He marched off towards the shore.

Billy looked around him as they went. Were it not for the purple hues of the grass, just visible in the moonlight, and the fact that this moonlight came from three moons (the other three being below the horizon), he might have been on Earth, taking a stroll by the seaside. Suddenly, the very similarity of the landscape to a typical Earth vista made him feel even further from home. He put the thought from his mind and marched on, onto the dunes of the beach itself.

– *Careful,* said Pktk, *you're walking right towards—*

Billy's nose impacted hard against something cold, solid and quite invisible. He fell to the sand.

– *—it,* said Pktk.

Billy clutched his aching proboscis. – *Typical,* he said, his eyes streaming, *I'm the one who walks into it and I'm one of only two of us who've got noses. What is it, anyway?*

– *Just a moment.* Pktk smiled, feeling along the invisible surface. He found a gap in the shape, and vanished inside. I'm actually getting used to seeing people do that, thought Billy.

There was a crackle of energy, and the shape appeared in front of them. Terra gasped in horror.

It was a giant blue sphere. A G'grk battle sphere. She'd ridden in one before, a captive, being taken to what she'd feared would be – what, by any logic, should have been – certain death. She'd seen hundreds of similar spheres laying waste to her home city, hovering above the skyline, belching grav-rockets and pulse-cannon bursts, raining death. She shuddered violently.

Pktk's head emerged from the hatch. - *Our own G'grk battle sphere! Isn't it brilliant?*

- *NOT the word I would have used,* said Terra, beginning to recover a little. The very sight of Pktk emerging from the sphere, rather than ranks of armoured G'grk drones, immediately made it far less threatening a presence.

- *I found it a couple of cycles ago,* said Pktk happily. *It must have been left behind during the retreat. It's still powered up and everything. The controls are so simple – well, they were designed for G'grk to use.*

Terra frowned. That sort of cheap disrespect for the G'grk was supposed to have ended with the peace treaty. It angered her to hear Pktk throwing it into conversation like that. She resolved to have words with him in due course but not right now. - *Can you fly it?* she asked instead.

- *Oh yes, easily,* said Pktk airily. *Come on in!*

They clambered through the hatch, first Terra, then Fthfth and finally Billy. Billy looked sadly at the sphere's interior. Strannit's dinghy had been full of padded, upholstered seats. This sphere didn't seem to have anything to sit on at all. Even the pilot was meant to take a standing position at the controls, as Pktk now did.

- *Invisibility shield back on!* reminded Fthfth. *We can't let them see us coming.* Pktk looked at the battle-sphere console and tried to remember the intitialisation sequence. Simple though the controls were, he always found it hard to concentrate this early in the morning. If only he'd been able to make himself some FaZoon soup, he thought sadly. You just couldn't get the ingredients in Lsh-Lff . . .

Pktk jabbed at the controls in what he thought was the right order; to his relief, the gravity engines started to grind away noisily and the sphere juddered into the air . . .

They might not see us coming, thought Terra, but they'll probably hear us. She looked at Billy. He was sat cross-legged on the floor, and seemed to be chuckling quietly at some private joke. 'What's so funny?' she asked him.

Billy looked up, smiling. 'I'm just thinking about my mum,' he said. 'Her big worry since I became a teenager is that I'll start hanging out with the bad lads from off the estate and go round nicking cars all night. Always on about it, she is. "You come straight home from the pictures, our Billy; I don't want you hanging out with the bad lads and going round nicking cars." She was so pleased when she found out my best friend was a girl, she was like, "Well, she's got daft hair, but at least it'll mean he's not off nicking cars with the bad lads off the estate."' Billy laughed out loud.

'What?' persisted Terra. Billy, hardly able to talk through his laughter, grinned at her.

'In the past few days hanging out with you, I've nicked three spaceships and a battle sphere.'

And Terra laughed with him.

3.6

Colonel Hardison had his eyes on Professor Steinberg's holographic star-chart and his Pktk-adapted field radio in his hand. I know some extremely clever people, he thought to himself. He spoke into the radio, in English.

'It hasn't changed course, Preceptor. Still headed this way. Professor Steinberg says – what? Oh, for—! Professor Steinberg says HELLO. There, I said it, happy now? He also says it's definitely being guided, it's not drifting. And according to his projections, it'll pass right by us – inside the orbit of the six moons – in another two days' time.'

Preceptor Shm's voice came through the radio; Professor Steinberg's cube, sitting on the desk in front of Hardison, translated as Shm spoke.

- *It all fits with the legends. The Black Planet was said to pass close to inhabited worlds, there would be some sort of transfer of matter or energy and the inhabited world would be left scoured and lifeless.*

Hardison nodded grimly, then remembered that Shm couldn't see him, and replied, 'I know. I've told Grand Marshal Zst'kh. I've never seen him so happy.'

- *Happy?* said Shm, then, thoughtfully, *Yes, I suppose he must be. Do you have any idea what he has in mind?*

Hardison glanced around the command centre. The Grand Marshal himself was elsewhere (working on who-knew-what), but a few drone officers were milling around. He lifted the radio close to his face and went on in a lowered voice, 'Not so far. He's just told me the matter's in hand. I think he reckons this is his chance to fulfil his destiny or something.'

Preceptor Shm's sigh was audible over the radio.

– You know, I do wish people would stop worrying about their 'destinies' for a while and just get on with living in the present … Well, see what you can find out. There's not much I can do about anything from here, I'm afraid. Oh, that reminds me. I don't suppose you've heard from the Ymn girl again, have you?

'Terra?' asked Colonel Hardison. 'No, why?'

Another audible sigh from Preceptor Shm. *– She and her little band of friends have gone missing. I've a horrible feeling I know where they've gone. Everyone here is more than a little concerned, as you can imagine. In particular I'm getting all sorts of complaints from young Pktk's parents.*

Hardison smiled. He'd met Pktk's parents. Shm went on:

– If you hear from her, tell her …

A pause.

'Tell her what?'

– Tell her to be careful, that's all.

'I will,' said Colonel Hardison, and put the radio down on the desk.

'What was that all about?' asked Professor Steinberg, looking up from his calculations.

'Terra and her pals are missing. Think she's gonna try to liberate Mlml on her own,' said Hardison, with a knowing smile.

'Best news I've heard all day.' Steinberg smiled. 'If anyone can do it, she can.' He looked up at his star-chart and his face fell. The Black Planet was now clearly visible, a circle of pure darkness. 'I wish I knew what Zst'kh was cooking up,' he muttered.

'Me too,' said Hardison.

3·7

Terra shrugged. - *I did warn you*, she said.

Fthfth was gazing round the Preceptorate in utter despair. Terra had never seen her so distressed. Looking at Fthfth's face, she wouldn't have been surprised if her Fnrrn friend had spontaneously evolved tear ducts just in order to have tears in her eyes.

- *But ...* Fthfth began, *but who would DO this? Why? What's the point?*

They stood in front of the pile of smashed interfaces. Pktk put an arm round Fthfth's shoulders, and said thoughtfully:

- *All dictators need to control access to information. First thing you do when you take over. Also, if you're basing your claim to power on some sort of supernatural authority, a prophecy or divine commandment or something, you need to clamp down on anything which might be able to disprove your claim. Close down the libraries, round up the scientists ...*

- *Burn the books*, muttered Billy.

- *Books?* asked Pktk.

- *Never mind*, said Billy.

They'd landed the sphere, still cloaked in invisibility, next to the statue that wasn't of Tnk any more. Terra had forced herself not to look up at the statue's face; to see that grinning idiot's visage where Tnk's noble expression belonged would have so consumed her with indignation that she wouldn't have been able to think about anything else. She needed her wits about her now.

Foolishly, they'd left the two white New Believer robes aboard Strannit Zek's dinghy; they were lost somewhere inside Lsh-Lff now, along with the dinghy itself. Terra and Billy felt horribly exposed – the only Ymns in Hrrng – but fortunately the Preceptorate was every bit as deserted as they'd left it.

Fthfth took a moment to collect herself, then stood up very straight and announced in a clear voice, - *Right! I need to access the Extrapolator. What's the best way of doing it?*

Pktk thought. - *Well, in every instance I've ever heard of when the Extrapolator actually responded to someone, they were standing in the main council chamber. So that seems like a good place to start.*

- *Well, off we go, then!* said Fthfth, striding off towards the quartz dome. She'd gone a few steps before she realised that Terra and Billy hadn't moved at all. She looked back and saw Terra, standing stock-still and ashen-faced, a worried-looking Billy by her side. Fthfth was about to ask what the matter was, when it dawned on her.

- *Oh, Terra,* she said, *I'm so sorry. I forgot ... You don't have to.*

- *What's the matter?* Billy's question was directed more at Fthfth than at Terra, but it was Pktk who answered him.

- *The last time Terra was in the council chamber, it ... it wasn't ...*

Terra looked up at Billy, tearful and trembling. Billy didn't know what they were referring to specifically, but he got the idea. Something terrible had happened to Terra in that place. Fthfth took both of Terra's hands and looked her in the eyes.

- *Terra, don't think of that day. Think of the first day we saw the inside of the dome. Our first day at the Lyceum ... Remember Preceptor's Shm's speech? You nearly dozed off, remember? I definitely heard you snoring.*

Terra laughed in spite of herself, a smile breaking through her fear.

- *Well, Preceptor Shm's bored another two classes half-asleep since then in that dome, and it's all thanks to you,* said Fthfth, grasping Terra's hands tightly. *Terra, that dome isn't the place where you nearly died, it's the place where you saved us all.*

Terra grimaced a smile and sniffed. Fthfth was the kind

of friend you only found once in a galaxy, she thought to herself.

Fthfth grinned. – *Now let's get in there, 'cos it's MY turn to save everybody,* she said. She turned and marched off towards the dome. Terra took Billy's hand and set off after her.

3.8

This is actually pretty good fun, thought Colonel Hardison. Maybe I should apply for some black ops assignments if I ever get home.

Nah, he reminded himself, you've always been a full uniform stand up and salute kind of guy. Not the sneaking around type.

Still, he thought to himself, looks like you might be pretty good at sneaking around anyhow.

He'd made it unnoticed out of the command centre barracks in the dead of night. He'd waited for the Grand Marshal to emerge from his private quarters, accompanied by his personal bodyguards, and followed him to the barn-sized building which stood at the far end of the complex. He'd remained outside, unseen, for at least an hour, while Zst'kh did … whatever he was doing in there.

Hardison watched from the shadows as, Zst'kh and his guards emerged, marching back towards the Grand Marshal's quarters, but he did not follow them. He wasn't interested in the Grand Marshal's movements. He was intensely interested in seeing what was inside that barn-sized building.

A single G'grk drone stood guard in front of the building's entrance. Hardison looked around on the ground for something heavy. Finding a rock about the size of his fist, he picked it up and, thoughts of high school baseball flashing through his mind, hurled it into the darkness. It landed with a clattering noise about fifty yards away. The drone, hearing it, ran off to investigate.

I canNOT believe he fell for that, thought Hardison. Hasn't he seen ANY old prisoner-of-war movies?

No, of course he hasn't, Hardison told himself, as he tried the door. Finding it unlocked, he slid it open, slipped inside and closed it firmly but silently behind him.

The interior of the building was in darkness. Hardison took a moment while his eyes adjusted.

There was something there; a single vast object occupying the whole length of the building. Shiny, cylindrical, lying on its side, the end nearest him tapering to a point, the far end – he could just about make it out – finned and flared. He'd been an Air Force officer long enough to know exactly what he was looking at.

The room was flooded with light. A familiar voice came from behind him.

- If you wanted to know what we were building, Ymn, you should have asked us, said Grand Marshal Zst'kh.

- I DID ask, responded Hardison, *many times over. You said you'd tell me when the time was right, remember?*

- Indeed I did, said the Grand Marshal, gesturing to his guards to lower their pulse-orbs. *And now you have finally taken the initiative and found out for yourself, the right time has arrived. Keeping secrets,* Zst'kh said, with a dismissive sneer, *is not the G'grk way.*

- But building giant missiles behind closed doors is? challenged Hardison. *How long have you been working on this thing? Steinberg only detected the Black Planet yesterday. There's no way you put this monstrosity together overnight.* He approached the Grand Marshal and looked him right in the face. *So who were you going to use this thing on? Dskt? Mlml?*

- Hopefully, neither, said Zst'kh. *This –* he gestured toward the missile – *was Marshal Sk'shk's creation. He had our Dsktn hosts work on this weapon during the occupation. If Dskt had rebelled against us, or Mlml had proved impossible to subdue, then an example would have been made of the unruly nation, in order to pacify the other. Don't look so shocked, Hrrd's-nn,* he said, registering the Colonel's disgust, *your planet's history is full of instances of such actions being taken by conquerors*

against the conquered. Was it not your own people, he said, fixing Hardison with a stare, *who vaporised two whole cities full of civilians in order to offer just such an example? Even in our own history, there is nothing so ... uncompromising.*

Hardison's jaw clenched. - *That was different,* he said, although if pressed, he wasn't sure he could explain exactly how at that moment. Fortunately, Zst'kh went on.

- *But then, the ... curious events ... in Hrrng unfolded, and the war ... ended,* he said uncomfortably. *All work on this project was suspended. Few even know of this weapon's existence. I was only informed myself upon my investiture. So when St'nn-brkhh warned us of the Black Planet's approach – and the Mlmln scientist identified it as the dreaded destroyer of legend – I ordered the missile to be completed. The warhead is almost prepared. If St'nn-brkhh is correct about the time of the Black Planet's arrival, then the weapon will be ready to fire with just moments to spare.*

Colonel Hardison studied the gleaming rocket; it certainly looked powerful. Would it be accurate enough? Did the G'grks even understand the technology that had gone into creating it? Might they destroy Fnrr in their attempt to save it?

Grand Marshal Zst'kh, it seemed, harboured no such doubts. - *So you see, Hrrd's-nn, the Occluded Ones are indeed wise.* He smiled. *They have denied us our place as Fnrr's rulers in order that we might become its SAVIOURS.*

Hardison hoped the Grand Marshal was right.

3.9

'**A** re you all right?' asked Billy quietly.
Terra breathed hard and nodded.

She'd clenched her eyes shut as she'd passed into the domed chamber but opened them soon after. There was something so distinctive about the way sound reflected off those curved quartz walls that there was no mistaking where she was, even without looking.

With a deep breath, she'd opened her eyes. The dome looked more like the way it had the first time she'd seen it, on that first day at the Lyceum. The holographic portraits of long-dead Preceptors had been restored, the damage done during the invasion repaired. There were no blue G'grk banners fluttering from the ceiling, although her mind's eye was treacherously painting them back in.

Fthfth was looking at her slate. - *There,* she said, *I've loaded all the files I could gather about the Black Planet up onto the Source.*

Terra was surprised. - *You managed to get onto the Source?*

Pktk held his own slate up. - *The Source is still accepting submissions of information; it's just blocking requests to READ information. I suppose the Gfjk didn't think there'd be any danger in people telling him things, just in them finding stuff out. But it means I can figure out what he's done and maybe even how to undo it.* Pktk smiled quietly. *Idiot,* he muttered. *I would have totally thought of that.*

Fthfth coughed and went on. - *I've ALSO loaded an astroscopic plan of the trajectory of the Black Planet. Hopefully the Extrapolator will ... well, extrapolate something.*

Billy looked around. The dome reminded him of the circular reading room in the big Central Library back home, only shinier. He remembered being told about a curious acoustic feature of the reading room whereby the tiniest sound would travel diametrically across the room, so you could have a whispered conversation from a great distance as long as you sat directly opposite each other. He and Lydia – sorry, TERRA – had tried this once and it had worked, much to their amusement. He thought about suggesting trying it out in this room but decided against it. It wouldn't have gone down well, he suspected, and he wasn't sure how Terra would react to being reminded of home.

No, not home; Earth. He could tell that Earth wasn't really home for her any more and at that moment, he realised, it didn't feel THAT much like home to him either...

There was a moment's silence.

- *So now what?* asked Billy.

- *We wait,* said Fthfth, staring at her slate.

Another moment's silence.

And another.

- *For how long?* pursued Billy. *I mean I don't want to hassle you or anything, but between the mad dictator and the planet of doom up there, we're kind of against the clock here.*

Terra stared daggers at Billy, but Pktk spoke up. - *No, he's right,* he said, *we can't just wait for the Extrapolator to respond. We have to try to contact it directly.*

- *But no one knows how!* protested Fthfth.

- *Wait a minute,* said Billy. *You said that this room had some sort of connection with the Extrapowhatsit, didn't you? That it replied to people who were standing in this room? Wasn't that why we had to come in here and scare the p'zk out of Terra?* Interesting, thought Billy, I'm even swearing in Mlmln.

- *Well, yes, but—* began Fthfth.

- *HELLO?* bellowed Billy towards the ceiling. *Are you listening? Can you hear us? Only this planet's in trouble, and if I've got it right, if the planet goes, you go with it, so ARE YOU RECEIVING US?*

Billy's voice echoed around the dome for what seemed to Terra like about half an hour. - *Brilliant,* she snarled at him. *Just brilliant. You remember we're supposed to be sneaking around unnoticed, right? I don't know if the Extrapolator heard you, but I bet somebody did!*

- *No ... wait*, said Pktk. *Look!* He held up his slate.

The symbols meant nothing to Billy, but Terra read them instantly. - *'Yes, I hear you.' I don't believe it!*

Billy smiled.

- *I think we have the Extrapolator's attention*, explained Fthfth, looking delighted.

Pktk's fingers hovered over his slate. - *What do we say?*

- *Ask it if it's seen the Black Planet and if it understands the threat*, said Terra. Pktk tapped away on his slate.

- *Well?* asked Fthfth. Pktk peered at the slate.

- *It says 'I am aware'*, he said.

- *What can we do?* asked Fthfth.

There was a pause. Pktk stared at the slate as if in disbelief. - *It says 'Survive. Consume. Reproduce.'* He stared blankly at his companions.

Billy coughed. - *I think*, he ventured, *that might be a computery way of telling organic life forms to go about their usual business.*

Terra was furious. - *But we can't go about our usual business! If the Black Planet reaches our space, we WON'T survive. Does it know that?*

Pktk tapped, then read. - *It says 'I am aware' again*, he said.

Fthfth had another thought. - *Ask it if it knows what's going to happen. Not WHAT'S going to happen – it'll never tell us – just if it KNOWS what's going to happen.*

Pktk tapped. A longer pause, then, - *It says, 'The outcome has been predicted.'*

This seemed to animate Fthfth. - *So if it KNOWS what's going to happen, and it's not willing to intervene or tell us what to do, that must mean it's confident that everything will be okay, mustn't it?*

- *Maybe not everything*, corrected Pktk, *it might just*

mean it thinks IT's going to be okay. We don't really know how bothered it is about what happens to US.

Terra decided to cut to the chase. - *If the outcome has been predicted, does that mean everything will be okay whatever we do, or do we still have to think of doing whatever it is it thinks we're going to think of doing?*

Everyone stared at Terra blankly. - *I don't know if the Extrapolator would understand that, but I certainly didn't,* said Pktk.

- *I did,* said Billy. *Will everything sort itself out, or is it still up to us to save everyone?*

- *Thank you,* said Terra.

Pktk was about to tap this simpler version of the question into his slate, when he paused. - *It's already answering,* he said.

- *Told you it could hear us.* Billy beamed.

Pktk looked up apologetically. - *It just says, 'All events are proceeding as anticipated.' I don't think we're going to get anything out of it, do you?*

Terra thought. - *If the Extrapolator's right, we've got nothing to lose by TRYING to figure out how to stop the Black Planet. If it all turns out okay without us, then fair enough, but I don't think we can ASSUME that's going to happen.*

Fthfth sighed. - *So where do we start?*

Terra pondered a moment, then spoke, - *The Black Planet should be close enough now to get a proper look at it. If we can figure out what it's made of, or what's controlling it, we might be able to think of a way to stop it.*

- *The astroscopy lab, then,* said Pktk. *Or whatever's left of it.*

They turned to go. At the doorway, Fthfth turned and shouted, - *You're about as much use as the FaZoon, you know that?* She left, slamming the door.

If Pktk had been looking at his slate as he hurried towards the astroscopy lab, he would have noticed that it displayed, yet again, 'I am aware.'

3.10

'He's calling it the Lance of the Occluded Ones,' said Colonel Hardison over the radio. Preceptor Shm gave a groan of distaste that he knew would be clearly audible in T'krr.

- *Named for the broken lance of office, of course.* Shm's guts (located, like all Fnrrn's, in his chest cavity) turned at the memory of the last time he'd seen the actual lance. Protruding from poor Lbbp's shoulder, his blue blood staining the floor of the council chamber. Shm had seen how that lance had met its end; snapped in half by its last owner, the now-retired Grand Marshal Z'ksht, to enable Lbbp to be carried away for treatment. The old warrior's destruction of his own sacred emblem had saved young Lbbp's life. (And where was he now? – Shm didn't like to contemplate.) That act had sealed the unexpected accord between G'grk and Mlmln, ending the war, but it had caused distress and alarm among the more hardline elements of his own people.

'I guess Zst'kh just didn't feel like a real Grand Marshal without one,' mused Hardison, echoing Shm's thoughts exactly.

- *The real question is, will it work?* wondered Shm.

'Well, it's certainly big,' came Hardison's reply, 'and if the specifications of the warhead's yield I've read are correct, it might be powerful enough. How accurate it is … Well, your guess is as good as mine on that one, Preceptor.'

Shm had fleeting visions of the missile's engines failing during take-off, the rocket falling back to Fnrr. He pushed the image from his mind, and asked, - *Will it be ready in time?*

'Just barely – the explosive elements which make up the

warhead are being enriched right now – it's a chemical process which can't be sped up. If Steinberg's right about the planet's ETA – and he's usually right about that kind of thing – they'll be loading the warhead onto the missile with minutes left on the clock.'

After a moment's delay (the translation cube had a little difficulty with the Rrth acronym 'ETA' and the expression 'on the clock' but figured them out after a blip or so) Shm responded. – *I'm not sure whether I'm more worried about the Black Planet or the G'grk's solution to it,* he grunted.

'What about the crazy dictator?' asked Hardison.

Shm blinked and sat down. – *To be honest, I'd rather forgotten about him,* he said.

3.11

- *No, no, that's not the idea at all, said Lbbp. You're still thinking in terms of how you can make yourself LOOK mighty and important, when you need to think about how you can actually BECOME mighty and important.*

- *Oh*, said the Gfjk-Hhh, disappointed. He'd rather liked his idea of carving his face into the surface of each of the six moons, so that even after his death (assuming he DID ever die, of course; that was by no means a given) he could gaze down smilingly upon his beloved children. Still, he could always do that as well, he supposed. *So what sort of thing do YOU think I should do?* he asked.

Behind him, Wffk waited, scroll in hand, ready to take notes. Wffk wasn't sure what made him more uncomfortable – being in the dank cell, or the dread presence of His Luminescence's arch-nemesis. Why exactly His Luminescence had come to consult the Deceiver on his course of action, Wffk couldn't begin to fathom, so he didn't try.

- *Well, think back to the last time*, said Lbbp soothingly. *What makes you proudest? What do you remember most fondly?*

The Gfjk cast his mind back. It was strange, but when he thought about it he COULD remember his previous incarnation. How ridiculous, he thought, that he'd once believed he was faking his identity! Images passed through his mind; throngs of robed Fnrrns crowding into the Forum square to hear him ... cheering as he passed through the streets in his jewelled chariot ... he could see it all so clearly now.

His reverie was disturbed by the voice of the Deceiver.

- *Okay, here's a suggestion*, said Lbbp. *In your previous* incarnation, you were famed for your justice and fairness. You were ruthless but also merciful. This time around, if you don't mind my saying so, Luminescence, you've certainly got the ruthlessness together, but the mercifulness ... not so much.

- *I see*, said the Gfjk thoughtfully, *so I should be showing mercy to who exactly?*

- *Well*, began Lbbp, *for a start, how many political prisoners do you currently have detained?*

The Gfjk mulled this over. - *Not as many as you'd think, actually. I've arrested LOADS of them, but I don't tend to detain them for very long, if you get my meaning. I only hold them until I find space for them in the gshkth pit. There's a BIT of a waiting list but—*

- *There you go*, said Lbbp. *That's a perfect way to demonstrate your mercy. You could offer amnesty to all your political prisoners. That's a proper wise and noble leader gesture.*

The Gfjk's face fell. - *No more Scary Gshkth? The people will be SO disappointed.*

Lbbp gave a shrug-wobble of his head. - *We all have to make sacrifices for the good of society, Luminescence*, he said solemnly.

The Gfjk sighed. - *I suppose you're right. Wffk, write this down. Scary Gshkth to be suspended indefinitely, amnesty granted for all political prisoners.* Yes, both of them, the Gfjk thought to himself. It was a VERY short waiting list. He stood up and stretched. *Ah! You know what, I feel nobler and more merciful already! Thank you Deceiver, you've been most helpful. I'll be back in the morning.*

The Gfjk got up and turned to leave, Wffk bustling after him. As he approached the cell door, he turned and addressed Lbbp.

- *Oh, wait, you didn't think ... You weren't expecting me to release YOU, were you? Oh dear me, no.* He went back to the crystal. *You're not a political prisoner, Deceiver, you're my most trusted adviser.* The Gfjk smiled coldly, then tapped the crystal. *Well, I SAY trusted ...*

He turned to go. - *Don't worry, Deceiver*, he said as he

strode to the door, *my mission will soon be revealed to me. I feel it in my ... my ... that place where you feel things.*

The Gfjk-Hhh and his scrivener swept out. As the cell door clanged shut, Lbbp sat down. He hadn't really thought it would be that easy. Worth a shot, though.

3.12

- *Well? said Pktk.*
    - *It's black,* said Fthfth.
- *Brilliant,* said Pktk, pacing up and down in the astroscopy lab. The lab had been as quiet and deserted as the rest of the Preceptorate, but unlike some of the facilities on the lower floors, it hadn't been vandalised. Good job the Gfjk's thugs were as lazy as they were stupid, Terra had thought. It had meant they could remote-activate an orbital astroscope, and Fthfth was now perusing its readings on one of the lab's visualiser screens, her brow furrowed.

- *No, seriously,* said Fthfth, *it's BLACK. As black as it's possible to be. The surface is completely non-reflective, either to visible or invisible light frequencies, or any sort of long-range scan. It's like a gap in space, a ball of nothing.*

- *If only it were,* said Terra. *Keep trying. As it gets closer, you might spot something.*

- *Yes, and my last words will be 'Oh look!'* Fthfth smiled anxiously.

Pktk stopped pacing. - *I think we may be going about this the wrong way,* he mused.

- *How do you mean?* asked Billy.

- *Well, if there's no information to be had from looking at the planet itself, then maybe there's information to be found elsewhere.*

- *Such as?* asked Fthfth, looking up from the screen.

- *History,* said Pktk.

Fthfth groaned. - *Not you and your history texts again! Not all wisdom is to be found in your crumbly old military memoirs, you know! This problem is happening here and now, not on some battlefield in the twenty-fifth era!*

- Not military history this time, said Pktk, *natural history. There's a database of every planet that has ever been surveyed – by this Preceptorate or any other institution that came before it, going back for eras and eras and spanning the whole galaxy. There are records of the position, dimensions, mass, composition, every physical detail of every planet in existence or that's ever BEEN in existence.*

- How will that help? squeaked Fthfth.

Pktk pointed at the image of the Black Planet on the screen. *- Whatever that is, if it is actually a planet, then it's on that database somewhere. If we can find out WHICH planet it is, then we can figure out what happened to it to turn it into that ... thing. Then we might actually know what we're dealing with.*

- And what if it's not a planet? said Billy quietly. *What if it's just some vast planet-sized weapon, left over from some ancient space war? It certainly seems to work like a weapon.*

- Well, if it's not in the database, we'll know, won't we, said Pktk simply. *Process of elimination.*

- It's a start, said Terra. *And it's the closest thing we've had to an actual idea all day. How do we access this database?*

- Difficult, said Pktk, *if we can't request it from the Source.*

- Yes, frowned Fthfth. *Is anybody else getting REALLY annoyed about the Source being down?*

3.13

*G*o away, *murmured the Gfjk–Hhh.*

The door to his chambers tinkled again. The Gfjk thrashed around in his sleep-well. - *I said GO AWAY, or I'll have you thrown into the Gshkth . . .*

Oh yes, he thought. No more Scary Gshkth, by order of me. Gzzks.

Miserably, the Gfjk deactivated his sleep-well and unlocked his door. It was Wffk. Of course it was Wffk. He was getting a bit tired of seeing Wffk.

- *I'm so sorry to disturb you, Luminescence, but I thought you should see this,* stammered Wffk.

REALLY tired of seeing Wffk. What to do with him, in the absence of Scary Gshkth?

- *Several citizens reported seeing something odd in the night sky. I realise the observatory was closed down by Luminescent Decree, but . . .*

Feed him to something? Like what? Wild znks? How do I get hold of wild znks at this time of night?

- *I felt that the phenomenon merited closer investigation, so . . .*

No, far too much hassle. AND dangerous. Once the znks had eaten Wffk, then what, eh? See, when you're a leader you have to think about these things.

- *I found one of the College of Astroscopers in the Reformatory, Luminescence, and I set him to work . . .*

Shove him off the top of the Forum! That was it. Yes. Come up here a moment, Wffk. Now, look down there . . . Whoops! Splat.

- *. . . and he has reported that the object . . .*

No, no, not the Forum building, far too low. High

enough to do the job, obviously, but not high enough to be fun watching him go. Something higher.

– *Wffk, old thing, what's the tallest building in Hrrng?* asked the Gfjk chirpily.

– *What, Luminescence? I'm afraid I don't know. I could find out?*

Hang on, whatever that was that Wffk was on about, it sounded like it might have been a bit important.

– *I'm sorry, Wffk, I wasn't listening to a word you were saying. Could you repeat it, please?*

– *Certainly, Luminescence. A mysterious object has been sighted in the night sky. It appears to be a rogue planet. It is completely black and featureless . . .*

The Gfjk suddenly remembered how tired he was. – *And what does this have to do with me?*

Wffk coughed apologetically. – *Forgive me, Luminescence . . . but there is an old legend I recall hearing as a child.*

The Gfjk perked up. – *Legend, you say? Nothing wrong with legends, Wffk. Very useful things if used correctly. Let's hear this legend.*

Wffk related the legend that he remembered from his youth. And as the Gfjk listened, his eyes opened wider and wider.

- *W*ow. *That's actually very clever, mused Fthfth.*
    - *Well, we know he's not stupid,* said Terra. *Crazy, but not stupid. What exactly has he done?*

Fthfth was holding up her slate for the others to see. Reams of characters raced across it. Billy tried looking at the display and got an almost instant headache. Even if those had been Earth numerals, he wouldn't have been able to make any sense of the hurtling figures. As it was, he found himself unpleasantly reminded of the swirly colours you saw when you poked your fingers in your eyes.

- *What is it?* asked Pktk.
- *Look at this,* said Fthfth. *I sent a little data-parcel to zip round the Source as far as it will go. I can track it 'cos it's me who sent it; I'm not trying to extract any information. And wherever it tries to go, it's getting blocked. It's like the Source is full of tiny custodians, turning it away from every place it wants to get into.*

Billy had a flash of understanding and seized upon it. - *So the Gfjk's given the whole Source a virus or something?*

- *It's cleverer than a virus,* said Fthfth, *it's more active, more self-aware. It's some sort of artificially intelligent program, overriding all the security protocols it finds and substituting its own.* She looked up from the slate. *This explains why EVERYTHING has stopped, including all the long-range transmissions. Everyone's been trying to solve the wrong problem – they've been trying to figure out how the Gfjk was jamming the signals. But he wasn't; he'd just found a way to persuade the transmitters not to send the signals in the first place!*

Terra had been listening intently; so that was why she

hadn't heard anything from Fnrr for so long. With a stab of panic and guilt, she remembered Lbbp. In spite of her friends' doubts, she just knew that he was still alive, although at the mercy of the Gfjk. As soon as she could find an excuse to slip away, she'd set off to find him. She had no idea where to start, but she WOULD find him.

Fthfth went on, - *Of course, he probably didn't come up with this on his own. He'll have had the best programmers in the nation working on it under threat of punishment ... If we could find them, they might know how to get rid of it.*

Billy interjected. - *Erm, I don't want to be the voice of doom here, but I wouldn't have thought the Gfjk would take the risk of keeping them around. I reckon as soon as they were finished he'd have ...*

He let the silence hang.

Pktk had been deep in thought but now spoke. - *He missed one of the nation's best programmers, though, didn't he? My father. Let me show you some REAL programming.* He produced his own slate. *Here,* said Pktk. *This is what my father was working on just after the G'grk withdrew. Remember why they'd invaded in the first place?*

Terra remembered. She would always remember. Sh'shk's shrill voice, declaiming, - *We will harness your space-bending technology and make it our own. We will set out and take the G'grk's gifts of purity and death to all the worlds of the universe!*

- *To achieve interstellar travel and invade other planets,* she said simply, although Billy noticed her shudder.

- *Right,* said Pktk. *And it was decided that we couldn't allow that to happen at any cost.* He turned to Terra. *The thing is, after you went back to Rrth, it was a tense time. No one was sure if the ceasefire would hold. So the Forum authorised a secret project. And this was it.* Pktk held up his own slate now. It showed a spiral of characters, twisting around itself.

- *This,* said Pktk, *is called the Off Button. Just a few lines of three-dimensional code. If it's loaded into any system anywhere, it rips right through the whole Source in a matter* of blips, smashing through security protocols and wiping out EVERYTHING.

Terra's nose wrinkled. - *Why have you got a copy of it, then?*

Pktk smiled. - *I helped Father out with some of the programming*, he said.

Billy thought he might even be keeping up with this bit. - *So in case of an invasion, you upload that, and it destroys the whole inter— I mean, the whole Source?*

Pktk beckoned him over. - *Yes and no*, he said. *Look here, at the penultimate spiral of code. It's the REALLY secret part. It wipes out the whole Source — but only for ONE ORBIT. The Source would look dead, but it would just be dormant. After one orbit — by which time, the idea was, the invaders would have given up and gone home — everything restores itself.*

Fthfth was amazed - *Why didn't I know about this?*

- *That's what secret means, Fthfth*, said Pktk. *Nobody knew.*

Fthfth frowned. - *I HATE not knowing things.*

Pktk had begun tapping away on his slate. - *Now, if I can just isolate that penultimate spiral, and change one thing...*

- *Which one thing?* asked Terra.

- *The time frame*, said Pktk, his brow furrowed with concentration. *I'm taking 'one orbit' out and replacing it with 'sixty-four blips'.*

Terra's eyes lit up with excitement. - *So we load this into the Source, everything goes blank for sixty-four blips then comes back? And the Gfjk's blocking program?*

- *Should be purged during the restarting process*, said Pktk. *We'll have control back.*

Billy snorted. He stifled a titter. He couldn't contain himself. He guffawed. The others stared at him in confusion.

- *Are you all right?* asked Terra.

- *Yeah I'm all right*, said Billy, weeping with laughter, *it's just...*

- *What?* demanded Fthfth.

- You're going to switch it off and switch it back on again, hooted Billy, before collapsing, helpless with mirth.

- Why is that funny? asked Pktk.

3.15

- Where are you taking me? asked Lbbp. No reply came.
Lbbp hadn't been able to take more than three or four steps in the same direction for an orbit, so when he awoke to find himself being hauled to his feet by two custodians, shoved through the cell door (the crystal barrier having slid silently away) and dragged along the dark corridor, his legs had great difficulty keeping up.

The spiral staircase posed a problem, dragging-wise; after a moment's thought, the custodians decided on a push-pull technique; one going ahead of Lbbp and pulling him upwards, the other shoving him from behind. After that there came another corridor, then a heavy door, and then ...

- Welcome, Deceiver, to MISSION CONTROL!
Lbbp blinked at the perfectly normal – but to him, blinding – light. As his eyes adjusted, he began to make out his surroundings. Wait, he thought, have I been right underneath the Forum the whole time? And why is there a dungeon under the Forum?

As the room swam more clearly into focus, Lbbp saw that it wasn't really the Forum any more. The shell of the building was still recognisable, but that was about all. No delegates, no Chancellor, just an assortment of bizarrely dressed courtiers and off-duty custodians lounging on the benches. At the far end of the central aisle, there stood what had been the Chancellor's chair, but which had now been decorated with seemingly random bits of precious metal and gemstones, turning it into a gaudy throne.

On this throne sat the Gfjk-Hhh, semi-resplendent in his now rather shabby green and gold robes and lopsided brass helmet. He beckoned Lbbp towards him; Lbbp, still in the grip of his two escorts, had no choice but to advance.

In the centre aisle itself, a curious jumble of computers and other machinery was being installed by nervous-looking technicians. And above all this, dominating the room, a huge visualiser screen was hanging precariously from the ancient stonework.

Lbbp blinked and answered the Gfjk. - *Mission Control, you say? Dare I ask what the mission might be?*

The Gfjk leapt to his feet and bounded over to meet him. - *I did say, didn't I? I did say my mission would be revealed to me?*

Lbbp thought back to their last conversation. - *I do seem to recall that*— he began.

The Gfjk cut him off. - *BEHOLD!* he cried, gesturing triumphantly towards the giant visualiser.

Nothing happened.

- *I said BEHOLD!* repeated the Gfjk, casting a steely glance at one of the nervous-looking technicians, who frantically activated the screen.

There's another one for the Gshkth Pit, thought the Gfjk. Oh NO, no Scary Gshkth, NO SCARY GSHKTH any MORE. Must remember that. Mind you, he thought on, once I pull this off I'll be able to have Scary Gshkth twice a day, as well as Scary Dfsh, Scary Dks-Wks, Scary Pretty-Much-Anything-I-G'shbbing-Well-Like, and they'll LOVE me for it, because I …

The Gfjk became aware of the fact that Lbbp was standing waiting for him to say something, so reluctantly he yanked his mind back to the here and now.

- *From the stars, Deceiver. Revelation from the stars. See, my quest got impatient waiting for me. My quest sought ME out! How about that?* He gestured again towards the visualiser.

Lbbp peered up at the giant screen. It showed a view of deep space, and in its centre – what? A disc of pure blackness. What was that?

- *The Black Planet*, said the Gfjk reverentially. *The celestial harbinger of death. The destroyer of worlds. It's found me, Deceiver. It's found me. The one it's been looking for all these eras. Its journey is over.*

Lbbp's mind, still adjusting to so much stimulation after cycles of darkness and silence, struggled to assimilate all this new information. He had a vague recollection of reading about an ancient legend that told of a rogue Black Planet which brought devastation to any world which encountered it.

As Lbbp looked, the screen switched from a live image of the planet to a diagram showing its distance from Fnrr. It was less than a day away.

– *What do you think, Deceiver?* asked the Gfjk.

Lbbp pondered for a moment, then replied, – *What do I think? I think I've had just about enough of ancient legends.*

The Gfjk-Hhh smiled. – *I wanted you to be here, Deceiver. You have to witness the completion of our project. I couldn't have done it without you, you know.*

Lbbp said nothing.

– *In a few moments,* said the Gfjk, *I will address my people. I will tell them that death is coming for them, for this whole world, but that they must not fear, for I, the Gfjk-Hhh, Champion and Defender of Fnrr, Commander of the Platinum Legions, the Past and Future, the First and Last and Always, have been returned to life at this time to save and protect them! And once I've done that* – the Gfjk turned to Lbbp, his tone becoming icy – *I will*—

When suddenly ...

– *What's happened?*

– *I can't see!*

– *Has it started?*

– *Save us, Luminescence, save us!*

The chamber had been plunged into darkness. Every light had failed, every screen gone blank. In the impenetrable gloom – actually quite a relief to Lbbp's dazzled eyes – he could hear courtiers stumbling around, bleating in panic, technicians fiddling with their equipment, muttering in confusion, and above it all, the voice of the Gfjk, calling for calm, insisting he was in control and there was no cause for alarm. Lbbp was annoyed to notice that, despite the turmoil, the two custodians who held him firmly by the arms had not relaxed their grip one little bit.

After only a short while – it felt to Lbbp like about sixty-four blips – the lights began to flicker on, the screens glowed again, the machines hummed back into life. A general sense of relief passed around the room.

The Gfjk collected himself, then addressed the assembly.
- *See?* he said, smiling. *Nothing to worry about, it's all . . .*

The Gfjk's smile faded. No one was listening to him. They were all gazing up at the visualiser. He turned to look at it himself.

The screen showed a face. A round, pink face, with a button nose, slightly stuck-out ears and a fringe of oddly coloured hair poking out from under a curiously striped item of cloth headgear.

As the crowd in the Forum-turned-Mission-Control looked on in confusion, the face spoke, in perfect accentless Fnrrn.

- *My name is Terra.*

3.16

A cross the whole city, across the whole nation, the young Ymn's voice was heard.

It was heard in the homes of the oppressed and frightened population, gathered around their visualisers, surprised not to be seeing the Special Address from His Luminescence that they'd been ordered to watch.

It was heard in the stations and barracks of the City Custodians, many of them tiring now of their part in the climate of brutality and fear, realising they'd been forced to choose between their leader and their own people, wondering if they'd chosen wisely.

It was heard – but not by many – in the all-but-deserted lectoria and libraries of the Preceptorates, Lycea and PreAcademies.

And in the hall of the old Forum, so misused, so befouled, it echoed around the stone walls to the confusion of the courtiers, the fury of their false emperor – and the absolute delight of his prisoner.

– *My name is Terra. I'm not from this planet, but it's my home – as much my home as it is any of yours.*

I'm here to tell you about two dangers we all face. One you already know about, the other you maybe don't, yet.

Some of you will already have noticed a black shape in the sky. We believe that this is the Black Planet, as mentioned in an old legend some of you may be familiar with. The legend says that whenever the Black Planet visits another world, everything on that world dies.

This brings me to the other danger you face. You know him as the Gfjk-Hhh. This is not his name. I don't know what his name is, but he's not the Gfjk-Hhh. The Gfjk-Hhh has been dead for twenty eras. The present ruler of this nation is a fraud, a pretender, an imposter with forged ancient scrolls wearing a dead emperor's stolen robes.

In less than a day, the Black Planet will be here. The Gfjk-Hhh can't save you, and not only that, he has taken away from you the things you need to save yourself. He closed down the Source, so you couldn't inform or educate yourselves or find solutions. He closed down the communication system, so you couldn't work together or consult with each other.

I have given these things back to you. You'll find the Source is working again, and all communications have been restored. The Gfjk-Hhh – or whoever he really is – will tell you that he can defeat the Black Planet, but he has nothing to offer you but myths and stories. If this world is going to survive, then we'll need something real. I'm now calling on all the scientists, the astroscopers, the engineers, the xenologists and experts in all ... those ... sorts of things, to come together now, to work – as my friends and I are doing – to find a way to deflect the planet, or destroy it, or cancel out ... whatever it is that it does. We don't have much time. We're going to need each other. Every one of us.

And I have a message for one person in particular. If you're still alive – and I'm sure you are, I don't know why, but I'm sure you are – then I'll find you. Stay as safe as you can. I'm coming to find you.

Good luck, everybody.

The face disappeared.

3.17

Lbbp, still a prisoner, still bound, still a lunatic's whim away from death, had never been happier in his life.

He felt a fierce love and a fiercer pride. If the Gfjk-Hhh had struck him dead at that moment, his last thoughts would have been ones of gratitude that he'd lived long enough to know that feeling.

How had she done it?

She looked so grown up.

His Terra, his brave, brilliant Terra.

Weird hair, mind you, but still.

A sound crashed into Lbbp's thoughts. A shrill, sustained shriek of fury. The kind of anger of which only gods are supposed to be capable.

- *NnnnnnnnnnnNNNNNNNNNNOOOOOOOOOOoooooo!*

Lbbp turned his head to see the Gfjk-Hhh. He had slid from his throne onto his knees. As Lbbp watched, the Gfjk tore the brass helmet from his head and began to slam it repeatedly into the stone floor, denting and deforming it a little more with each impact.

- *SHE*
- *RUINED*
- *EVERY*
- *THING*
- *SHE'S*
- *SPOILED*
- *EVERY*
- *THING*
- *STUPID*
- *LITTLE*
- *BEAST*

- *SHE*
- *SPOILED*
- *MY*
- *BIG*
- *SPEECH*, yelled the Gfjk, in rhythm with the clanging of the helmet against the floor. He collapsed, as if exhausted, then sprang to his feet, hurled the bizarrely shaped remains of his helmet in no particular direction, and started pacing around in a hunched position, his hands clenching and unclenching.

His courtiers, who habitually hung around the Forum desperately trying to catch the Gfjk's eye in the hope that he might bestow on them some favour or other, now averted their eyes and edged away, terrified that his gaze might fall upon them.

Someone did catch the Gfjk's eye. It was Wffk. Standing faithfully behind his master's throne, he hadn't budged during the blackout and ensuing panic, or during the young Ymn's unexpected address.

The Gfjk lunged at Wffk and grabbed the front of his garment. He pulled his scrivener's face up to his own and bawled at him.

- *Why did she do that, Wffk? Why? I was going to tell them all about the Black Planet! Me! That was my job! She spoiled my speech!* He released his grip on Wffk, sank to the floor and sat down, his legs splayed, his head lolling on his chest. *She spoiled my speech*, he sobbed.

- *Erm ... Luminescence?*

The Gfjk looked up to see who had addressed him. It was the Deceiver.

- *This is exactly what we NEEDED to happen, Luminescence*, said the Deceiver soothingly.

- *What ... what do you mean?* asked the Gfjk. He became aware of the indignity of his position and struggled to his feet, smoothing down his robe.

- *The Ymn has challenged the authenticity of your claim, Luminescence. She says you're a fraud, an imposter.*

The Gfjk was nonplussed. – *A lot of people say that,* he said.

– *Yes, but not out loud, not in front of the whole nation,* said the Deceiver. *You've received a direct challenge in a public forum. This DEMANDS a response, and today you have the perfect response ready! You can banish any lingering doubts about just who – and WHAT – you are for ever.*

– *Yes, I have the perfect response ready. What is it?*

– *Why, Luminescence* – the Deceiver smiled – *your grand plan for saving Fnrr from the Black Planet!*

– *Ah yes, yes . . . Erm* – the Gfjk's brow furrowed – *what IS my grand plan for saving Fnrr from the Black Planet?*

– *We'll discuss it now,* said the Deceiver. *And it really is perfect. You are to be congratulated, Luminescence, I couldn't have come up with a better one myself.*

– *Of course, of course,* panted the Gfjk. He smiled at the Deceiver. *You are, after all, my most trusted adviser.* The Gfjk-Hhh looked over his shoulder. *Wffk?* he said.

– *Yes, Luminescence?*

– *You're fired.*

Wffk froze. He'd been present when the Gfjk-Hhh had 'fired' underlings before. There was always more to it than that. Always humiliation, and often death. He tensed and shuddered, awaiting whatever cruel trick his master had in mind to spring on him.

The Gfjk-Hhh turned back to the Deceiver, and soon the two of them were deep in conversation.

Wffk didn't dare move. He could feel the eyes of everyone in the room upon him. They all wanted to see what happened next as well.

After a moment, in which the Gfjk did not turn round but carried on talking to the Deceiver, Wffk began to edge towards the door, backwards, not daring to turn his back on his former master.

He reached the door. Fumbling behind himself, he opened it. He could sense the general disappointment in the room.

Wffk slipped backwards out of the Forum, then turned, and ran, ran as fast as he could.

* * *

Back in the Forum, the Gfjk-Hhh had a question for the Deceiver.

- *Deceiver, I'm confused ...*

You said it, thought Lbbp. - *In what way, Luminescence?* he asked with concern.

- *Why are you advising me on how to beat the Rrth child? When she's the source of all your ... skills?*

Lbbp measured his response, then smiled. - *Today is a day for transcendence, Luminescence. I have surpassed her achievements. There's nothing more she could teach me about deception.* Quite true, in fact, thought Lbbp. He went on, in a conspiratorial whisper, *I don't NEED her any more, Luminescence. And before today is done, you won't need me any more either.*

The Gfjk seemed content with this answer.

In fact, thought Lbbp, if all goes well, by the end of the day you won't need much of anything.

3.18

Terra switched off her slate, sat back in her chair and exhaled hard. She looked at her friends' faces. She didn't ask what they'd thought of her address. Their smiles told her enough, and it was too late now, anyway. So instead she asked:

- *How long do you think it'll take them to trace the signal back here?*

Pktk looked blankly back at her. - *There's no way to tell,* he said. *If they know what they're doing, it shouldn't take them long, but it's more than likely that they DON'T know what they're doing. No one's made an unofficial transmission for an orbit, and the kind of creeps and lackeys the Gfjk's surrounded himself with may not have any idea how to deal with it.*

- *That's true,* said Fthfth. *Anyone who knows anything about science has either been arrested or is hiding out in a different country, like us.*

- *Like we're supposed to be,* reminded Pktk.

- *Well, if I get a vote in this,* said Billy, *I say we don't hang about here any longer than we have to. What's the next move?*

Pktk had already made his next move; he'd accessed the database of all surveyed planets and was running through it, looking for a planet of the same mass and diameter as the Black Planet – these being the only halfway meaningful measurements they'd been able to take of it. He was watching the list of planets rush across his slate. Pktk was SO glad to have the Source back. He felt like he'd just regrown a missing limb (a friend of his had actually done that once; Pktk made a mental note to ask him how it had felt – if they ever met again).

- *Right,* said Terra. *We've started the bdkt rolling. There are people all over Fnrr working on the problem now, or I hope so, anyway. And the Source is up again, so we can be mobile. We can use our slates to access whatever information we need. I say we move out. We can find another empty apartment to hide out in. There are plenty of them,* she added grimly.

There was no dissent; the band of friends began to pack up their various odds and ends in preparation. Just as they were about to leave, there came a great blaring, trumpeting sound. It came from everywhere, from the streets, from the sky, from their slates.

Fthfth looked at her slate and groaned. Billy looked over her shoulder.

– *Well, look who it isn't,* he muttered.

The Gfjk-Hhh's grinning face filled the slate, and also the screens of all the astroscopy lab's computers.

– *Beloved children!* it said. *Well, that was an interesting little speech by the Ymn, wasn't it? I'm sure we all found it very entertaining. Like so many of the st'rss and f'k-shnns she brought to us all those orbits ago. Because always remember, that's what Ymns are. Deceivers. They have a word for it, you know. Lies, they call them, lies. Untruths, told to mislead us, to confuse us, to HURT us. Ymns are the bringers of lies! Let me hear you! Ymns are the bringers of lies!*

To Terra's horror, she heard the Gfjk's words echoing around the city. People were chanting, – *Ymns are the bringers of lies!*

– *Yes, yes they are. And, beloved children, do not let an alien's lies discourage you! We have come so far together, haven't we? We've cast aside the old ways, the ways of division and conflict, and moved forward into a new age of unity and common purpose ...*

– *Well, that's one way of putting it,* snarled Pktk.

– *Shh,* said Fthfth.

– *And we have done this by placing our confidence not in the arid, dusty, STERILE ways of the scientists, the CYNICS. We have done this by placing ourselves in the hands of Fate!*

Fate itself, which chose me to lead you! Fate, which returned me to life in your time of direst need! Exactly as promised!

Terra and Fthfth exchanged anxious looks.

- For was it not written that I should return to you, as Death itself came upon us from the skies?

- Was it? asked Billy.

Terra gave a despairing shrug. *- Oh I don't know,* she said, *he's just making it up as he goes along now.*

- But do not fear, beloved children! Do not doubt! I shall, this day, do battle with Death itself! The Gfjk's voice rose to a scream. *I will stay its path with my very word! The evil which bears down upon us will flee my radiance!*

- And I thought he'd lost it before, said Billy. *He is well and truly off with the pixies.*

- The what? asked Pktk.

- Tell you later, said Billy.

- Stay by your visualisers! Gather in the meeting places! You will witness my triumph! My ascension! My VICTORY!

The Gfjk-Hhh's face disappeared, replaced by Mlmln text reading LOVE AND GLORY TO THE GFJK-HHH. To Terra's horror, this chant could be heard echoing through the city.

- I don't believe it, said Fthfth. *They're not actually going for that, are they?*

- Sounds like some of them are, said Terra quietly.

- But WHY? said Pktk, despairingly.

Billy had some thoughts on this. *- I've got some thoughts on this,* he said, *but let's walk and talk.*

- Go on, then, said Pktk as they exited the astroscopy lab.

- Well, began Billy as they passed along the corridor, *some people just ... like to believe. Somebody comes along with all the answers, it's easier just to sign up and swallow it all wholesale than to think things through for yourself. Saves effort. Understand?*

- I think so, said Fthfth as they found a functioning grav-chute and stepped into it.

- The other thing you have to remember, said Terra to Billy

as they descended, *is that until not so long ago this society had no concept of fiction, let alone deception. The idea of something being made up is still quite new, so the thought that someone would deliberately and maliciously make something up just for personal gain is . . . well, alien to them,* she concluded as they arrived at ground level.

- *Literally unimaginable,* pondered Billy as the strode to the exit. *Tell you what, when I get a minute I'll have a word. Talk them through it.* He winked at Terra as they passed through the door into the deserted street. *Where to now, then?*

Pktk was about to reply when a pinging noise interrupted him. For a moment he was confused, then he said, - *Of course! My comm! My comm is working again!* He rummaged in his bag for the gadget; finding it, he looked expectantly at the screen. His face paled, and his jaw dropped.

Terra had never seen Pktk look so stricken. - *What? What is it?*

Fthfth peeked over Pktk's shoulder and smiled. - *It's his mother calling,* she said.

Billy patted Pktk on the shoulder. - *Better answer it, mate. Get it over with.*

Pktk turned away, in search of a little privacy. Fthfth chuckled at his predicament, then suddenly fell silent. - *Look . . .* she said feebly.

Billy and Terra looked.

Above the city spires, like a dark second sun, the Black Planet hung in the evening sky.

Not a word passed between the friends, but they each knew what the others were thinking: we haven't been taking this seriously enough. We've been treating it like a game, like it's all about getting the better of the Gfjk-Hhh. But it isn't. We might all be dead by the morning. There may not even BE a morning. This could be the last day this planet sees.

This could be the end of the world.

They walked on in silence.

3.19

*- S*o talk me through this 'Mission Control' of yours, Luminescence – who are all these people and what do they do?
  - They're here to control the mission! The Gfjk-Hhh grinned.
My mission! My mission to save my people!
  - I see, said Lbbp thoughtfully. He looked around the
equipment that had been loaded into the Forum. On close
inspection, it looked to be a pretty random selection of
hardware. Just how much of it would be of any use when
co-ordinating a space mission, he didn't care to guess. Lbbp
was fairly certain that at least one of the bulkier machines
was in fact one of those big old-style protein manipulators.
He turned to address the Gfjk. *And how do you intend to do
this, Luminescence?*
  *- Isn't it obvious? I shall take to the stars! I shall confront
the Black Planet! We will meet as equals. The destroyer and the
saviour. Death itself, and the immortal redeemer, face to face.
I think you'll agree that this will stand as my finest moment,
in this life or the … other one,* said the Gfjk, his vocabulary
failing him at the last moment.
  Inwardly, Lbbp was punching the air in victory. Out-
wardly, he looked admiringly at the Gfjk. *- Magnificent,
Luminescence. Just magnificent. When will you be, erm, taking
to the stars?*
  The Gfjk paused to consider this, then, *- Why, immediately, of course! Why keep history waiting?* He turned to one
of the technicians. *You! What's your name?*
  - M-me? stammered the technician. *My name is Fshnk,
Luminescence.*
  *- Very good, Fshnk. Send word, I will take off as soon as
possible. Prepare my ship.*

An awkward silence.

- *Ship?* asked Fshnk.

Another awkward silence.

- *I have GOT a ship, haven't I?* said the Gfjk quizzically.

Fshnk looked anxiously around him at the other technicians. They gazed blankly back at him.

- *Um ...* began Fshnk. *Not as such, no. Not one of your own, anyway, Luminescence.*

The Gfjk, who had been striking a suitably heroically erect pose, slumped. - *No ship?* he said weakly.

- *Well,* said Fhsnk, his mind racing to think of a solution while the Gfjk's temper held, *we could see if the Space Navy have one, but they're all ...*

Lbbp coughed. This oversight couldn't be allowed to stall things, not when he was so close. - *Er, Luminescence,* he said, *I've got a ship you can borrow.*

3.20

Colonel Hardison, shielding his eyes against the glare of the setting sun, gazed up at the Lance of the Occluded Ones.

It had been hauled to the launch pad by a hundred-strong team of G'grk drones, using ropes and rollers, like something from an old movie about the building of the Egyptian pyramids. Hardison had watched with more than a little amusement. He was sure the G'grk had some sort of GravTech contraption somewhere around the place which would have made the job much easier. But of course, he thought to himself, the G'grk do enjoy their ceremonies (especially when the Occluded Ones had been invoked, of course), and even when they used advanced technology they seemed uneasy, even suspicious of it.

The Lance itself, after all, had been built not by G'grk technicians (Hardison assumed that the G'grk did have technicians, although now he thought about it he hadn't met any) but by Dsktn scientists, under circumstances which didn't bear thinking about. The fact that the scientists might have known that their own country was one of the missile's possible targets couldn't have made the work any easier. Hardison wondered if they'd thought of sabotaging the weapon, and if so, would the G'grk have been able to spot it?

So, he summarised to himself, basically, our only hope for survival is an enormous missile, built by resentful slave labour, which is about to be fired by technophobic tribal warriors in the vague direction of the ghost planet which, should the rocket miss, fail to detonate, or just turn out not to be powerful enough, will kill us all before the morning.

An even more sobering thought was, it now occurred to him, that this still wasn't the craziest strategy he'd ever been a party to. He'd got mixed up in much dumber situations back on Earth. He shuddered at the memory.

Somewhere behind him, back in the command centre, the warhead was 'brewing'. Hardison squinted as he looked up at the black disc in the sky.

What ARE you? he wondered.

3.21

The people of Mlml, it seemed, had missed the Source almost as much as Pktk had. Ever since it had come back online, it had been ablaze with activity.

Debate was raging on every discussion site or conversation page over whether the Gfjk was truly the reborn saviour of Mlml or a demented fraud. Reading her slate, Terra was encouraged to note that a slight majority seemed to be coming down on the 'demented fraud' side.

She and her friends were in Pktk's family apartment. The Gfjk had, as yet, no reason to suspect Pktk's or Fthfth's involvement in Terra's little insurrection; as such, Terra had reasoned, his custodians wouldn't think to watch Pktk's old residence. They'd opened the door with Pktk's key tube and made themselves at home.

The place was comfortable at least, and extensively decorated; Fthfth had been giggling almost non-stop at the sheer quantity of holographic portraits of Pktk dotted about the rooms and corridors: baby Pktk; Pktk's first steps; Pktk's first day at the PreAc; Pktk's first go with a gravity pod … Pktk registered Fthfth's mirth but did not respond; he just shuffled past her, his head lowered, muttering crossly, - *Not my fault, I didn't put them up.*

Terra, catching Pktk's eye, said, - *So tell us again about this thing the G'grk have built.*

Pktk's tense comm conversation with his mother had not consisted entirely of frantic admonishments, fretful pleas to come back to Lsh-Lff and mumbled apologies. Almost entirely, but not entirely entirely. There had also been time for Pktk and his mother to bring each other up to date on what was being done about the ongoing Black Planet situation.

- *Well,* began Pktk, *they've constructed a massive rocket called the Lance of the Occluded Ones.*

Terra flinched at a sudden flash of memory – the ugly steel shaft protruding from Lbbp's shoulder, dark blue blood, so much blue blood …

Terra contained her distress; Pktk didn't notice it and carried on. - *They say it'll be ready to fire at the Black Planet just before it arrives.*

Fthfth snorted. - *How do they know? There are no detailed scientific records of what actually happens when the Black Planet does whatever it does. We don't know how close it has to get! We don't know whether it smashes right into you, grazes the atmospheric lid or whether it can wipe everything out from half an optical away!*

Billy shrugged, - *Well, it's a start, isn't it? And even if it doesn't blow the Black Planet up, it might slow it down, or blow it off course, or … something. And it's more than anyone else has come up with.*

- *Give it time,* said Terra. *We've got the whole scientific community of Fnrr on our side now. Someone will think of something. Someone HAS to think of something.*

- *Somebody DID think of something,* said Billy. *The G'grk thought of blowing the thing to bits. Not exactly Nobel Prize-winning stuff, I'll grant you, but if it does the trick I bet you won't be complaining this time tomorrow.*

Pktk looked up from his slate. - *It'll never work,* he muttered. *The G'grk won't have built it themselves, they wouldn't know where to start. They'll have stolen it from somewhere. They probably don't even know how it works. They're more likely to blow themselves up with it than—*

- *You know what I think?* said Billy, his temper starting to fray a little, *I think you and all your clever mates just can't stand the idea of the stupid, primitive G'grk being the ones who actually get their act together and save everyone, that's what I think.*

Terra, Fthfth and Pktk exchanged embarrassed glances. They weren't going to admit it out loud, but Billy had a point.

No one was sure what to say next, so it came as a great relief to everyone when both Pktk's and Fthfth's slates started making high-pitched pinging sounds, one after the other. They both checked their devices excitedly.

- *The database search is complete!* announced Pktk.

- *I've got a message! From the Ff-Shkrr observatory!* said Fthfth delightedly.

- *The what?* asked Billy.

- *It's another Preceptorate – university, sort of thing – on the other side of Fnrr. They were the first ones to notice the existence of the Ymn race, for what it's worth.* Terra smiled. *Perhaps they've figured something out about the Black Planet.*

Terra went to read over Fthfth's shoulder. This normally annoyed Fthfth intensely, but on this occasion she was too excited to notice.

- *It's from Senior Postulator V-Kst V-Shft, head of the Ff-Shkrr Astroscopy Hub! Wow! She's amazing! I read this fantastic article she wrote about the atomic decay of—*

- *What does it SAY?* Interrupting Fthfth in full academic enthusiasm flow was always a bit of a risk, but Terra felt it necessary, what with the impending end of the world and everything.

- *Oh, yes ... Hmm. She's sent me a recording. They were scanning the Black Planet for any signals it might be giving off—*

- *There aren't any,* grumbled Pktk. *We checked.*

- *—and SHE SAYS,* continued Fthfth, ignoring him, *that they picked something up. Here you go, listen to this.* She tapped her slate to activate the sound file.

A faint hiss was heard. Pktk was unimpressed.

- *That's nothing,* he said. *Background static. Stellar radiation, reflected from the sun.*

- *I thought you said it didn't reflect the sun?* said Terra thoughtfully. Pktk fell silent. Fthfth went on:

- *This is it, slowed down sixty-four times.*

A lower-pitched hiss, sounding oddly like breath.

- *Still nothing,* said Pktk. *What are we listening for?*

Fthfth held up a not-now hand and said, - *And this is that sound slowed down ANOTHER sixty-four times.*

The sound was no longer a hiss. It now resembled a heartbeat. Pktk's eyes widened.

- *That's not stellar radiation. It's too uniform.*

- *Sounds like a pulse,* said Billy quietly.

- *It's a signal,* conceded Pktk. *That's a signal. Something is communicating with something else.*

Terra turned to face him. - *Communicating? Communicating how?* she asked eagerly.

Pktk's interest had clearly been piqued but his enthusiasm did not yet match Terra's own. - *No way to tell, really. Could be some sort of automated system; a relay between...*

- *But something could be ALIVE up there?* Terra interrupted. *Something intelligent? Even if it's just artificial intelligence?*

Pktk was still cagey in his response. - *Terra, just because the signal seems to have some sort of pattern, it doesn't...*

Terra was unfazed. - *But communication implies intelligence, doesn't it? Who could they be trying to communicate with? Us?* She had hopeful visions of messages being exchanged, language barriers being broken, accords being reached ...

But Fthfth shook her head. - *The signal's far too weak. Postulator V-Kst said their scanners only just picked it up at their maximum sensitivity.*

Terra paced the room, her mind racing. - *So they're not trying to talk to us, but they are talking to each other ...* she said. *There are things on that planet that are talking to each other.*

She wheeled round to talk to the others. - *If they're talking to each other, then we can talk to them. We can communicate with the planet.*

- *What's that going to achieve?* queried Pktk.

- *I don't know!* shouted Terra. *But it's got to be worth a try! We could warn them about the G'grk rocket, persuade them to turn the planet round . . .*

- *What makes you think they're controlling the planet, anyway?* asked Pktk crossly. *And who ARE they? We have no idea what we're dealing with.*

- Woah, woah, calm down, said Billy, sensing the mounting tension. *There's something we're forgetting about here. Pktk, you said that database search-thing you had on the go had come up with something. Have you even bothered to check what?*

Pktk's irritation abated. He lowered his eyes. - *Not yet,* he mumbled.

- *Well, then,* said Billy, *off you go and sort that out. Fthfth,* he turned to her, *if that IS some sort of communication network up there on that planet, can we hack into it? Listen in, maybe even get a word in ourselves?*

- *I . . . might be able to work out what frequency they're using,* said Fthfth.

- *Sounds like a plan,* Billy said encouragingly. *Get cracking.*

Billy exhaled and turned to Terra. She was smiling. 'What?'

'I'm glad you're here, Billy Dolphin,' she said.

So am I, thought Billy. He went to the window. The Black Planet dominated the darkening sky. Unbelievable as it may seem, thought Billy, so am I.

His thoughts were interrupted by Pktk's voice. - *Hm. Perfection.*

- *What is?* asked Terra. There were many words she could think of with reference to their current situation and 'perfection' wasn't one of them.

- *The planet. Or it might be, anyway,* said Pktk, reading from his slate. *Its mass and diameter are an exact match for the planet Perfection, which disappeared eras ago.*

- *Perfection?* chuckled Billy. *Bit pleased with themselves, weren't they?*

3.22

'How long?'

Colonel Hardison and Professor Steinberg were standing in the centrifuge lab at the G'grk command centre. The vast, vibrating metal drum in front of them contained the combination of volatile elements which would, once 'brewed', become the explosive core of the warhead which the Lance of the Occluded Ones would deliver – hopefully – straight through the crust and into the very heart of the Black Planet.

Professor Steinberg checked the time on his slate. It showed local Central Plains time, but he thought it would be easier to answer Hardison using comforting old Earth units.

'Couple of hours.' He shrugged.

Hardison shifted his weight anxiously from one foot to the other. 'Do we even HAVE a couple of hours?'

Steinberg consulted his slate. He still got a bit of a kick from using Fnrrn gadgets. And to think how impressed he'd been by some of the stuff they had back home.

'Just barely, I think. Nobody knows what the planet's destructive range is. Nobody even knows exactly what it does – just what's left after it's done it.'

Hardison stared uneasily at the centrifuge. 'Where did they even get this thing? Do they know how to use it?'

'It was built at the same time as the rocket,' said Steinberg matter-of-factly.

'In Dskt?' asked Hardison. 'How do you think they got it all the way back here?'

Steinberg shrugged. 'It's amazing what you can achieve

when you have a rigid caste system and a completely servile underclass of a hundred million or so.'

Hardison nodded grimly. He shifted his weight again and checked his watch. It hadn't worked for weeks and had no way of showing local time, but he checked it, anyway.

3.23

Lbbp, flanked by his usual armed escorts, stood on the upper balcony of the Forum and watched the ship's progress with a mixture of unease and admiration. It's amazing what you can achieve with half a country's worth of fawning acolytes, he thought glumly.

They'd found his trusty old lemon-shaped spaceship where he'd said it would be – in a little hangar just behind the Life Science Hub – and loaded it onto a low-energy grav-platform. Now they were towing it along through the streets, dozens of them in their ridiculous white robes, while hundreds more stood by and gave out hissing cheers.

It would have been far easier, of course, for him to pilot it back to the Forum, but in spite of his new-found status as the Gfjk-Hhh's 'most trusted adviser', the Gfjk seemed reluctant to let Lbbp out of his sight. Obviously not that 'most trusted' yet, thought Lbbp. We'll have to work on that, in however long we've got left, he concluded, casting an anxious glance skywards. The Black Planet hung over the city, a larger disc than any of the six moons, larger even than the sun appeared at the end of the day.

So the plan now was for the ship to be towed back to the Forum, where Lbbp would override the biometric security measures before handing it over to the Gfjk, so he could set out on his quest for glory. That way, Lbbp would never be left in sole charge of the ship. That way, he couldn't just blast off to freedom on his own.

Odd, thought Lbbp, that they should take such precautions to prevent me from escaping NOW, when escape is the last thing on my mind. The absolute last thing.

He became aware of the Gfjk's presence at his side.

- *Is that it?* the Gfjk said sourly.

- *I did say it wasn't very big,* said Lbbp, *but so much the better for your purposes, Luminescence.*

The Gfjk turned to Lbbp, a quizzical expression on his face. - *Explain?*

- *Well, Luminescence,* began Lbbp, *ANYONE can set off for battle in some hulking great warship, heavy with armour and bristling with weapons. Any fool, any MORTAL can defeat an enemy by outgunning it. But to set out unarmed ... to face such a terrifying threat as this* – he indicated the Black Planet hanging above them – *and thwart it JUST BY THE POWER OF HIS WORD, why those are the actions of ... of a ...*

- *A God,* said the Gfjk quietly.

- *Indeed, Luminescence,* said Lbbp reverentially. A blip passed, then another. That's right, thought Lbbp. Believe it. Believe it, and doom yourself.

There was a weighty pause. Eventually the Gfjk spoke, but the words he uttered were NOT anything Lbbp was expecting, or hoping for.

- *Is there actually going to be room in there for both of us?*

3.24

- *So let me see if I have this right*, said Billy. *Once upon a time, there was a planet where life was so blissful it was actually called Perfection, and then one day it just disappeared? And now we think – or at least HE thinks – he pointed to Pktk – that it didn't just vanish into space but somehow turned into the wandering Death Planet up there?*

- *Erm, yes*, said Pktk.

- *Fair enough*, said Billy. *Just wanted to get it sorted out in my head.*

- *Is there NO explanation as to what happened to Perfection?* asked Terra. *Not even a clue?*

Pktk fiddled with his slate. Fthfth cast an anxious glance out of the window. Was that really Perfection? The long-lost planet of peace and beauty? What had happened? And how long did they have to work it out?

- *There's one version of the legend here, it's in a particularly obscure old dialect. The slate's taking its time translating it ... Come on, come on*, said Pktk impatiently, bashing the slate with his free hand.

Hey, look at that, thought Billy, people do that here too.

- *Right, here we go*, said Pktk, and he read:

- *'Crowds gathered on the steps of the Temple–Palace of Sha'ha–las at dawn. The philosopher–priests and the scientists emerged together to rapturous cheers. They carried before them a great golden urn, a sealed vessel within which the Deliverers were contained. At the appointed hour, the urn was opened and the Deliverers were released to carry out their task. To preserve. To perfect ... The Deliverers sprang forth, and began to un-weave Perfection. Cell by cell, molecule by molecule, they took the planet apart.'*

Pktk looked up from his slate. - *What's a Deliverer?* he asked.

The only thing which came to Billy's mind was the image of a bloke on a moped bringing him pizza. He didn't really think it was worth mentioning this.

- *Nanites* ... said Fthfth quietly.

- *Nanites?* asked Terra.

- *Teeny tiny sub-microscopic intelligent machines, smaller than cells. My mother uses them at the nosocomium.*

Terra experienced a flashback to her first day at the Lyceum. There was little Fthfth, proudly describing her parents' occupations. '- *My father's name is Knkt-sh-Dstnk-sh-Hbf and he is EXTREMELY clever. He is Director of Applied Science at the Hrrng GravTech Research Hub. My mother is called Hskth-sh-Fnl-sh-Gskt and she is EVEN CLEVERER. She is Chief of Cellular Surgery at Hrrng Nosocomium.*'

- *Cellular surgery,* said Terra. Registering Billy's bewildered expression, she went on. - *Nanites are like incredibly small robots. They can be injected into diseased or infected cells and they can actually repair the cells individually.*

- *That signal!* said Fthfth. *That signal YOU thought* – she shot a look at Pktk – *was just background radiation – it must be the nanites communicating with each other. The nanites my mother programmes at the nosocomium use just the same kind of incredibly high frequency* ...

- *So what if you made – nanites, was it?* Billy asked. Terra nodded. Billy went on. *What if you made nanites, and programmed them to destroy rather than repair?*

- *They would dismantle living tissue,* said Pktk. *They'd turn it to dust.*

- *How could one urnful destroy the whole planet, though?* Billy frowned.

- *If they were self-replicating nanites, they'd recycle the consumed matter and make copies of themselves,* said Pktk. *There'd be enough to destroy everything in about a spectrum.*

- *But why?* asked Fthfth in distress. *If their life was so perfect, why did they do this to themselves?*

- *The legend said they were obsessed with KEEPING their life perfect. Once you're at the top, the only way is down. Except it isn't,* said Billy. *There isn't just down. There's OUT!*

- *They destroyed themselves rather than risk becoming flawed and ordinary like every other planet in the universe,* said Terra angrily. *What is the matter with people?*

Billy shrugged. - *Once people decide they're always in the right, it's amazing just how wrong they can end up being.*

- *Fine,* said Fthfth, *but once the stupid g'shbks had destroyed their own planet, shouldn't that have been it? Why is it wandering about trying to do the same thing to everyone else?*

- *Bad programming,* said Pktk. *You have to be very careful when you're giving instructions to machines. They're very literal. They don't use intuition to work out what you mean, they just go by what you say. EXACTLY what you say.*

- *You think the Deliverers are still following their original directive?* Terra said thoughtfully. *If they were just programmed to destroy all life, they wouldn't know that they were supposed to stop after one planet's worth ... But how is the planet moving?*

Pktk went to the window. - *What if there's no planet left? What if they consumed the whole thing? What if the object up there is just a planet-sized clump of nanites? Shuffling through space under some sort of propulsion system the nanites are generating between them, looking for life to destroy ...*

Pktk stared up at the black orb, in awe and not a little admiration at how far the nanites had surpassed their makers' expectations. Suddenly his eyes opened wide, his jaw fell open and his skin became the palest grey ... He turned back to his friends.

- *The G'grk! Their rocket! We need to stop them! We need to stop them firing their rocket!*

3.25

Lbbp's feet scampered down the Forum square steps, and his mind scampered in search of a way to convince the Gfjk that taking his adviser along on his sacred mission was really NOT a good idea.

The Gfjk was already striding across the square, towards the little lemon-shaped spaceship which had been set up on a podium. He waved regally at the crowd of supporters who had come to see him off.

What to say? What to say? He'd come so far – he'd almost persuaded the Gfjk that he was invincible, almost got him into the ship, blasting off on his suicidal quest – and now it turned out that the Gfjk was expecting him to come along? How could Lbbp talk him out of it?

As Lbbp's eyes darted around the Forum square, an idea began to form in his mind.

- *Luminescence,* he called to the Gfjk, who now stood at the foot of the podium.

The Gfjk paused mid-wave and turned towards him. - *Yes?*

- *I was just wondering – which of these plinths would be the best one to put our statue on?*

The Gfjk blinked. - *OUR statue?* he said.

- *Yes!* said Lbbp happily. *They're bound to make one of us, aren't they? After we save them all. I reckon* – he looked slowly around the square – *THAT one. In that corner. It gets the most sun. We can get rid of . . . whoever that is.* He waved dismissively at the statue currently occupying the plinth, and in truth, he didn't have the faintest idea who it was supposed to be.

- *Erm . . .* said the Gfjk uneasily.

- *You'll be in front, obviously, Luminescence. Hmm, I am*

slightly taller, but we can make sure they make you taller.

The Gfjk-Hhh squirmed at the thought of sharing plinth-space with this grovelling mortal. He liked the idea of being a statue – he'd had that silly hovering one re-modelled with his face – it had been one of his first acts as Gfjk – but so far there hadn't actually been a proper statue made specifically in his honour. He didn't like the thought that the first one, the first bespoke statue of the Gfjk-Hhh, would not depict him standing alone, but as part of some bizarre double-act. That just wouldn't do. The Deceiver would be disappointed; should he let him down gently?

G'shb gently. Gently is for those with something to fear. Gently is not for Gods.

– Actually, Deceiver, I'm going on my own. Sorry, but that's how it is. That spaceship is dreadfully cramped and I am NOT going to save my people while sitting on someone's lap. I trust there are no objections?

Careful, thought Lbbp. I have to act just crestfallen enough to be convincing, but not so much as to change his mind. Lbbp made his biggest saddest face and said, *– If you think that's best, Luminescence.*

– I do. Now stand over there. I must address my people.

The Gfjk-Hhh climbed onto the podium. Hissed cheers and applause (you learned that from Terra, you cheeky f'zfts, thought Lbbp) echoed around the square. The Gfjk raised a hand and the clamour subsided.

– Beloved children! he began. *Above, you see the destroyer, the eater of worlds, the bringer of death whose coming was foretold ...*

Apparently, thought Lbbp. Not sure where, or by whom, but never mind.

The Gfjk went on. *– But my coming was also foretold! Death is coming, and I am ready! Ready to destroy the destroyer!*

Oh, just get in the ship, thought Lbbp. There must be a way I can speed this up. Once he's ... out of the way, there might just still be time to find a way to actually stop that planet, but not if he stands there making speeches until the thing is actually touching the ground.

Lbbp glanced up at the Black Planet. It all but filled the dawnward half of the sky.

An idea came to him. Just as the Gfjk was about to begin reciting another glowing tribute to his own wonderfulness, Lbbp roared, - *LOVE AND GLORY TO THE GFJK-HHH!*

The crowd, ever mindful of the necessity of appearing at least as loyal as the next Fnrrn, took up the chant immediately. The Gfjk's words were drowned out. He raised his voice, but the impossibility of making himself heard became obvious. So, with a final regal wave, he climbed through the open hatch and entered the spaceship.

The chanting faded away.

There was a moment's pause. The crowd began to look around, anxiously.

A voice came from inside the ship.

- *Deceiver ... ? Come here a moment.*

Lbbp looked expectantly at his two escorts. They marched him to the podium and helped him climb through the hatch.

Inside the spaceship, the Gfjk-Hhh was sitting in the pilot's chair and staring at the array of controls in front of him. Registering Lbbp's arrival, he waved a hand in the direction of the console.

- *How does all this work, exactly?*

3.26

Colonel Hardison hadn't expected a positive response from the Grand Marshal, but the fury his request had provoked startled him.

- NO, Ymn. Do you think we are fools? Do you think we are animals? The weaklings in Mlml and Dskt thought so, and it cost them dearly. It should have cost them their lives.

Hardison had received Terra's panic-stricken message a few minutes earlier. His relief at finding the long-range communication network live again dissipated as soon as he heard what she'd had to say. Now he was trying to convey that information to his G'grk hosts, and it was NOT being well received.

- If you fire that rocket of yours, cried Hardison, *not only will it NOT save Fnrr, it could doom this planet and every other inhabited world in this spiral arm!*

Hardison found himself pinned to the spot by two of Zst'kh's bodyguards, who grasped his arms tightly behind him. He'd made no threatening moves towards the Grand Marshal, at least he didn't think he had – but the heated tone of the conversation was obviously enough to convince the guards not to take any chances. The Grand Marshal turned away and consulted with an armoured, war-painted drone officer. Hardison called out to him.

- That thing up there, it's NOT a planet. It consists of tiny destructive robots, killer machines which shred all living things upon contact. If you fire your missile, the sphere will shatter and the machines will be scattered through space! Fnrr will be covered in the robots immediately. Everything will die. Then the machines will drift through space, reproducing. There will be

hundreds of Black Planets! No world will be safe! You HAVE to listen to me—

- And if we do not fire the Lance? What then? asked Zst'kh. *We wait for the Black ... whatever it is ... to descend upon us? What do we have to lose by firing the Lance? What other solution is there?*

Hardison calmed himself, then answered the Grand Marshal. *- Terra says she thinks there might be a way to communicate with the planet, that it might actually be conscious, that if we—*

- TERRA? snapped Zst'kh, cutting him off. *That is the source of your information? The Ymn child? Tell me, Hrrd's-nn, just how many times does the child think she can humiliate us?*

Hardison closed his eyes and sagged, despairingly. Mentioning Terra by name. Big mistake. The Grand Marshal drew close and hissed, *- She might have worked her alien tricks to cloud my grandfather's mind, but not me. Oh no, Ymn, not me.* He turned and barked at a waiting officer. *The warhead! Load it! Now!*

Zst'kh turned back and addressed his bodyguards. *- Confine Colonel Hrrd's-nn to his quarters.* Seeing that Hardison was about to protest, he went on. *Unless there is somewhere else you would prefer to stay, Hrrd's-nn? The stockade, perhaps?*

Hardison blanched. He'd seen the inside of the G'grk stockade.

- Good. Be content, Ymn. You will have a good view of the launch from your quarters.

- At least let me contact Terra! Hardison pleaded. *Let me tell her I've failed. Let me tell her you're going ahead with launching the Lance—*

The Grand Marshal smiled, a thin lipless smile. *- I think she will know,* he said.

3.27

Terra stared glumly at her comm. Her inert, silent comm.
- They're not going for it, are they? They're going to fire that thing.

- What did you expect? sneered Pktk. *It's the G'grk. Any excuse to blow something up.*

Terra turned on him angrily. *- STOP it, Pktk! Stop it with all the G'grk stuff! They're NOT stupid. They had us BEATEN, remember? They'd WON. The only reason we're not all G'grk child soldiers now is because old Grand Marshal K'zsht decided he'd had enough of war! If the G'grk are dumb animals, then who are we? Who are OUR people? We're the ones who let dumb animals conquer us!*

Pktk stood up. *- What do you mean, 'our people'? This isn't your battle, Terra! This isn't even your world! Why did you even come back here?*

Fthfth and Billy looked at each other with alarm. This wasn't good.

- I came back because I was worried about you! said Terra, wide-eyed and red-faced with fury. *I was worried about all of you! I'd lost contact with you and I was scared that something might have happened, and something HAD happened, and I dragged myself all this way across space to try to HELP, and I STILL can't find Lbbp, and we're all going to die before the morning unless we can stay friends and find a way to stop that thing in the sky so WE DON'T HAVE TIME FOR THIS!*

A leaden pause.

- I'm sorry, Terra, said Pktk humbly.

- And anyway, said Fthfth. *Billy's right. It's us in clever old Mlml who are currently being buried under ancient prophecies*

and superstitions while at least the G'grk are doing something. It's just a shame it's something so ... G'grky.

Terra decided to change the subject. - *Fthfth*, she said, *any progress on finding the frequency the nanites are using?*

Fthfth gave her an equivocal look. - *Good news and bad news on that one. Yes, I've established the frequency, but the signal itself is, well, it looks like a—*

Pktk cut in, - *It's a psychic frequency. The nanites communicate telepathically.*

Terra thought this over. - *Makes sense. They're thinking as one. Like individual cells in a planet-sized brain. So can we talk to them? I mean ... think to them?*

Pktk grunted in frustration. - *I've already made a telepathic transmitter, it's how I sent you that dream message. But I left it in Lsh-Lff ...*

Billy perked up. - *Since you've built one already, how long would it take you to make another one? Not long, surely? This is you we're talking about, Pktk.*

Pktk frowned. - *It's impossible. I could rig up the transmitter and the signal booster, but we've got no way of plugging in, of getting my thoughts into the system ... I used an interface in Lsh-Lff and there are no interfaces left in Hrrng! Remember? They've all been smashed!*

Terra stood up. - *Not all of them*, she said. *Come on, we've got to move again.*

3.28

- *There, Luminescence. All programmed and ready to go.* Lbbp stepped back from the console of his little ship. He'd overridden the biometric security system (well, it was his ship; his presence on board had been enough) and had programmed an intercept course with the Black Planet. He took a sorrowful look around at the ship's interior. They'd had some good times together. He'd been right over there when he'd heard that sound. Pip p-pip. The sound that had led him to her.

He hoped she was somewhere safe.

He remembered that nowhere was safe.

- *Thank you, Deceiver,* said the Gfjk, sitting back in the pilot's seat. *You have been a ... good friend.*

Lbbp paused. He didn't think he'd ever heard the Gfjk use the word 'friend' to describe him, or anyone. - *Thank you,* he said, almost reflexively.

The Gfjk smiled warmly. - *No really,* he went on. *I couldn't have done any of this without you. And I know how hard it is for people to be themselves around me, I do. All the 'Love and Glory' this and 'Luminescence' that. But I feel I've really got to know you, Lbbp.*

His real name now? Not 'Deceiver'? Curiouser and curiouser.

The Gfjk went on, softly. - *And more than anyone else, Lbbp, I think you've got to know me.*

Lbbp peered at the ridiculous robed figure sitting in his pilot's seat. Is there hope for you? Is there still a residual quantum of decency in there somewhere? Is it just the power that's sent you so crazy? Could you be saved?

Lbbp felt a glimmer of sympathy for the damaged

individual he saw before him, and a twinge of guilt at his betrayal. The Gfjk spoke again.

- *Will you do something for me while I'm away?*
- *Of course,* said Lbbp.
- *Will you make sure the custodians don't slack off in finding that Ymn child? She very nearly ruined my special day. I'd like very much to meet her and her little friends. I'm going to make them watch while I turn her slowly inside out.*

No, thought Lbbp, you're a thoroughly irredeemable little sh'znt and I'm going to be happy when you're dead.

- *I will, Luminescence. Love and glory!*
- *Yes, yes, love and glory,* said the Gfjk with a wave. He turned back to the console. Lbbp could hear the gravity engines warming up. He climbed out of the hatch and slammed it shut.

Lbbp backed away from the ship as it rose silently into the air, to the sound of rapturous hisses from the loyal onlookers. He watched as it dwindled into a dot in the deep red evening sky. He felt his two escorts grip his arms, and smiled at them.

- *Back to Mission Control then, boys?*

3.29

- *B*ack! Back! There's someone there! hissed Terra.
  - *I knew there would be,* whispered Pktk.

They had scampered through the streets, ducking from doorway to doorway, across the short distance from Pktk's home to the tower where Lbbp had raised Terra from infancy. Terra had fumbled in her rucksack and found the keytube that released the front door of the building. She hadn't used it for two years; occasionally, back on Earth, she'd held it in her hand and looked forward to the day when she might use it again. She'd never imagined using it under circumstances like these.

The rest of the little gang had glanced around nervously while Terra rummaged. The streets were deserted, but a visualiser set into the wall next to the door showed them an image of the Gfjk-Hhh's grinning face (along with the Mlmln text 'Love and Glory'), as if to remind them of their vulnerability.

Once safely inside, they had found the grav-chute and ascended to floor 6-green, being careful not to bash their bag full of equipment against the sides. Now, peering round a corner, they saw a white-robed figure standing guard in front of Apartment 4.

- *New Believer, not a custodian,* mused Terra. *Wonder why?*

- *It sounded like there was something going on in the Forum square,* said Fthfth as quietly as she was capable of being, which was quieter than Pktk expected. *Maybe all the custodians are there.*

As the robed figure turned, looking first one way down the corridor and then the other, they saw a pulse-orb, holstered on a belt around his waist. Custodian he might not have been, but he was armed nonetheless.

- *What do we do?* whispered Billy.

- *I don't know,* said Terra, watching the figure intently. *Maybe we could ... Wait! Is that—?*

To the alarm and confusion of her friends, Terra stood up straight and walked round the corner.

- *What are you doing?* whispered Fthfth.

- *Come back!* said Pktk.

Terra walked slowly towards the robed figure. She took her hat off. - *Yshn,* she said. *It's me ... It's Terra.*

Startled, Terra's old schoolfriend lowered his hood. He gazed at her wordlessly for a moment, then fumbled with the comm on his belt.

- *No, don't,* said Terra calmly. *Wait.*

- *I have to report you!* said Yshn. *I have to report you to His Luminescence!*

On hearing this, Fthfth groaned quietly.

Terra's friends emerged from their hiding place and stood behind her as she continued:

- *Listen to me, Yshn. He lied. He lied to everyone. He's not who he says he is. He can't do what he says he can.*

- *He can!* insisted Yshn. *It's all happening like the prophecy said it would! It's the moment of his ascension! It's happening right now and I'm having to miss it because I have to guard your stupid apartment!*

- *Same old Yshn,* snarled Pktk. *Still whining.*

- *Quiet, Pktk,* spat Terra over her shoulder. She turned back to Yshn. - *Give me the comm, Yshn. And the pulse-orb. You might get me, but you won't get all of us. I've played dfsh with you; you're not that fast.*

- *I'm one of his now!* said Yshn proudly. *One of his elite! And I'm proud to be one of his. The old leaders were weak! You were here – they let us get invaded! He'll never let that happen again.*

- *Er, it occurs to me that there's no point not getting invaded if in order to not get invaded you have to make things worse than if you HAD been invaded,* observed Billy.

Yshn hadn't noticed Billy until now. - *Who's THIS? Is this another Ymn? Why is there another Ymn here? Ymns spoil everything! They're the bringers of lies!*

- *I wouldn't come by our planet if that's how you feel, our kid.* Billy smiled, sidling up to Yshn in a friendly manner. *Place is crawling with them.*

Yshn, said Terra, *come with us. You don't belong to him. You don't belong to anyone.*

Yshn's eyed darted from one of his old friends to the other in turn. His mouth opened and closed silently, then he grabbed for the comm.

Yshn managed to shout, - *They're*— before Billy slapped the comm from his hand. With his other hand he shoved Yshn back against the door. Pktk piled in, grappling the pulse-orb from Yshn's belt and handing it to Fthfth, who looked at it like he'd just handed her a dead sknth.

- *They'll be coming,* sneered Yshn as Billy pinned him to the door, *they'll be coming for you.*

- *We'll be ready,* said Billy.

Terra shook her head, tears in her eyes. - *Oh, Yshn,* she said. She wished she could feel more shock and disappointment at her old classmate. All she felt was pity and a hint of disgust. *Get him inside,* she said to the others.

The gang of friends bundled their hostage through the door.

Terra stood in her childhood home.

Everything was much as she remembered it.

There was no layer of dust over the furniture as there would have been in a long-deserted Earth house – the building's air filters were far too efficient – but it was immediately obvious to Terra that no one had set foot in the apartment for a long time. She missed Lbbp more keenly than at any time since she'd returned to Fnrr. His not being in the one place he really OUGHT to be … Somehow his absence now felt total. For the first time, Terra found she wasn't sure that he was still alive after all.

'Terra.' Billy interrupted her thoughts. 'We've got stuff to do.'

Terra blinked and went into her old room. What she saw in there made her jump with alarm, giggle with amusement, and then feel rather guilty at having giggled.

Yshn, his wrists and ankles sealed in binding gel and his mouth stuffed with a torn-off piece of his own robe, was rotating, upside down and weightless, in her old sleep-well. Fthfth and Pktk were watching him revolve, admiring their own ingenuity.

- *Well, that's one way of keeping him out of mischief,* said Terra. *Where did you get the binding gel?*

- *It's his,* said Pktk, grinning. *It was on his belt.*

- *Well, that's poetic justice, I suppose,* murmured Terra. She walked over to her cupboard and went inside.

After a moment, she emerged, triumphant. - *Told you,* she said.

In her hand, she held an interface. Her own, personal, Ymn-friendly interface. It had been made specially for her after her unfortunate experience with one of the standard models. Shortly before her return to Earth it had been delivered, along with her other belongings, to the apartment. There was no point leaving the interface at the Lyceum; no one there could use it. It had been missed during the Gfjk's purge of its fellows.

Billy smiled. - *Let's get to work,* he said.

3.30

The Gfjk-Hhh looked around the inside of the space-ship. He had no idea what any of the controls did. But it didn't matter. He was in the hands of Fate now. Fate had appointed him. Fate had guided him. Fate had preserved him. And now, Fate had brought the Black Planet to him, that he might defeat it and take his rightful place among the gods.

If Fate could do all that, then surely Fate could be trusted to pilot a spaceship.

The ship's forward visualiser showed the Black Planet. Silent. Implacable. Unstoppable. Until now.

On the console in front of him, a small communication screen flickered into life. He saw – what was his name again?

– *Can you hear me, Luminescence?* asked the face on the screen.

– *Of course,* replied the Gfjk. *But can the people hear me? Can they see me? They must witness this! They must all witness this!*

– *Yes, Luminescence,* said the face.

The Gfjk smiled contentedly. This was going to be the best day EVER.

3.31

*O*h, *what now?* snapped Pktk impatiently.

He was kneeling on the floor of the main room of Terra and Lbbp's apartment, trying to assemble the equipment he'd brought. He had wired up the home-made transmitter (he'd made that as a Lyceum project the previous orbit) to the signal booster he'd cannibalised from the visualiser in his parents' apartment, and was now trying to hook up Terra's old interface to the resulting jumble of cabling and circuits. The last thing he needed was the big visualiser on the wall suddenly springing unexpectedly to life, and the last thing he needed to see on the visualiser was the enormous grinning face of the Gfjk-Hhh in unpleasantly tight close-up.

- *How's he done that?* wondered Fthfth. *I thought that thing was switched off.*

- *Probably some sort of override system for use in cases of national emergency or something. Who cares? Turn it off, I'm trying to concentrate,* grumbled Pktk.

- *No, wait!* said Terra. *We need to see this. We all need to see this. Billy, get Yshn in here – he needs to see this most of all.*

Billy shrugged and left the room.

- *I think one of our troubles might be about to take care of itself,* said Terra.

3.32

Lbbp, with his armed escorts, walked into 'Mission Control'. The old Forum building was a hive of activity. Technicians – or at least Fnrrns dressed as technicians – bustled around the haphazardly installed machinery. Some of them even looked as if they knew what they were doing.

Above all this, the newly installed giant visualiser crackled into life and the Gfjk-Hhh's beaming visage loomed massively over the room. A thrill passed through the crowd of courtiers and acolytes. Lbbp sighed. Ah well, he thought, not long now.

– *My beloved children!* said the Gfjk-Hhh. *I feel your fear! I sense your apprehension! But worry not! Now is the moment! We ascend together! You will be witnesses! Witnesses to my ascension and your deliverance!*

Gzzks, thought Lbbp. Utter gzzks from start to finish. He's making it up as he goes along. Does he even know he's making it up?

– *I speak to you now to invite you all to join me in our moment of common triumph!*

Wonderful bit of syntax, thought Lbbp. I'll almost be sorry when this is over. He looked around. The guards who had escorted him to the Forum were no longer watching him; their attention, like everyone else's, was fixed on the visualiser, rapt smiles upon their faces. Their hands remained on his arms, but their grip, he noticed, had finally relaxed …

3·33

- *What's he doing?* asked Fthfth, her brow furrowed as she stared at the visualiser.

- *I think he's attacking the Black Planet on his own,* said Terra.

- *Well, this should be interesting,* said Fthfth. She found a chair and settled down to watch.

Billy entered the room, Yshn over his shoulder like a sack of potatoes. He flopped the captive acolyte onto the sofa-thing. It didn't look much comfier than the one he'd tried to sleep on.

Yshn righted himself grumpily, then sat bolt upright upon seeing the visualiser. He said something like, - *Lmmnffnf!*

- *That's him,* said Billy.

Pktk continued to tinker intently, and did his best to ignore the goings-on going on around him.

Billy went to the window. The Black Planet seemed almost to be touching the tops of the city's highest buildings.

It occurred to Billy that maybe it wouldn't be such a disaster if the Gfjk-Whatsit DID turn out to be a reincarnated demi-god after all, because just at that moment he couldn't see another way out ...

3·34

On board the little lemon-shaped spaceship, the Gfjk-Hhh stared at his forward visualiser. The black orb all but filled the screen. Yes, he thought. Yes, keep on coming. I'm here. The one you've been searching for. The one who will end this.

He addressed the comm device, - *Distance to target?*

The voice of the technician – what WAS his name? – answered him. - *Sixteen by sixteen and closing. It's approaching you as fast as you're approaching it, Luminescence.*

- *I must speak to it. Open a channel!* said the Gfjk with an authoritative wave of his hand.

There was a pause. - *Erm ... A channel to what, Luminescence?* said the voice. (Fmsk? Was that it?)

The Gfjk-Hhh did the wave again. - *To the planet! The black ... orb thing! I must speak to it now!*

A longer pause.

- *No one knows how to communicate with it, Luminescence,* said the voice. (Fmgst?)

- *Well ...* The Gfjk-Hhh pondered this a moment. *Open all channels! The planet WILL hear me. ALL planets will hear me!*

The Gfjk drummed his fingers on the console expectantly. The Black Planet loomed ever larger on the visualiser ...

3·35

His Luminescence's order had caused a degree of confusion and consternation in Mission Control. No one seemed sure how to comply with the Gfjk's command, or indeed if it were within their ability to comply.

Lbbp sensed the suspense and bewilderment in the room. Nothing could alter the course of events now, but he didn't want to put the Gfjk off in any way. He turned to his escorts. - *May I?* he offered politely.

The custodians barely seemed to register his question, so intent were they upon following the events unfolding on the big screen. Lbbp shrugged off their hands with no resistance and went over to the machine that looked like a protein manipulator.

Lbbp began merrily punching random buttons and throwing switches. The machine beeped satisfyingly and a convincing amount of light-blinking resulted. Lbbp looked over at Fshnk, his face triumphant.

- *Tell His Luminescence all channels are open!* he announced.

Fshnk nodded and conveyed this information to his master.

No idea what I just did, thought Lbbp, but you're still going out live to your people, and that's what matters, Luminescence.

3.36

The Gfjk-Hhh received the news gratefully from Fshnk. (Yes! Fshnk. That was it. Good old Fshnk) Now he could get on with the business at hand.

He drew himself up to his full height, bashed his head on an overhead control panel, muttered a curse, hoped no one had heard him, cleared his throat and began.

- *This is the voice of His Luminescence the Gfjk-Hhh! Champion and Defender of Fnrr! Commander of the Platinum Legions! The Past and Future! The First and Last and Always! I command you to TURN! TURN, pestilence! Turn, destroyer! Leave this world in peace!*

The Gfjk stared at the little ship's forward visualiser. The Black Planet filled the screen now. Its surface seemed to swirl and pulse. He spoke again.

- *Turn! Depart!* Was there another way to say go away? Oh yes. *Desist!* That meant stop it rather than go away, now he thought about it, but it was the same thing really. Still the black sphere drew closer.

The Gfjk-Hhh was not worried, of course not, but suddenly he felt that perhaps his beloved people down on the planet's surface might be. He looked towards the little communication screen and gave them all a reassuring smile.

He became aware that he was gripping the lip of the control console very tightly. He looked down at his hand. He saw that his fingers were indeed clenched around the edge of the panel, his knuckles pale with tension. He stared at the hand. Skin. Bones. Tendons. Flesh. Blood.

A great freezing chill rushed up his spine. His eyes darted left and right. His knees quivered. His vision swam and then cleared, and it was clearer than it had been in a long time.

He saw the black orb, filling the whole frame of the little ship's visualiser. Wisps of black dust began to reach out from the surface, towards his ship, towards him. His mouth opened, but no words came.

The ship juddered.

The snub prow of the little ship, visible at the bottom edge of the image, seemed to blur and shimmer. As the Gfjk watched in horror, the prow dissolved away.

The Gfjk-Hhh found his voice, and it came from him in a shrill, strangulated cry.

- *I'm not the Gfjk-Hhh! I made it all up! My name's Bfgsh! I'm a cleaner! I work at the Preceptorate!*

The ship shook violently. The visualiser crackled and died. Bfgsh — for that was indeed his name, and always had been — turned to look through one of the little ship's portals, and saw the Black Planet. Clouds of black dust were billowing towards him.

- *I'm nobody!* he screamed. *I want to go home! I want to go—*

3·37

The Forum's giant screen, which had been showing an extremely tight close-up of Bfgsh's terror-stricken face, went blank. Silence.

Lbbp looked around him. Everyone else in the room was staring at the inert visualiser, mouths and eyes wide open in dumb shock. Technicians – if that was indeed what they were – sat frozen at their stations. The courtiers were no longer lounging on the benches but sitting upright and rigid. The custodians stood, arms limp, jaws slack.

Lbbp waited a moment for someone to speak. No one did. So he spoke himself.

– I really liked that ship.

No one reacted. Lbbp went on.

– Right, well, things to do … I'll be off, shall I?

Lbbp strolled towards the exit. Nobody tried to stop him. His escorts, like everyone else in the Hub, were staring aghast at the visualiser, their pulse-orbs in their holsters, their arms helpless at their sides.

Lbbp strolled, unimpeded, to the exit. As he opened the door, he had a thought. He addressed the mute throng.

– Listen, if he reincarnates again, you will let me know, won't you?

Some of the assembled acolytes turned to look at him, but their horrified gaping expressions did not change. Lbbp winced.

– Too soon?

No one replied. They gazed at him in blank, wordless confusion and despair. Lbbp slipped silently out of the room. He was not followed.

Lbbp exited the building and strolled into the now

deserted Forum square. The crowd that had seen the Gfjk off had doubtless hurried home to follow events on their visualisers. Warm evening air enveloped him and he breathed deeply.

It was impossible not to feel a tingle of grim satisfaction at Bfgsh's (was that what he'd said his name was? Didn't matter now) downfall. He'd been steeling himself for a rush of remorse at how mercilessly he'd manipulated the dictator along the road to his doom. Hadn't happened so far. I'm probably still in shock, thought Lbbp. He decided to give the grieving process time to work and deal with the guilt when – and if – it hit him.

But as Lbbp looked to the sky, and saw the black orb hanging above the city, tendrils of black smoke twirling around its outline, he reflected that if he was lucky, he might just get half a spectrum or so to feel smug about his victory.

He hoped the Gfjk hadn't been the only one with a plan, that somewhere out there someone had a plan at least vaguely grounded in reality.

That was the thing about reality, thought Lbbp. However far you ran from it, it would always find you in the end.

Lbbp heard what sounded like distant screams. Either rage at the Gfjk's fall, or the sudden realisation that Fnrr was helpless against the Black Planet had just dawned on someone.

The screams multiplied. It was, as the Rrth expression so colourfully put it, kicking off.

Lbbp cast one last glance up at the Black Planet, and with not much idea what else to do, headed for home.

3.38

Terra stared at the visualiser. Fthfth stared at the visualiser. Billy stared at the visualiser. Yshn stared at the visualiser. Even Pktk, intent as he had been on his work, stared at the visualiser.

- *Well*, said Fthfth. *That was ... unpleasant.*

- *Couldn't have happened to a nicer bloke, though*, opined Billy.

Yshn sat bolt upright and rigid. He trembled. His face was one of abject despair. Into his gag he said softly, - *Lmmnfnff...*

Terra looked at him sadly. She couldn't help but pity him. She knew many others would be feeling the same anguish, and many, she expected, would be feeling more than a little angry, even if they didn't yet realise with whom.

Pktk snapped himself out of it. - *I've got to get this finished!* he said. *We're almost out of time! We've only got about as long again as it took the Gfjk's ship to reach the Black Planet before it reaches us!*

Billy and Terra stared at each other in alarm.

They had minutes.

And that's when they heard the sound from the street below.

3·39

*I*diot.
    Grand Marshal Zst'kh wasn't much of a fan of slates or other such technological baubles, but something had told Professor Steinberg that the warlord would want to see the Gfjk-Hhh's single-handed assault on the Black Planet.

Zst'kh watched the imposter die without a flicker of emotion and handed the slate back to the Ymn scientist.

    - It is of no consequence. Proceed with arming the warhead.

Steinberg had watched the warhead being loaded into the cone of the rocket a few minutes previously. Now, as the radiation meters on the display in front of him surged into the red, the Lance of the Occluded Ones was finally ready to fly.

Steinberg glanced around him. Where was Colonel Hardison? He'd thought his colleague would have wanted to be here for this.

Zst'kh gazed up at the Lance. He hadn't shared the Ymn warrior's bizarre theories about the Black Planet with the Ymn scientist. He didn't want to cloud St'nn-brrkh's mind with doubts at such a moment as this.

Steinberg looked at the display. In the middle of the console there was a screen showing a single symbol. Rhythmically, the symbol changed.

Steinberg's knowledge of the G'grk numeration system was a little sketchy, but he knew a countdown when he saw one.

3.40

- *What's going on down there?* asked Pktk.
      - *Never mind that, you just get on with ... whatever that is,* said Billy, pointing at Pktk's ever-expanding technological creation.

They'd ungagged Yshn out of sympathy, and were beginning to wish they hadn't.

- *It's the others, isn't it? The other New Believers. They got my message. They've come for Terra.* Yshn smiled.

Billy looked at the street below them. There was a crowd gathering, some of them clad in those white robes. They were hammering on the door of the building. It was locked, being a private residential block, but as the crowd grew in numbers and anger, Billy wasn't sure how long the door could hold.

- *Let me speak to them,* said Terra.

- *No,* said Billy, *in a minute Pktk will have his gadgetoid ready, and then you're up.*

They had already realised that once Pktk's telepathic transmitter was functional, it would indeed have to be Terra who used it. Her interface had been especially designed for Ymn use; Fthfth and Pktk's Fnrrn skulls wouldn't even fit into the dome. Billy had never used an interface before; this wasn't exactly the moment to try it out for the first time. So Terra's job it was.

Billy thought for a second, then said, - *I'LL talk to them.*

- *YOU?* chorused everybody, including Yshn.

- *Yes, me,* said Billy. *You've all got things to do, and besides, I think I might be able to offer them a new angle on things. Terra,* he said urgently, *whatever it was you did that time you spoke to, like, everybody ... do it again.* He handed Terra her slate.

245

It had in fact been Pktk who had set up that particular stunt, but the slate had stored the process in its memory. Terra looked back through the last couple of days' activity, found the program and ran it again.

– *There,* she said. *Just tap the screen when you're ready.*

Billy took the slate and went into the servery. He needed a bit of privacy. And perhaps a bit of configuration 6.

Pktk looked up.

– *It's ready,* he said. He looked at Terra.

– *Are you?* he asked.

3.41

Billy swallowed a chunk of configuration 6 and gripped the slate tight. He looked straight into the screen, as Terra had done. He tapped the slate.

Down at the entrance to the building, Billy's enormous face replaced that of the late Gfjk-Hhh on the visualiser next to the door.

He was also seen on the giant screen in the Forum; his sudden appearance roused the courtiers and technicians from their stunned torpor.

His face popped up on visualisers in homes and work-places throughout Mlml.

After a blip or so, he spoke.

- People of Hrrng ... erm ...

Lend me your ears? They didn't have any. What then? Listen to me? Bit weak. It'd have to do.

- Listen to me! My name is Billy Dolphin, and I'm sorry about the Gfjk-Thingy, and look, I know you're all feeling a bit disappointed at the moment, but—

From the street below, he heard cries of, - *It's another one! Another Ymn!*

- That's right, he said, *I'm a Ymn, and that means—*

- Ymns are the bringers of lies! screamed a voice from below. This was taken up by the crowd. - *Bringer of lies! Bringer of lies!*

- Yes, said Billy. *You're right, Ymns are the bringers of lies. The Master Liars. Biggest fibbers in the galaxy, that's us. We can lie bigger and better than anyone. But you know what else Ymns can do?*

A drop in the clamour as the crowd pondered Billy's question.

- We can tell lies from truth! We can figure out what's a lie and what isn't! We learn it at a very early age because we have to! Life on Rrth would be impossible if you couldn't!

The battering at the door ceased. Billy had their attention. He went on.

- When you're a Ymn, you get lied to from the moment you're born! As soon as you can see and hear, all you see and hear is lies! They lie to you at home, at school, in church, at work ... Every show on TV is full of lies and the adverts between them consist ENTIRELY of lies. Massive bare-faced whoppers, all of them.

The crowd listened intently.

- Even the people you love lie to you! My mum said I'd be thin by now! My dad said playing rugby wouldn't hurt! And the only girl who ever said she fancied me turned out to be a shape-shifting insect bounty hunter who tried to suck my brains out, so don't tell me I don't understand disappointment!

A few titters at this.

- But what you do, when you're a Ymn, is you listen to what people tell you and you figure out whether it's LIKELY to be true or not. Okay, example ... if an advert tells you that, say, this new shampoo gets your hair clean, that's probably true. If it says this new shampoo will make you rich, handsome and irresistible, it's probably NOT true. Follow me?

Silence.

- Right, bad example, you're all bald. Billy slapped himself. *All right, try this: what's more probable: that two thousand orbits ago, someone successfully predicted the future – which you used to think was scientifically impossible, remember – and said he'd come back from the dead – ALSO impossible – while somehow forgetting to mention the part where he turns out to be a total jerk and then gets himself killed when things get a bit serious ... OR, that some guy made some stuff up to make himself look good?*

A different kind of silence. A sheepish, awkward silence. Billy let it bed in for a second and then continued:

- Now here's the thing; Terra's in here working on a way

of stopping that big black thingy. If you give her time to sort it out, then there's a CHANCE we'll all see tomorrow. But if you break in here and stop her, then WE WILL ALL DIE. Like, NOW. You've got literally nothing to lose. Just give her time. Meanwhile, if I'm wrong, and we're all going to die in a minute, don't you have better things to do with your last moments? Aren't there people you'd rather be with?

The crowd exchanged glum, guilty glances. The ones at the back of the group shuffled away first; soon all had dispersed.

Billy slumped to the floor. He let out a great, deep sigh. After a few seconds he got up, rubbed his face vigorously and walked back into the main room.

- *Told you I'd have a word*, Billy said to Pktk. *So, where are we up to?*

Pktk gestured at Billy to be quiet. He pointed to the middle of the floor.

In a kneeling position, her hands on her knees, Terra was there. In front of her stood the interface, its glass dome glowing gently.

Terra breathed hard.

- *If you're going to do this it has to be now*, said Fthfth, looking at the darkening sky.

Terra looked across at Billy. She smiled but there was fear in her eyes. He smiled back, and she saw no fear in his.

'You really think I can do this?' she said.

'I really think you can do anything,' he said simply.

Terra jammed her head into the dome. - *Do it, Pktk.*

There were three blips, and then ...

3.42

Terra opened her eyes.

She stood on the surface of the Black Planet.

This isn't real, she thought to herself. I couldn't survive if I were actually here. It's just a visual representation my brain's creating.

She looked to the sky. It was dominated by the disc of Fnrr, orange-green, huge, beautiful.

She looked to the ground. Black dust. It swirled and pulsed.

- you YOU are not NOT US not deliverer WE ARE we DELIVERERS are why are WHY you WHY ARE why WHO are who ARE why are you HERE here?

A thousand whispering voices inside her head. It was true. They were intelligent.

And anything intelligent could be reasoned with.

That was the theory, anyway.

- HOW how do you HOW CAN you can WHO ARE you be BE HERE?

- I've come to talk.

- life form LIFE form FORM YOU you are ARE a LIFE life form you YOU must be PERFECTED perfected PERFECTED

- You'll get a chance in a minute. I'm actually on that planet up there. I've projected myself telepathically into your communication system. Like I said, I'm here to talk.

- all ALL LIFE life forms FORMS are imperfIMPERFECTect IMPERFECTIONS must MUST be perfected PERFECTED deliverers DELIVERERS we are

- Why?

- the mission THE PURPOSE the purpose THE

250

MISSION purpose PURPOSE it is IS OUR PURPOSE deliver DELIVER PERFECT perfect remove REMOVE all trace TRACE life

All trace of life, thought Terra. That's why they erase the cities as well as the people. The people of Perfection didn't want their culture to crumble and decay without them, they wanted it all gone.

- CORRECT correct

Oops, forgot they can hear my thoughts, thought Terra. Better keep asking them questions before they get too good a look inside my head.

- Who gave you your mission?

- The PERFECT perfect ones ONES THEY sought SOUGHT preserve TO PRESERVE THEIR perfection PERFECTION no NO DECAY decay NO decline DECLINE perfection PERFECTION preserved for ever FOR EVER PRESERVED FOR EVER delivered them WE DELIVERED THEM them

- Your creators were life forms, but they were perfect? I thought all life forms were imperfect.

- WE PERFECTED perfected them THEM THEY ARE are perfect PERFECT NOW they are THEY are perfect now delivered DELIVERED PERFECTfect

So much for that line of attack, Terra thought. That had been Billy's idea.

She looked up; Fnrr looked so close, she felt like she could reach up and touch it. The ground beneath her swirled more actively; tendrils of black vapour started to snake up around her ankles.

We must be nearly close enough, she thought. Any moment, these tendrils of dust will reach out towards Fnrr. The transfer will begin. That's how it happens.

Terra didn't know how she knew this, but she knew it absolutely.

Hey eye was caught by a sudden flash from the surface of Fnrr. From her old cartography lessons, she recognised the place. It was the Central Plains.

The Lance. The G'grk had fired the Lance. It would take maybe two minutes to reach the Black Planet. When it struck, the Deliverers would be scattered through space. Fnrr would die in seconds and then the curse of the Black Planet would spread to all worlds. There would be hundreds of black planets!

Wait a second ...

Why weren't there *already* hundreds of black planets?

If the Deliverers were self-replicating, why did they leave their victim-worlds scoured and lifeless? Why didn't they stay and convert them into roaming weapons, as they had done Perfection? Hundreds of wandering Black Planets, becoming thousands, millions ... Surely that would enable them to complete their mission much more quickly?

Terra found that she knew the answer. I can hear their thoughts too, she realised.

There must be only one Black Planet; one engine of deliverance. The Deliverers must be unified. If it were otherwise, if there were many Deliverer-worlds, the scattered and divergent populations could come into conflict. The rival black planets might hunt each other down, the Deliverers destroying each other before their mission could be completed ...

A faint glimmer of another idea came to Terra. But just a glimmer. Her mind surged. Panic could seize her at any moment. She fought to keep it at bay and maintain focus, trying to force the idea to coalesce into something useful. She gazed up at Fnrr. It was teeming with life. Precious, fragile life.

Life ...

– *So now your mission is to wander space in search of life forms to perfect?*

– *WE search for SEARCH life we LIFE and PERFECT perfect it PERFECT IT*

– *How do you decide what ORDER to perfect them in?*

– *WE find them THEM and we WE perfect AND WE PERFECT THEM deliver them THEM*

- As soon as you find them? You perfect the nearest life form?
- yes YES
- So if there were a life form nearer to you than the ones on the orange-green planet, you'd have to perfect them first, or you'd be in violation of your mission, correct?
- CORRECT correct
- How do you define life? What makes something alive?
A pause.
- LIFE life REPRODUCESproduces life EVOLVES evolves LIFE has HAS a PURPOSE purpose

Terra could see a glinting object above the planet's surface. She had seconds.

- You define life as reproduction and evolution with a purpose?
- it IT IS is a SUFFICIENT sufficient definition DEFINITION
- You're surrounded by life forms! Right here! All around you!
- explain EXPLAIN
- You ARE life forms. The Deliverers. You're alive! You may have been engineered and created, but for centuries you've been reproducing and evolving to fulfil your purpose! This planet is teeming with life forms, and they need to be perfected! They need to be delivered! NOW!

There was no reply.

They're not going for it, thought Terra.

She looked up; a silvery dot was now visible. The Lance will hit any second, she thought. I've failed.

The ground trembled. It shuddered.

It shook violently. Terra wondered why she hadn't fallen over, then remembered that she wasn't really there at all.

Cracks appeared in the surface; fissures, faults, crevasses, opening, widening into gorges, canyons.

It's working, thought Terra. It's working. They're turning on each other.

The sound of a thousand distant voices. Tiny voices. Whispering voices. Screaming. All screaming.

253

Switch the interface off, thought Terra. Switch it off ...
Switch it off, NOW ... I don't want to see this ...

The planet's surface quaked, pulsed, bucked and heaved.
The black dust blew and surged, a dark sandstorm blotting
out the sky, obscuring Fnrr.

Switch it off, switch it off, PLEASE switch it off ...

The ground fell away beneath her; she was drifting in
a blinding, whipping maelstrom of dust, which thinned,
faded, cleared to reveal a gleaming missile bearing RIGHT
DOWN ON HER ...

Terra fell to the floor. A solid, cold, hard floor.

She rolled over. Bright lights and faces.

– *You did it.*

She blinked. Her vision swam, blurred, focused.

– *You did it!*

Terra sat up, aching. Billy was behind her, propping her up. She looked around her.

– *It's gone?*

– *Come and see,* said Billy.

He helped her to her feet. Unsteadily, she shuffled across to the window.

Terra looked into the sky. Stars, twinkling peacefully. Three of the six moons, shining serenely. Even – unusual for Hrrng – a couple of clouds, pale patches in the inky sky.

And nothing else.

– *It just … sort of … folded in upon itself,* said Pktk.

– *I know,* said Terra weakly. *I need to sit down.*

Suddenly, the area of sky where the Black Planet wasn't any longer was lit up by a distant flash. It reminded Billy of how the star of the nativity was depicted on Christmas cards.

– *The Lance,* muttered Pktk. *The G'grk must have remote detonated it. I wonder if they've worked out what happened?*

– *I'm rather looking forward to telling them.* Fthfth grinned.

– *I REALLY need to sit down,* said Terra urgently.

– *Move yourself, you,* said Billy, shoving Yshn sideways off the sofa-thing.

– *Let him go,* said Terra. *There'll be some solvent for the binding gel in his belt.*

Pktk found the little phial and poured a drop onto the

gel binding Yshn's wrists and ankles. It evaporated away.

Yshn got to his feet. - *Terra*, he said, a terrible emptiness in his eyes, *Terra, I'm*—

Terra held up a hand. - *Not now, Yshn. Just ... go home.*

Yshn looked at the stern faces of Terra's companions. Without a word, he turned and walked away.

They heard the door close.

Billy looked at Terra's face. - *What's the matter? We won. You saved everyone*, he said.

- *Again*, added Fthfth.

Terra took a deep breath and exhaled, shuddering. - *It was horrible*, she said, her eyes dampening. *They tore each other to pieces. I could feel them, I could hear them ...* She looked imploringly at her friends. *Did we do the right thing?* she said tearfully. *They were just obeying their programming. I wiped them out. They were more or less a species in their own right and I wiped them out. What gave me the right to do that?*

Fthfth put her arms round her. - *If they were a species, then they were one that was moments away from destroying every species on this planet and which had already wiped out every species on countless other planets. They certainly didn't have the right to do that.*

- *But nobody has*, sobbed Terra. *There should have been another way ...*

- *Well, spider-friends*, said Billy, *that's been the recurring motif of the day, hasn't it? Nobody's perfect. Nobody's ever perfect. And whenever anyone forgets that, whether it's the population of the Lost Planet Smug, or some bloke who decides he's a god, things go wrong. Really wrong.*

They heard the door open and close again.

- *Oh no, has he come back?* groaned Pktk.

- *Probably forgot his thumbscrews*, Billy grinned.

The sound of footsteps in the corridor. Terra turned her face away. The last thing she wanted was to have to face Yshn again. She couldn't face the effort of forgiving him. She needed all her energy to forgive herself.

A curiously excited hush had descended upon the room.

Terra looked at her friends. Fthfth and Pktk's faces had lit up with smiles; Billy just looked confused, as he often did.

A voice from behind her.

- *Terra?*

Terra almost didn't dare turn around, just in case it wasn't who she thought it was.

Terra turned round.

There, in the doorway, looking pale, drawn and even thinner than usual, was Lbbp.

Terra leapt to her feet and flew into his arms.

Lbbp clung to her like he'd never ever let her go.

They didn't say a word to each other. They didn't have to.

PART FOUR

Pick Up the Pieces

4.1

- *I can't BELIEVE they're taking credit for it,* huffed Fthfth.

She was peering crossly at her slate, reading the news. For the first time in a couple of orbits, the ACTUAL news.

- *It doesn't matter,* said Pktk, *if it makes them happy, let them.*

- *But everybody SAW it!* she said, getting up and stomping across the room to the window. *The planet IMPLODED before the Lance even got there! They blew up the rocket in empty space! How can the G'grk be claiming they saved Fnrr? And why is ANYONE believing them?*

- *If we've learned anything, it's that there's no telling what people will believe,* mused Pktk through a mouthful of configuration 5.

They were in the servery of Pktk's apartment, to which his parents would soon be returning. All the exiled academics who had been hiding out in Lsh-Lff were on their way home. The Chancellor, who had been lying low in a remote village in the hills above Jfd-Jfd, was returning to resume her duties, and those delegates who had been tracked down – and who WANTED to return – were also on their way back.

Pktk and Fthfth were supposed to be cleaning and tidying up the apartment in advance of his parents' arrival, but so far all they'd done was eat breakfast and argue about the news.

- *People remember things wrong, anyway,* reflected Pktk. *People remember what makes sense to them, even if it's not what actually happens.* Seeing Fthfth's confusion, he went on:

– *Look, here's the actual sequence of events: the planet's there, the planet's gone, then big explosion. That makes no sense, unless you know what we were doing, which nobody except us does. So what everyone remembers is: the planet's there, big explosion, the planet's gone. Now that makes sense. It's not what happened, but it makes sense, so that's how people are remembering it. Understand?*

Fthfth glowered. – *Doesn't make it right, though. Terra was the one who saved everyone! People should be thanking her!*

– *Have you asked Terra how she feels about that?* asked Pktk. *The last time she saved everyone it turned her life upside down. Maybe she's happy to let the G'grk take the credit for it.*

Pktk took another bite of configuration 5, then said thoughtfully, – *Where is Terra, anyway?*

4.2

Preceptor Shm looked around his reading room. It was all still here.

He'd had horrid visions of his scrolls lying torn and scattered around the room, his historic artefacts smashed, rude slogans daubed on the walls. But the place was exactly as he'd left it all those cycles ago.

Apparently the Gfjk-Hhh and his followers had had no interest in academia. But then, considered Shm, they didn't seem to have been interested in learning things at all.

The Preceptor sat in his old chair. It felt as if he'd never been away.

The aftermath of the fall of the Gfjk-Hhh – or whatever his name had been – would be long and messy. No doubt some sort of commission would have to be set up. Tasked with deciding what punishment, if any, should be meted out to the Gfjk's surviving followers. How responsible should they be deemed, legally, to have been for their actions? It would be a thorny question. Are you doing wrong if you sincerely believe you're doing right?

Shm rubbed his temples and grunted.

A lot of them HAD believed they were doing the right thing. But that, he reflected, was because they hadn't thought about what 'the right thing' was. They hadn't exercised any personal judgement. Working out what was right, Shm decided, would ALWAYS be an individual's responsibility. Whatever leader they were following, and whatever authority that leader claimed.

There would be difficult times ahead.

With regards to the Black Planet, young Fthfth had told him the truth: how the Rrth child had contacted the nanites and persuaded them to self-destruct. Shm had managed to convince Fthfth, who was still angry, that it would be far the wisest course of action to let the official story – that Fnrr had been saved by the G'grk and their rocket – go unchallenged. For all sorts of reasons – practical, political, but principally because that's how Terra wanted it.

Preceptor Shm got up, walked to his window and looked out across the city.

Where was Terra, anyway?

4·3

'**Y**ou were right, you know, James. About the Black Planet.'

Professor Steinberg and Colonel Hardison looked out across the vast, purplish expanse of the Central Plain. Upon being released from confinement after the destruction of the Black Planet, Hardison had decided he needed some air. He'd set out for a hike across the plain, and invited Steinberg to accompany him. Steinberg had struggled to match Hardison's determined pace, and was taking advantage of a brief sit-down to have a private talk with his human colleague. This, he felt, was probably why Hardison had wanted to come out here.

'I know,' said Hardison. 'Terra told me.'

Hardison had received Terra's message upon his release. It had read, in English:

'Thanks for trying. We sorted it out. Let them take credit – it's easier that way. Thanks T x'

'So what do we do?' Steinberg continued.

'Do?' replied Hardison, his eyes scanning the horizon. 'We do nothing. The peace process between the G'grk and their neighbours isn't a done deal, Dave. It could collapse, and that crazy fool being in power in Mlml all that time didn't help. Part of the accord was that the G'grk were put in charge of protecting the planet against any threats from space. If the rest of Fnrr thinks that the G'grk have succeeded in doing this, it'll smooth things over.'

Steinberg was briefly taken aback by hearing Hardison call him 'Dave' rather than 'Prof'. He was not quite convinced by Hardison's position. 'Doesn't seem fair, though.'

Hardison sighed. 'First rule of politics, Dave ... Fair's got nothing to do with it.' He stood up and stretched. 'Where is Terra, anyway?' he asked.

4·4

- There. Send that. And Drone Major ...?
*   - Yes, Grand Marshal?*
- No one else is to see that message. Understood?
- Of course, Grand Marshal.

The Drone Major turned and strode away towards the communications room.

Zst'kh sat back in his seat. Apart from the cold metal bed, it was the only furniture in his quarters.

Zst'kh had composed the message extremely carefully.

He had thanked the Ymn child for her help in the matter of the Black Planet, while never exactly specifying what that help had been. He added that he was aware of her difficulties with certain rogue dissident elements from within his own nation and promised to devote his time and energy towards tracking these malcontents down and ensuring that she was no longer inconvenienced in this way.

Zst'kh had been quite sincere in this; he'd sacrificed much to cement the peace process and secure his own position. He wasn't about to let all his good work be undone by a rabble of discontented exiles. The Walkers of the True Path would not find Terra. He would make sure of that.

Come to think of it, thought Zst'kh, where was Terra, anyway?

4.5

In its bunker below the Preceptorate, the Extrapolator followed the events unfolding up on the ground, and beyond.

The false emperor's rule had ended, just as the Extrapolator had known it would. The arrival of the Black Planet had been unexpected, but once its presence was factored into the Extrapolator's calculations, its place in the course of events had become clear.

The Extrapolator was aware that an inaccurate version of events was being circulated. It would not seek to correct this. It knew that the Ymn child had been responsible for preserving Fnrr. She had almost fulfilled her role in the planet's destiny. Almost.

The Extrapolator continued to monitor communications on the surface. It appeared that no one knew where Terra was.

The Extrapolator knew.

4.6

- *I didn't think I'd ever see this again.* Lbbp gazed out across the rainbow sand to the pink sea. The waves lapped gently, soothingly.

- *I didn't think I'd ever see YOU again,* said Terra.

Silence that might have lasted three blips or half a day.

- *I ... did things I'm not proud of,* said Terra quietly.

- *So did I,* said Lbbp. *I took a fragile, vulnerable individual and exploited his weaknesses until he destroyed himself.*

- *I found a unique, distinctive species and talked them into exterminating each other,* said Terra.

Another silence.

- *That's something you learn as you grow up, though,* said Lbbp. *Doing the right thing isn't always nice.*

- *Growing up,* muttered Terra. *It's overrated. Think I want to stop here, if it's okay.*

Lbbp smiled. - *I think you're doing a fine job growing up so far. Why stop now?*

A short distance away, further up the beach, Billy looked back towards his friend and her stepfather. He'd give it another minute, he thought. Give them a bit more privacy. He could tell they had a lot to talk about, and he knew they'd talk about it a lot more easily if he wasn't listening.

Rfk was certainly living up to Terra's description of it, Billy thought. He could see why it had been her favourite place on Mlml when she was growing up here, and he understood entirely why she'd insisted on coming here now.

The journey had been fun, certainly. Billy wasn't sure he had the 'knack' of using a gravity bubble yet, but he'd made it here in one piece without being towed, so that was progress, he supposed.

He looked at Terra's comm, blinking away quietly in the palm of his hand. He'd asked to borrow it soon after they'd arrived at the beach. Now the extra-planetary communications array was functioning again, he'd wondered if he might be able to use it to phone home.

He checked his chunky digital watch. Absurdly, it still showed Earth time and the date back home. He'd been gone less than a week. It wouldn't be hard to get a lift back from somebody; he was owed that, he was sure ... He could be back there in a couple of days, could just pick up where he'd left off. Even his absence from school could be explained away.

He looked at the comm. It had configured its screen into a phone keypad again.

Billy dialled his home number, remembering to include the international prefix.

After a moment, Billy spoke.

'Dad? It's me ... Yes, I'm all right. I'm fine. I'm—'

A pause.

'Listen, Dad, tell Mum: I'm NOT in any trouble, I HAVEN'T run off and joined a cult ... or a band (which would probably alarm her more, thought Billy), and I'm perfectly okay, but ... I won't be home for a little while longer. No, Dad, I'm not sure how long. I'm gonna say don't worry, and you shouldn't. I know you will, but ... you really shouldn't.'

Another pause.

'Yes, Dad, I promise I'll call. I'll call whenever I can. I love you. Tell Mum that as well.'

He switched the comm off. He stared at it for a moment, then walked back along the beach to where Terra and Lbbp were sitting.

Billy tapped the translation cube in his pocket, and smiled at Lbbp. - *How you feeling?*

Lbbp smiled back. - *Better. Much better.*

Billy handed Terra's comm back to her. 'You want to use it?' he asked.

'What for?' asked Terra.

Billy shrugged. 'To call your parents? Your human parents, I mean.'

Terra stared out to sea for a moment, then put her comm back in her bag. 'Not yet,' she said, 'I'll wait.'

'Wait until what?'

'Until I know what I want to say to them.'

Billy sat down on the sand. The orange sun was setting at the horizon, half visible above the line of the pink sea. And in the morning, it would rise again over the purple hills behind them.

'What happens now?' asked Billy.

EPILOGUE

Nowhere Man

The asteroid had no name. It was not marked on any star-charts.

It drifted among its fellows in the belt of rocks and ice which circled the star 62-13-440-09. Had anyone ever thought to take any energy readings of the asteroid belt, they might have noticed that one of the larger bodies was giving off a signal indicating some sort of fusion reactor buried deep below its surface. But no one had ever taken any such readings – there was no conceivable reason why anyone would.

The fusion reactor in question had been installed many eras previously by the victors of the war on the nearby planet of Quexis between the Tranta people and their rival nation, the Hifficks.

The plucky Hifficks had triumphed over the Tranta aggressors (that was how the history of Quexis recorded it, anyway; it is curious how often, when the history of a war is written, it's the vile aggressors who lost, and the plucky defenders who prevailed). The defeated Tranta leader, Yakus Yakus the Undefeatable, had been sentenced to life imprisonment in an asteroid gaol where the automated life support mechanisms (powered by the aforementioned fusion reactor) were designed to keep him alive, in total isolation, for as long as possible. When Yakus Yakus eventually died, many MANY years later, the asteroid prison had been abandoned.

Few nowadays knew it had ever existed.

Fewer still knew its location.

And no more than a handful knew that it had recently been reactivated, and was occupied once more.

The asteroid's current inhabitant had been there for just over two years, or nearly two orbits, as he would measure it.

The robot guards who brought his food, cleaned his cell and monitored his health did not speak to him. They had no speech circuits and, in any case, there was nothing to say.

The only voice to be heard in that place was the voice of the prisoner.

It resounded through the stone corridors, night and day – in as much as night or day can be said to exist in such a place.

The robot guards would come and go; they could hear the prisoner's words, but they did not react or respond in any way.

Still the voice went on. Quiet only when the prisoner fell into fitful, restless sleep. As soon as he awoke, the words would begin again:

– *Occluded Ones hear me; Occluded Ones guide me; Occluded Ones deliver me. Occluded Ones hear me; Occluded Ones guide me; Occluded Ones deliver me. Occluded Ones hear me; Occluded Ones guide me; Occluded Ones deliver me* ...

Nothing ever interrupted the prisoner's prayer. Until that night, if such a thing as night can be said to exist in such a place.

The prisoner had heard no voice but his own for nearly two orbits. But now he heard a voice, as clear as any he had ever heard.

– *WE HEAR YOU, SK'SHK*, said the voice. *NOW LISTEN TO US.*

Sk'shk clasped his hands together in gratitude and humility. He bowed his head, and closed his eyes.

And listened.

Acknowledgements

Thanks to Simon, Charlie, Genn, Sophie and the rest of the Gollancz massive; thanks as always to Fthf— er, I mean Greta, and Astrid (pickle). Many thanks to Ken & Liz Bartlett for continued use of the increasingly legendary Barn, and to Hilary Bartlett for so many things. Thanks to Budgie for editorial input and output; thanks to Mum & Dad and Our Rachel. Thanks to Ian Wilson, the galaxy's most patient manager. Thanks again to Neil Himself Gaiman, from whom all blessings flow, and most of all thanks to Clara Benn, without whom ... doesn't bear contemplation.

And, of course, huge thanks to everyone who read and enjoyed the first book, and ESPECIALLY those of you who then persuaded a friend to do likewise. You're my favourites.

M x